Sinking Sand

By Hazel Mattice The Books of The Chosen Five

The Green Door
Where there is no Whisper
Thirsty Ground
Sinking Sand

Sinking Sand

Grace,

for to set the mind on the flesh is death, but to set the mind on the Spirit is life and peace.

Hazel Mattice

This is a work of fiction. All of the characters, names, incidents, organizations, and dialogue in this novel are either the products of the author's imagination or are used fictitiously.

Cover by Anna Grotberg

ISBN (SC) 978-1-7351054-7-5
ISBN (e) 978-1-7351054-8-2

"And everyone who hears these words of mine and does not do them will be like a foolish man who built his house on the sand. And the rain fell, and the floods came, and the winds blew and beat against that house, and it fell, and great was the fall of it."

Matthew 7:26-27

Part I

April 25, 1975
Spiritwood Lake, North Dakota

Sheriff Casey Miller was in love with his best friend's wife.

Nearing the lake house, his heart kicked into high gear. A rumble of thunder in the distance promised the first storm of the season, renewing the exhilaration inside him at the memory of seeing Inga Pederson for the first time.

The charity event before Christmas at Saint James Basilica was one of many events the community expected him to attend as Stutsman County Sheriff. Inga Pederson entered the sanctuary, laughing.

Casey couldn't remember who else was there after that. He approached the woman with crimson locks and introduced himself. She smiled and turned his world upside down. Afterward, he had invited her to dinner and she said yes.

The next day, he told his best friend Bruce Solberg, who chuckled, "Case, you're in love with a new woman every week."

Then Casey introduced Inga to Bruce, and she was the one falling.

Bruce's laughter echoed in his memory as he turned down the drive leading to the elegant lake house, catching a glimpse of the pretty pregnant woman in the seat next to him.

Uncertain what to do with his love, the next night Casey had found himself at Elizabeth Martin's door, drunk as a skunk. She in turn invited him into her apartment and her arms.

At the front door of the lake house, he cut the engine and got out. Making his way around to the passenger door, he blew out a bitter breath. Now Bruce was married to Inga and Casey was stuck with Elizabeth.

Casey opened the passenger door and offered his hand.

Elizabeth took it and stepped out, a blonde ringlet falling across her forehead.

At the front steps, Casey reached over to ring the doorbell. Fiery locks and cherry-colored lips consuming his thoughts, he hoped to catch a glimpse of Inga in the window. Instead, his eyes caught Elizabeth gazing up at him with adoration. She had always loved him.

Guilt wormed its way inside his gut, reaching his heart.

The door opened and Bruce stood with a hand on the knob. "You're right on time."

***

Twenty minutes earlier

"Can I take this off now?" Inga Solberg slid a thumb beneath the bandana covering her eyes.

"Not yet," Bruce's voice was low and husky as he stepped over the threshold, and set Inga down. He took off the blindfold. "Okay, open your eyes."

She glanced around the room, eyes growing round.

Inside the lake house, plush dark orange carpeted the living area. The walls were a hint of yellow. The fireplace chimney was dark brown, disappearing through the tall ceiling. Large glass windows faced the lake. In the open living room, a gold sofa. There were glass end tables on either side of the couch, complete with matching lamps.

"What do you think?" Bruce's voice was spiked with excitement.

"This…" She waved her hand over the room, "must have cost a fortune."

"I got it for a steal. Andersons are moving down south to Arizona."

"I keep thinking it's all a dream."

"If it is, don't wake me," he said. Harold Klingensmith became a millionaire farming. At sixty-nine, he bought three colonies of honey bees. Bruce took to bees like the bees to honey, and Harold let him care for the honey bees. He died shy of a year ago. With no living relatives save a distant cousin, the wealthy bachelor left everything to Bruce.

"Well?" Bruce brought the conversation back around. "What do you think of the place?"

"Not sure," Inga withdrew slightly, "I'll need to see the bed."

How he loved this woman! "Casey's on his way. He's bringing Elizabeth Martin." He took her hand, drawing her toward the bedroom. "If you don't watch it, he'll run off with you and leave me with Elizabeth."

Inga laughed. "What's wrong with Elizabeth?"

"She's not you. Did you know she won't let Casey have a drink?"

"She's Catholic and a longtime family friend of the Millers," Inga said, "She's known them for years."

"Usually when someone makes a big deal about a drinking problem, they are the one who has it."

"There's nothing between Sheriff Casey and me. It was just one date."

Reaching the bedroom door, he stopped to face her. "One where Casey met his soulmate."

"And I met mine." She reached up and touched his cheek.

He led her across the threshold.

"It has a canopy." A sultry smile spreading across her lips, she tugged him toward the bed.

"You want to try it out?" Bruce grinned boyishly.

There was a twinkle in her eyes. "I guess I can't get any more pregnant then I already am."

Bruce laughed. "Yeah. Then…" he paused, catching her green gaze. "Wait. What are you saying?"

Reaching up, she flipped a shock of dark hair from his forehead. "I'm saying I'm going to have your baby, Bruce Solberg."

His dark eyes exploded with wonder. "I hope it's a girl with red hair."

"Don't forget eyes the color of dark chocolate," she said, pulling his head down, and pressed her lips to his.

His heart thundered in his ears. The doorbell chimed through the fog in his brain.

"If we're quiet, maybe they'll go away," Bruce groaned against her lips.

She broke away. "We'll continue this later."

"Let's pretend we're not home."

Inga pushed him toward the door. "Answer it."

He gave her puppy dog eyes as he crossed the room, and opened the door. "You're right on time."

Sheriff Casey Miller and Elizabeth Martin stood in the entryway.

"A summer home. You two have arrived," Casey removed his hat and hung it on his coat.

Elizabeth kept hers on.

Casey held up a bottle of Welch's grape juice. "A housewarming gift."

Bruce caught Inga's eyes.

Inga's twinkled.

Elizabeth held up a bottle of Gentleman Jack whisky. "Nice house."

Inga and Bruce exchanged another cagey glance.

"I'm pregnant." Elizabeth's eyes sparkled as she gazed adoringly at Casey.

"You're kidding," Bruce said.

Inga clapped. "That's fantastic."

Bruce clamped a hand on Casey's shoulder. "We are too," he chuckled. "That is, Inga I mean."

"I'm so happy for you both." Inga threw her arms around Casey, and turned to embrace Elizabeth. "When is your baby due?"

Elizabeth's starry eyes were on Casey. "Christmas Day."

"Ours is due December 15. They'll be the same age. How wonderful."

Bruce crossed over to the kitchen and pulled tumblers from the cupboard. "Case? I can't drink this whole bottle myself."

"I better not." Casey flicked a glance at Elizabeth.

"You're not pregnant, too I hope." Bruce twisted the cap on the Welch's sparkling wine, pouring four glasses.

"Funny," Casey reddened, running a shaky hand over his head.

"To friends," Inga said, reaching for her wine glass.

"A new home." Bruce held up his.

Casey's turn. "To beautiful wives."

Elizabeth's voice was quiet. "To a house full of children."

1
Mercy Hospital
Valley City, North Dakota
December 13, 1975

Inside the hospital nursery, side-by-side bassinets cradled two of five infants born that day.

One wrapped in pink, parents on the birth card: Mr. and Mrs. Bruce Solberg.

In blue: Mr. and Mrs. Casey Miller.

In another realm, Chief of Seraphs Michael assigned guardians to the warriors.

Outside the Catholic hospital, Sheriff Casey Miller stood alongside Bruce Solberg.

"Think those nuns will let us see our wives and babies before New Year's?" Bruce held a box of cigars, each wrapped in a ribbon of pink: *It's a girl.*

"He was in a hurry to get here, I guess." Casey loosened his tie and unbuttoned the top two buttons of his white collared shirt.

"How is she doing?" Bruce unwrapped a cigar and handed it to Casey.

"Good, considering." *A house full of children,* Elizabeth had wanted and now she was fighting for her life.

"What's his name?" Bruce handed Casey the pack of matches.

"Norman Elton, after my father." Casey lit the cigar with shaky fingers. His father would never meet his grandson, having died of prostate cancer last year.

"Ours is Florence Dawn. After Inga's grandmother. She'll want us to raise her Methodist, but my grandmother…"

At the mention of her name, an image of Inga, her crimson curls tied back with a bandeau, the most common way she wore it lately, flooded his mind. He forced his thoughts to his own wife, reminding himself that Elizabeth was much more agreeable. But would she be okay with a smaller family? What would happen if…

"She'll be raised Mormon," Bruce's voice cut through his thoughts.

Startled, Casey asked, "What?"

Bruce laughed. "Thought that'd get your attention. Where were you?"

Heat swept up his collar. Rubbing the back of his neck, Casey shook the fog from his brain. There was no point in dwelling on what could never be. Inga belonged to Bruce, and Elizabeth…

"Your dad tells me you quit the business," Casey said.

"Yeah."

"I got the feeling when I talked to him that you didn't like working for Solberg Plumbing & Heating."

Bruce shrugged. "I had an opportunity to own my own business."

"Don't want to be just a worker bee?" Casey chuckled.

"Funny."

"How many colonies of bees did you say you got?"

"There's two hundred and fifty plus the three from Klingensmith."

"You sure like bees."

"I sure like being my own boss."

"What will your dad do?"

"He's getting close to retirement age. Until then, Don will take over for me." Bruce's only less-than-dependable brother who thought sowing wild oats in your late thirties was debonair.

"God spoke to me last night," he said at last.

"Oh yeah?" Bruce mumbled, cupped his hands, lighting his cigar.

"Norman is the only child we will ever have." Casey's shoulders slumped forward.

"Elizabeth will get better." Bruce put the match out with the flick of a wrist. "You'll have a house full of children like a good Catholic."

Casey straightened. "He's the only child we'll ever need."

Bruce puffed his cigar in silence.

"Since he's been born, I feel lighter than I have my whole life," Casey said. "It's hard to describe the feelings Elizabeth and I have for each other."

"In that case," only one side of Bruce's mouth lifted, "I'm happy for you."

2

December 27, 1983
The Miller house
529 5th Street SouthWest
Jamestown, North Dakota

Norman

John Paul II pardoned a man who shot him—Mehmet Ali Agca, and Dad forgave Mother before we left for the Solberg farm.

Right after lunch, she had a drink.

Dad arrived home from work when she was on her third.

"Hello Norman. How was your day?" He hung up his coat and sat on the bench by the front door.

"Good."

He glanced at Mother. "You finish off the Christmas wine?"

"I don't feel well," Mother said, her blue eyes narrowing. "Don't give me that look. Even Paul in the Bible told Timothy he should have a glass of wine to settle his stomach."

"A glass," Dad said with emphasis, "not the whole bottle."

"I still get phantom pains like the ones I got right after I had Norman."

At the mention of my birth, Dad's eyes immediately softened. "Of course."

"Do we have to go to Solbergs? Norman is getting over a cold and this is your only night off."

"I wanted to show Andrew Optimus Prime," I cut in. Andrew was the oldest Solberg brother at six years old. Plus, going over there meant Dad wouldn't retreat to his room and novel and Mother wouldn't sit in front of the TV all evening.

Besides, the Solbergs lived on a farm near Spiritwood.

Our house was in Jamestown, population 16,000, and home to the World's Largest Buffalo and the National Buffalo Museum, and there was nothing to do.

Oh, there was if you were a tourist or had a driver's license. But as an only child with a mother who didn't like to go anywhere, the Solberg farm was the place to be.

Mother took a sip of wine. "Norman, I don't want you bringing your Transformers."

"Ah, Mother."

"Ah, Mother nothing. Those kids are rough. They'll break them. Have you found G.I. Joe's head yet?"

"We already decided John doesn't get to play with them after what happened last time." John Solberg, the youngest, was only three. "I suppose we could play outside." I went over to the coat rack. "Do you know where any gloves are?"

She shrugged. "They're wherever you put them last."

"I left them at school. Besides, Mrs. Schmidt said they aren't warm enough."

"A lot good they'll do at school." She set her empty glass on the kitchen counter. "I suppose your teacher thinks I'm not a good parent since you can't keep track of your things."

"She won't let me go out for recess if I don't have them."

"Everyone would blame me if we didn't show."

Dad sighed. "I could tell them I got called in to work."

"Fine, I'll go," Mother said, sucking all the joy out of the outing with three little words.

***

The Solberg farmhouse
Spiritwood, North Dakota

At the Solbergs, we were greeted by the aroma of sweaty fish.

Bruce Solberg clamped his hand down on Dad's shoulder. "Hey Casey. Inga's got lutefisk on the stove."

Braided rugs were scattered about the wood floor. There was a china cabinet full of painted dishes.

Inga Solberg was mashing potatoes by hand.

Their grandma was at the grill, unrolling lefse with a stick.

The four Solbergs were on the floor by a Christmas tree that took up the entire living room.

"Your Christmas tree is cool," I said. A closer look said it was real. We had a real tree only once. Mother said it ruined the carpet and that was the end of it.

"Yep," Florence said. Her hair was the same shade as a field of poppies beneath the afternoon sun—matching her momma's—and she had a map of freckles on her face.

Her three brothers, Andrew, James and John had unruly mops of brown hair like their dad, and were named after Jesus' disciples. Rowdy, naughty, and rough, I guessed they were nothing like the guys from the Bible.

"Did you bring your Transformers?" Andrew asked.

"I want to be Opmus Pime," four-year-old James shouted and leapt to his feet.

"I'll be Megatron," Andrew said.

"Megatron is the sworn enemy of Optimus Prime and the Autobots," I said. "He is the leader of the Decepticons."

"John, don't eat marbles." Florence fished around in her three-year-old brother's mouth.

"I didn't bring my Transformers." I shoved my hands into my pockets.

"Want to build a snow fort?" Florence scooped up the marbles, dumping them into a bag with tie-strings.

That's when I noticed Mother was close. Her eyes were on me. "That's up to you, Norman. Did you bring warm clothes?"

"Uh…" My face reddened.

Florence pushed to her feet. "We have lots of extras."

"If you're sure." Mother eyed me like I would disappear forever once outside. "Next time, maybe you'll remember your hat and mittens."

Florence, taller than me by at least two inches, took my hand and led me to the entrance. She started digging through a bin of winter gear.

Alongside us, Andrew, James, and John peered into the bin.

Florence pulled out thermal hats and gloves. "We won't be gone too long, Mrs. Miller," she said, passing them out.

Andrew held up a Thermos. "We even have hot chocolate."

Mother said nothing with her mouth. Her eyes on the other hand, said it all. *Absolutely not. Under no circumstances will you share their germs.*

***

The sun shone bright overhead, glistening across the snow. Tromping through the thick of it, our breathing broke the early winter silence. Reaching the tallest wave sculpted to a fine snowy edge by the prairie wind, Florence set her backpack on the ground.

"We'll make a nice size hole and shape it with kitchen spoons. This is for you," she dug in and handed me a spade, a trowel for Andrew, and garden rake for James. John sat in the snow with the backpack.

I sank the trowel deep.

"How come you don't have a hat and mittens?" Florence asked.

"I do."

"Doesn't your mother like it outside?"

"She just worries about me."

"Do you like to play outside?"

"Yes."

"How come you forgot your hat and mittens?"

Anger burst through me. "What's with all the questions?"

"I like sledding." Andrew moved in between us.

Silence ensued.

Twenty minutes later, the cave was big enough for the three of us plus the backpack. Florence pulled out the Thermos, poured some into the cup, and handed it to me.

"This is cool," I said, taking a sip.

"Look, Nowman," James said, smoothing the bed of the cave. "You and Flowie can be the pawents and we'll be the kids."

Flowie would have to serve wine in the Thermos. At that thought, I'd had enough. "No. This is dumb," I said, and crawled out.

"We could build a snowman." Florence hurried out after me. "I brought the stuff for them." *Zip*. At the sound of the backpack's zipper, I stopped and turned around.

"No raisins until we are done making the snowwomen," Florence told John.

I made a snowball and started to roll it. The snow was soft and sticky, perfect for snow people.

Florence started one of her own. The boys joined in.

Andrew reached for the Tupperware container. James and John moved in closer. Florence pulled the lid off, grabbed the carrots, and handed me one. She dug into her pockets and pulled out buttons. "Here you go. I couldn't put them in the plastic container or John will eat them. I'm going to put the pink one on my snow girl."

"Snowman," I said.

"Mine is a snowwoman." She shoved the tools and container in her backpack.

"Snowwoman?" I blinked.

"Where do you think the snow children come from?" She smiled. "And who better to make a difference? Change the world."

"Hold it right there." Andrew held a stick gun in both hands, aiming it at Mr. Snowman. "He's wanted in a bank robbery."

"He didn't rob a bank." Florence grabbed at the stick pistol.

Andrew was too fast, moving out of the way. "It's obvious. He's got a scarf with tags still on, and a brand-new Carhartt hat."

"Mrs. Snowman bought them for Christmas," she set her hands on her hips.

Andrew eyed the snowman. "Then why is there a bandana over his face? He's trying to hide who he is."

"He's a cowboy. It's what cowboys wear," I said.

Andrew dashed forward and yanked the bandana off, quarters plopping into the snow.

"You win," Florence said, plucking the quarters from the snow. "Again."

Florence picked up the bandana and peered closely at her snowman's cheeks. "Andrew, what did you do?"

"I did it," I grinned. "They're freckles."

"Freckles?" Her face turned as red as her hair.

"Oh come on, Florence. They're pretty obvious."

"I know." She studied the snow wife. "They're all over her face."

"Because they're all over yours." I slapped snow from my gloves on the sides of my snow pants.

Her face turned crimson. "Very funny," she said, pushing my chest with both hands.

I fell backward in the snow.

"That's what you get." She whirled around, and took the container from James. "Now for the mouths… James, you ate all the raisins! The snow family will be blind." And then she started to cry.

At the sight of her tears, panic licked my gut and I did the only thing I could think of. I put James in a full Nelson. "What did you do that for?"

"Me? Yow the one with the fweckles."

I rubbed the top of his head. "Say you're sorry."

He wiggled in my arms. "Sowwy!"

"Say you'll never do it again."

"I'll nevew do it again."

I glanced at Florence. "What do you think?"

"It's okay." She wiped her nose with the back of her hand.

"Really?"

James made another attempt to wiggle free.

"Really."

I let James go. Eyeing Mr. Frosty, I decided he was missing part of his wardrobe. I pulled off my scarf and draped it around his neck.

Whack. A wet slush ball slammed into the back of my head.

"Hey." I put a hand on the spot, turning around.

Florence was crouched down, forming another snowball.

"Snowball fight!" Andrew yelled.

I ran around Mr. Snowman. Florence got me with another on my back. Behind cover, I quickly formed a snowball, whipping it in her direction. It missed her head by an inch.

"Nah nah." She stuck her tongue out.

"James get over here and help me." I had three ready now.

"Come on John," Florence grabbed his hand, dashing behind a fallen log. "Andrew is on our side."

Florence had a fantastic arm and sharp aim. Countless snowballs later, she, Andrew, and John won.

Red-faced, she looked at me beneath slushy bangs dripping from her forehead, and thrust out her hand. "Good game."

I shook it. "Good game."

"Let's go inside for hot cocoa." She picked up her backpack, and headed toward the house.

"Florrie, you forgot your container," Andrew called, grabbing it off the ground.

Florence held John's hand. Walking alongside her, I draped my arm around her neck. Andrew slung his around her other shoulder. James around mine.

"Race ya." A burst of energy swept through me and I broke away.

"No fair," Florence said. "You're faster."

"You're the one to beat," I said. "You're the tallest. Besides, I'll give you a five-second head start."

We flew toward the house.

I was the first to reach the steps.

All four gathered around me, patting me on the back.

Florence stuck her hand out and shook mine. "Good game."

I smiled back. "Good game."

3
New Year's Day 1984

New York City transit fare rose from 75 cents to 90 cents, and I, Florence Solberg, only daughter of Bruce and Inga Solberg, raised the prices in my first candy store.

Wearing my momma's apron and daddy's golfing visor, I stood behind my Fisher-Price cash register and sold my little brothers leftover Christmas candy.

"Five cents!" Andrew cried when I rang up a chocolate Santa.

"You have three nickels." I pointed to his hand.

"Yeah, but I wanted candy canes and the LifeSavers storybook."

"Kids, we're about to leave," Momma called.

"Where are we going?" I called back.

"The Millers."

I was going to marry Norman Miller when I grew up, even if he didn't know it.

James jumped up and down. "Hooway. I'm going to bwing my Matchbox caws to play with Nowman."

"How about it, Florence?" Andrew held out his cash.

"Oh alright. One candy cane, the storybook, and the chocolate Santa for all your money." I hurried to the kitchen. "I love going to the Millers' house. I wish we could go over there every day."

In a bright red sweater and black slacks, Momma poured a cup of coffee. "It's hard for them, his dad being the sheriff. Plus, their house isn't as big as ours."

"So?"

"So, it's a lot of work for his mother." She sipped from her mug.

"Dad, tell me again about when you met Momma."

They exchanged a tender look.

"I knew the moment Case introduced us there was no one else for me."

"Me either," Momma smiled.

"I'm going to bring my Strawberry Shortcake dolls," I said. I'd gotten Purple Pieman for Christmas.

"I don't know if Norman wants to play dolls." Dad chuckled, drawing Momma into his arms.

She set her mug on the counter, turned, and slid her arms around his neck, kissing him on the mouth.

James came into the kitchen behind me. "I want to bwing Matchbox."

Andrew rushed in, John trailing behind. "When are we leaving?"

Daddy and Momma were still kissing.

Andrew said, "Let's get our coats, Florence."

"I'll bring extra hats and gloves along with snowpants in my backpack." I shuffled through the winter clothes bin. "Can I bring ice skates?" Momma had gotten us another pair for Christmas. It was no coincidence they didn't fit Andrew, and instead of returning them to the store, she said we could save them for when Norman came over.

"No."

"How come?"

"Because the Millers live in town. I don't know if there's a place to skate there."

At the Millers, Norman's mother greeted us in a cream color turtleneck and a long necklace with colorful beads and brown slacks. She was a reserved woman with large blue eyes and a blonde curly bob.

"Won't you come in?"

"I like your necklace," I said.

"Thank you," she smiled and turned to Dad. "How are the bees?"

"Good." Dad stomped his boots.

Momma came in behind him. "Hello Elizabeth."

"Hello Inga. How are you?"

The atmosphere grew tight.

Norman trotted down the stairs. He was wearing a blue and red-striped shirt and bellbottom jeans. His dark hair curled across his forehead. He was only a little shorter than me.

"Want to see my room?" he asked.

"Yeah." I followed him up the plush cream-carpeted stairs.

Norman's room was at the top, his bedroom door had a poster of Luke Skywalker. Inside, the walls were dark blue. The comforter on the bed was a Matchbox car. There were yellow stars and a moon on the ceiling.

"Cool." James plopped on the bed.

"Watch this," Norman shut the lights off and the stars and moon glowed in the darkness.

"That's so cool," Andrew said.

"Turn light on," John whispered.

Norman flipped the switch, lighting up the room.

"I brought bubble gum." I tore open the package, separating pieces. "Santa brought Hubba Bubba for Christmas."

"No such thing as Santa. Your daddy and momma gave it to you." Norman popped a piece into his mouth.

"There is too such a thing as Santa," Andrew nearly shouted.

John's lower lip quivered. "Santa's real."

Norman's eyes dropped to the floor. "Well, he doesn't come to my house."

"Do you get stockings full of presents Christmas morning?" I chomped on my piece.

"Well, yeah."

"Santa brings those."

"Mother says she got them. That way I don't forget to say thank you."

I didn't know what to say to that, so I said, "I love ice skating. How about you?"

He looked away. "I don't know."

"We'll go next time you come to our house."

"Want to play with Legos?" he asked.

"Yeah."

John grabbed the back of my shirt and stuck his thumb in his mouth.

"I bwought my caws." James unfolded his Matchbox airport.

"Are we gonna play with your Transformers?" Andrew asked.

"Yep. I got something for you, John." Norman handed him a toy phone with a red plastic cord. "Sort of a late Christmas present."

"Florrie, look." John pulled the phone around, giggles erupting as plastic eyes rolled up and down on the toy.

Norman ruffled his hair.

Yep. I was gonna marry him.

4
February 7, 1984

Norman

Identified only as David "the boy in the bubble," the Texas Medical Center's most famous patient David touched his mother for the first time at age 12.

That morning before school, I dodged my own mother.

Tiptoeing down the stairs, I heard her talking to Dad. "My back aches," she moaned. "I must have slept on it wrong. I can't even walk."

"I'll take you to the clinic. I work the three-to-eleven shift today," Dad's voice was clear.

"Will you call them and make the appointment?"

"Alright." A few minutes later, he said, "They can see you at two. I'll drop you off on the way to work."

"What about Norman? School will be out before we get back."

"He can take the bus home to the Solbergs' house. I'll call Bruce."

"See you later," I called, heading for the door.

After school on the bus ride home, Florence sat in the aisle across from me. "Shall we go ice skating?"

Heat swept up my collar. "My mother said no." I'd never skated before.

Her face fell. "How come?"

"Doesn't want me to get hurt."

"What if you didn't get hurt? What if you were careful?"

"Maybe." I shrugged.

She turned to Andrew sitting next to her. "You won't tell right, Andrew?"

"No."

When we arrived, James met us in the entryway.

"Momma, we're home." Florence called, digging through a built-in wooden box. "We want to go ice skating."

"You actually have a skating rink?" I asked.

She nodded. "It's a slough in the trees. Dad swept it off this morning for us before he went to the bee shed."

"I don't have skates." I shoved my hands into my pockets.

Florence lined her foot up next to mine. "Our feet are the same size. I've got an extra pair you can wear."

"Can I go ice skating?" James asked.

"Sure," Florence said, pulling out a pair of skates. "Momma, shall I take John too?"

Mrs. Solberg emerged from the kitchen. "I just put him down for a nap." She smiled at me. "Hello, Norman."

"Hi."

Florence handed me gloves and a hat, dove back in and came out with snow pants. "Here you go."

The winter sun glistened off snow-tipped waves.

In cold silence broken by the crunching of snow beneath our feet and the short visible puffs of breath from our mouths, we made our way out to the trees.

Andrew and James trailed behind.

When we arrived at the edge of the slough, Florence passed out skates from her backpack, handing each of us a pair.

On a fallen log near the slough, they worked on trading skates for their boots.

Lacing her skates, Florence glanced over at me. "You haven't even started."

My face flushed hot. "Yeah, yeah," I said, pulling off a boot. *How hard could it be?* I laced up the skates the way I'd seen them do it.

"Those don't look tight enough." Florence crawled over to me, untied my right skate and retied it, pulling tight.

"What difference does it make?" I asked.

"You'll see." She tightened the left skate.

I stood, wobbling. Andrew skated alongside me. Even James moved with a natural grace that was humbling.

My ankles gave way.

Florence grabbed my hand. "Stand up straight. Don't let your ankle go soft."

"I know."

"Come on, you're strong."

I straightened my ankles.

"That's it."

I straightened even further, pushing forward. The sound of blades clacked against the ice.

After a few minutes, she released my hand.

Scooting around, I started to feel pretty good.

Florence laughed. "You skate like my grandma."

"Do not." She was lucky I couldn't catch up to her.

Half hour later, I was gliding right along. "I'm a natural," I told her.

"Naturally slow." She stuck her tongue out.

"Take that back." I headed toward her.

"Make me." She skated backward, laughing. "You'll have to catch me first."

In the house afterward, their momma served us hot cocoa and cookies.

"Do you like hot cocoa?" James asked.

"Yeah. Do you?"

"I love it," Florence cut in, sitting down next to me. "What did you think about skating?"

It was my turn to smile. "I love it."

***

After supper, we donned our snowsuits, hats, and mittens and made our way back outside. All but John who had to go to bed.

A light lit the front yard, and we worked on a snow fort in the growing darkness.

At last, Florence spoke, "I had a dream we were married."

"To each other?" I nearly shouted.

She laughed. "Of course to each other, dummy."

"I don't want to marry you. Gross."

"Let's pretend the snow fort is our house." She climbed over the wall. "James and Andrew can be our children."

James pouted. "You aways want to pway house."

"I'm with James." I tugged the sides of my stocking hat down.

She shrugged. "Good guys against bad guys then."

Andrew began picking up sticks. "I don't want to be on a team by myself."

"You won't be." Florence produced handkerchiefs, blue with white paisley for us and red and white for them. "Norman and James against me and you."

"We're good guys, of course," she added.

"What makes us bad?" Andrew asked.

"You robbed a train." Florence tied her bandana Karate Kid-style.

"I have a train at my house," I said, pushing myself up on an oak tree. "My mother bought it for me for Christmas."

"You shouldn't climb that," she said. "It rained last night. The branches are slippery."

"I can." The ice was thick and the bark was nonexistent. *I had a dream we were married,* her words kindled fire inside me, propelling me up. My hand slipped and I fell on the hard, flat, merciless driveway.

"Are you okay?" Andrew asked anxiously.

James stood over me, "Did you get an owie?"

"I think I broke my arm." I groaned, flipping on my back.

Florence crouched down and peered at my forearm. "We better bring him inside."

Making our way toward the house, the three of them hovered around me like it was my leg that was hurt rather than my arm.

Florence cried the entire way.

I didn't get it. I was the one who fell out of the tree.

Girls. Who could figure them out?

5
February 22, 1984

Florence

David "the boy in the bubble," died from Burkitt's lymphoma at 12 years old. At eight, I was convinced I was going to die from swallowing bubble gum.

It was eighteen below, with a wind chill of forty below, Norman had broken his arm by falling from the tree, and we had to play inside.

Train tracks were set up in Norman's room, from the entrance to the spare room down the hall.

"Momma said we can have gum." I tore a square of Hubba Bubba from the wrapper.

Norman pulled out a package from his pocket. On the front was a baseball player with an enormous cheek.

"You have Rigleages Chew?" I asked.

"It's Big League Chew." He pinched a wad of shredded bubble gum and handed it to me.

I tucked it into my cheek.

"What did you do with the piece you were chewing?" he asked.

"I swallowed it."

His eyes widened in horror. "You swallowed gum?"

"Yeah. So?"

"So? Holy moly, Florence. Did you know it takes seven years for your stomach to digest a piece of gum?"

"Nah uh. Who told you that?"

"My mother."

"Maybe she said that to keep you from chewing it." I did a mental count of the pieces of gum I ate yesterday. And at Christmas. Then there was Halloween, and…

"I want to pway caws." James waltzed in without knocking.

"In a bit," I told him. "What makes it stay in your stomach so long? Preservatives?"

"Butyl rubber, which is used to make inner tubes."

Butyl rubber? "Nuh uh."

"Ya huh. Each manufacturer has their own recipe with the aim of getting the perfect degree of elasticity." His chin came up. "Mother says if you swallow too much of it, you'll never poop again."

"Poopy." James laughed.

"Poop." Andrew built the corners up on his log cabin.

"It was the first time anyway," I lied, reaching over to set a log on Andrew's cabin.

Enraged, James plowed through the village.

We fell back.

"What are you doing?" I cried.

"James, you jerk," Norman grabbed him, folding him beneath his arm. Andrew piled on them, John climbing on the top.

In the background, John Anderson was "Swingin'", *"Now Charlotte she's the darlin', she's the apple of my eye… I just can't believe it started on her front porch in this swang."*

And I sat trying to figure out how long I had to live.

6
March 7, 1984

Norman

The United States attacked San Juan del Sur in Nicaragua and Mother attacked me in our kitchen with only a look.

"I have homework." I kicked my shoes off at the entryway.

"Line your shoes up, please," Mother said.

"I'm starved."

"Shall we have spaghetti for supper?"

"What's in the Crock-Pot?" I searched the cupboards for a snack.

"Knoephla for the Solbergs. Dad wants to stop by there after Mass."

"I'll wait for supper then. You want me to set the table?"

Her eyes narrowed. "Why?"

"Isn't it almost suppertime?"

"Yes."

Not waiting for her to respond, I reached in the cupboard for a stack of plates.

"How was school?"

"Alright." I made sure to set the forks on the left, knives on the right and spoons next to the knives.

"You like going over to the Solbergs?"

"It's alright," I attempted to sound casual.

Dad arrived home from work early, whistling.

"Looks like Norman isn't the only one looking forward to getting away from me," Mother said with her back to him.

"You can come too." He sat down on the entryway bench and removed his boots. "It's time to take the bees out of the shed. I told Bruce we'd help."

"Bees are dangerous." Mother took a sip from her wine glass.

"A wives tale," Dad said, washing his hands.

"Inga showed them to me once and they attacked me."

Wiping his hands on a dishtowel, Dad caught my eyes.

We sat across from each other.

Soon, the scent of oregano filled the kitchen.

My mouth watered as Mother piled steaming noodles high on plates, topping them with meatballs in sauce.

Dad said grace.

I dug into my spaghetti, and was three bites in when I realized my mother was watching me.

Dad noticed it too. "Aren't you hungry, Elizabeth?"

She picked up her fork, then set it back down. "I don't mean to criticize, Norman, but if you twist the noodles on the spoon, you won't end up with so much on your face."

My face went hot.

"I don't use a spoon." Dad took a drink of water.

"I know you don't," she pinned him with a look.

Dad didn't respond.

I did my best to eat without the noodles slapping my face with their sauce.

"Norman." Mother's eyes were on me.

"It's impossible not to make a mess."

"It's not impossible. It just means you need to take your time."

Dad glanced at the clock, tossed a napkin on his half-eaten plate of spaghetti, and stood.

"Where are you going?" Mother asked.

"Mass." He arched his brow at her. "Unless you want to be late, we best be going."

Mother shot out of her chair. "Oh my goodness, I didn't realize the time."

Thank God for Mass.

7

Florence

In the basement, Dad finished converting two guest rooms into one big playroom. When I arrived home from school, Momma took my hand. "I want to give you something."

On the end table next to the couch sat her bedroom lamp. The lamp was gold molded into a sphinx.

The cream shade was missing. "Where's the shade?"

She held up one with the plastic still on it.

"Holly Hobbie," I cried, throwing my arms around her neck. "Thank you, Momma."

"Every night I shut it off, I think of my dad."

"Watching over you?"

"No, just memories. The God of the Earth watches over us."

"Jesus?"

"Yes."

The Millers arrived as we were finishing supper.

"Case." Dad stood and strolled over and shook Sheriff Casey's hand. "Can I get you something to drink?"

"I've got the tea on," Momma called from the kitchen. Her hair was pulled back with a black bandana and she wore a gold sweater with a gold belt.

"Perfect," Sheriff Casey said, his face reddened. "Suppose to be a beautiful day tomorrow."

"Mid-fifties all week." Dad shook Norman's hand. "I'm going to be taking the bees out of the shed."

"Can I help?" Norman asked.

"You have school," his mother answered.

"After school. Please?"

Sheriff Casey glanced at Dad. "What do you think, Bruce?"

"Sure. He can stick close to Florence. No one is better than her when it comes to bees."

Norman's mother handed Momma a Crock-Pot. She wore a red angora sweater with half sleeves and a shiner on her forehead.

"What happened?" I asked, studying the dark spot.

Her eyes narrowed. "What do you mean?"

"You have a bruise," I pointed out. "Did you hit your forehead?"

Her chin came up. "I went to Mass."

"What's Mass?"

"Florence," Momma gasped.

I snapped my mouth shut. It was rare for her to shout. When she did, I knew I'd done something wrong.

The next day after school, I asked Norman about it in the back seat of the truck on the way to the bee shed.

"It's ash," he said. "*'For you are dust and to dust you shall return.'* It's from the book of Genesis in the Bible."

Norman went to St. John's Academy in Jamestown. We were Methodist and went to school in Spiritwood.

"My dad said Catholics are devoted to Mary," I said, and was reminded there was no way Dad would ever let me marry a Catholic. "Is it true you make shrines of her?"

"No."

"She was just a woman, you know," I said, my breaths emerging from my lips in icy puffs. "Mary was special because she was chosen to have Jesus, but no more better than me or you."

"Better," he corrected. "Father Paul talks about Jesus."

"Well, I guess that's good, but…oh. I forgot to tell you," I nudged his arm. "Even though you can't digest gum, that doesn't mean it stays in your gut for seven years."

"What?"

"It doesn't wind itself around your heart either."

He frowned. "I never said it did."

I searched his eyes. "You swallowed some too didn't you?"

He nodded. "Once."

"I don't chew it anymore. It's sort of a bad habit."

"Yeah."

"Swallowing lots of gum isn't good, but if you have eaten an occasional piece, you won't die. If it's small enough, it should make it through your stomach."

"Okay, Florence," Norman mumbled.

A tawny eagle touched down in the distance. A black vulture lifted off its carrion.

"I bet that's the one I saw yesterday." I pointed as it soared, foraging for carrion. The eagle hopped, squawked, and took to flight.

Dad and Sheriff Casey began pulling boxes from the truck bed and placed them on ready pallets.

"The bottom box is the nest," I told Norman. "That's where the queen and nurse bees are. The queen lays the eggs, and the nurse bees feed them the jelly."

Dad put screens on the top of the boxes.

"Those are to keep the queen in the bottom box," I said. "If you let her, she'll lay eggs in all the boxes. Sanitary bees clean up the dead bees. Drone bees are for mating. Then the drones are gone.

"The bees begin as larvae, and after three days they look like a crescent."

Norman's gaze was glued to the bee boxes. "Don Cook got the World Record in 1982 for a bee beard. He taped the queen to his neck and they didn't sting him. There were twenty-one thousand."

I scowled. "The queen is fragile. I bet she didn't get to return to her colony."

"I never thought of that." Norman worked the smoker.

"Did you know nurse bees regulate how big or small the bees get?"

"Cool."

"What do you think about bees?"

"I love them," he said, focused on the task at hand.

"Me too."

8
May 8, 1984

Florence

The Soviet Union announced it would not participate in the Los Angeles Summer Olympics in retaliation for the American boycott of the 1980 Moscow Olympics.

In our backyard, Norman told us his mother didn't allow him to eat hot dogs at our cookout.

Norman's dad dropped him off at noon on his way to work. Sheriff Casey stopped to talk to Momma who greeted him with a smile. After placing his hat back on his head, he left with a last wave at Norman.

The four of us rushed Norman.

"I didn't know if your mother would let you come," I said. "Let's listen to records in the living room until it's time to eat." I led the way to the sunlit room, crossed over, and flipped over the record.

After I set the needle, the music began to play. *"Theeere'll be bread in the city tomorrow…"*

Norman flopped down on the couch. "I never heard this before. Is this country?"

"It's Andrew Culverwell." I handed him the record sleeve.

"It's Flowie's favowite." James plopped down next to him.

"Me too." John crawled up on the other side of him. Reaching up, he took hold of Norman's ear and held it.

Norman flicked me a glance.

"That's John's new thing. He likes cuddles and ears," I said. "Right, John?"

"Ears," John echoed.

Norman frowned. "Wait. Why will they be dead if they don't believe about the bread?"

"It's a Bible stowy," James said.

Dad appeared in the living room archway, scooped John up, and threw him over his shoulder. "Burgers are ready."

"Me next." James was off the couch, jumping up and down.

Dad set John down and reached for James, swinging him around. He glanced at Norman. "Hey bud, you got the Frisbee?"

"Check." Norman held it up.

Momma packed two bags of marshmallows, two boxes of graham crackers, and a jumbo package of Hershey's chocolate bars in the Igloo. There were liters of Pepsi and sandwich cookies, both vanilla and chocolate.

Not that we needed cookies when we had s'mores.

After throwing the Frisbee back and forth, we gathered sticks while my brothers grilled Norman about the hot dog rule.

"How come you aren't allowed to eat hot dogs?" Andrew asked.

"Thew my favowite," James added.

"Hot dogs," John said.

"I like them fine," Norman peeled bark off a stick. "My cousin Mark choked on a hot dog and died."

Another thing that could kill you and no one warned you about, like gum.

"I don't want to die," Andrew said.

James said, "Hot dogs won't kill me."

"It'll be fine if you don't tell." I reached for the package of marshmallows. "One time last summer, Momma told me I couldn't go to the gas station when I was at my friend's house. We went anyway and I didn't tell her. She never found out." I left out the part where guilt had eaten away at me until I threw up.

We stabbed marshmallows with our sticks.

Momma and Dad stood close, kissing.

The rest of us kept our distance.

"Okay, I'll hand out the ingredients for s'mores." I dug into the cooler.

"Me first," James held out his hand.

"Say please."

"Please."

I handed him the items.

When it was Norman's turn, he held out his hand.

"Say please," I told him.

"Hand it over."

I held it out of reach. Being slightly taller, I had the advantage. At once, he grabbed my arms and before I knew what was happening, he had me pinned on the ground.

"Let. Me. Up," I ordered.

"Not until you say I'm the best person in the world."

"I'm the best person in the world."

Then he hocked up a wad of phlegm above me.

"No," I shouted, twisting my head to the side. "Mom! Dad! Make him stop." I shook my head back and forth while my brothers cheered him on.

The wad of spit hung in midair over my face.

"Okay okay! Norman is the best person in the world."

He sucked the wad of spit back up, pushed away and stood, grinning triumphantly.

I scrambled to my feet, my eyes flashing fire. "I hate you."

He glared. "You're a hothead."

"Say you're sorry," Andrew ordered.

Norman's eyes dropped. "Sorry, Florence."

Andrew turned to me. "Now you say sorry, Florence."

"I've nothing to be sorry for." I crossed my arms and stood my ground.

"Don't you want to set a good example for James and John?" Andrew's voice was urgent.

"Fine. Sorry."

Norman held out his hand. "Truce?"

I shook it. "Truce."

9
June 8, 1984

Florence

"Ghostbusters," American supernatural comedy film, directed and produced by Ivan Reitman, starring Bill Murray, Dan Aykroyd, Harold Ramis, and Ernie Hudson was released.

Thunder rumbled in the distance, dark clouds rolled over our house, and Momma called us to come inside.

The patter of raindrops on the roof meant we wouldn't be going back outside today.

"Let's play hide and seek," John said.

I scowled. "I don't want to play hide and seek. I always have to be it."

"That's because you don't come up with good hiding places," Andrew said.

"I've got a new game we can play," said Norman.

We moved in closer with excitement.

"It's called Sardines."

"How does it go?" asked James.

"The person who is it hides and everyone else has to find them."

I rolled my eyes. "Reverse hide and seek."

"Sort of. Only when you find them, instead of calling them out, you hide with them."

Anticipation crept through the group.

"But we'll get squished," I said.

Norman shrugged. "Whoever is it will just have to find a good hiding place. The last person to find the group is it the next time."

"Who's it?" Andrew asked.

"Not me," I said. "I hate having to find a place to hide."

"We'll play hot potato." Norman held a fist out.

The rest of us made fists.

"One potato, two potato, three potato four…"

After a few rounds, John was it.

"Ah," James growled. "He's too little. He'll give himself away."

"I'll be it first." Norman held up his hand. "You guys cover your eyes, and count to fifty."

"Okay."

Norman started to leave. "Oh, and when you come looking for me, split up. That way it'll last longer."

We covered our eyes. "One, two, three…." I heard him leave and we counted on.

At fifty, I said, "Okay, split up."

"We know," James cut in. "Norman told us."

We scattered.

I headed upstairs, tiptoeing through the hallway to the bathroom. I opened the linen closet and found Norman curled up on the floor next to a pile of towels. "Gotcha."

"Shhh." He held his finger to his lips. "Get in here and be quiet."

I crouched, slipped over next to him and sat down. "Now what?"

"Now we be quiet."

Long minutes followed where the only sound between us was our own harsh breaths. Sitting in close proximity was a sort of conspiratorial fun.

I asked, "Is your mother going to be mad about you being here during a storm?"

"Shhh."

"Sorry."

He shifted next to me. "Yeah, she'll be mad."

"Doesn't she like us?"

"She likes you fine."

"Then how come…"

"She just gets a little mad sometimes," Norman's voice dipped to a whisper.

At the sound of footsteps, we stilled. I held my breath. We exchanged glances.

The door opened and Andrew stood there. "Found you."

Behind him were James and John.

Norman sighed. "I guess this game wasn't intended for kids under six."

I smiled. "It was fun. I'll be it this time."

"Okay."

The four of them closed their eyes. "One, two…"

Dashing downstairs, my heart thumped hard in my ears. I had the perfect hiding place.

10
July 10, 1984

Norman

Prolific studio drummer Jim Gordon was convicted of murdering his mother and sentenced 16 years to life in prison.

My own mother sat in front of the TV. "Norman, can you bring me my pills?" she laid a hand across her forehead.

"Sure." I grabbed her pill box. "What do you want to wash it down with?"

"What do we have to drink?"

I opened the fridge. "Milk, orange juice, water…"

"What about Black Laslo?"

Diet Coke. I dove back in. "Nope."

"I don't mean to criticize, but you didn't wrap the liner around the rim of the garbage can after you took the garbage out. It keeps slipping off."

"I'll fix it." I strolled over, wrapping the bag around the top. It was way too small and I struggled, spilling some of the garbage in the process.

She came over, sighing loudly. "I'll do it."

"I got this," I said, working on the corner.

She swiped at my hands, pushing me aside. "I said I'd do it."

Dad walked in the door.

Mother quickly backed away.

"Hi Dad," I smiled to clear the air. "How was work?"

"Hot." Dad crossed over to the sink, flipping on the faucet, his gaze shifted from me to Mother. "How are things here?"

"Will you be a dear and run out and get Diet Coke?" Mother asked. "I would go, but I have such a headache."

She always called it by the right term with Dad. Black Laslo was a term only known between the two of us.

"Did you take something for it?" He scrubbed his hands beneath the water.

"I'm just tired," she sighed. "I'm sorry I'm such a bother."

"You're not bothering me." He flipped off the faucet, and reached for the hand towel.

Mother reached for the clicker. "You didn't even say anything about how I look."

I slowly backed toward the door.

He glanced over her. "Oh yeah. Did you get a new shirt?"

She scowled. "No. I did my hair different."

"Oh yes," he said, "Very nice."

"You don't care," I heard her say when I reached my room. "You never cared."

I shut the door. Their voices carried.

"That's not true."

"You work all the time. I'll change if it'll mean you're around more."

"You know I think you're perfect the way you are."

I flipped the tape over in my stereo and pressed play.

"I know I'm not as pretty as…"

"I can't fight this feeling any longer…" REO Speedwagon drowned out whatever else she had to say.

***

Florence

Dad and Momma were gathering honey and I was watching my brothers.

Heat radiating from the ground, humidity crept into our pores, sucking energy and life.

"I'm hot," Andrew said on the other end of the teeter-totter.

Chessy, the shed Siamese momma cat, rolled over, rubbing herself in the grass.

Our green Ford pickup drove into the yard.

Dad and Momma were home. Norman was with them.

"Hi Norman," we called, got off the teeter-totters, and ran over to him.

"Here Chessy," Momma said, stroking her head. "Good kitty."

"Did you pick us up a treat?" I held my hand against my forehead, shielding my eyes from the sun.

"Yes," Dad's eyes twinkled. "Come see."

We went over to the truck bed where Dad took the tailgate down. I searched for toys, a wagon or a doll…a doll would probably be in the cab.

"What do you think?" Dad asked proudly.

"About what?" I blinked.

"The bee suits." He fist-bumped Andrew's shoulder. "There's one that should fit you perfectly."

Andrew ran off, stopping when he saw a stick. He picked it up and sliced it through the air.

Norman's eyes were on the protective equipment.

"What do you think, Norman?" Dad asked.

"Can we go gather honey now? I'll run the smoker."

Momma's forehead crinkled. "Bruce, maybe we should check with his mother."

Dad nodded, running a hand down the back of his neck. "I'll check with Case." He arched a brow. "Next time?"

Norman smiled. "Yes sir."

After lunch I laid on the kitchen floor in front of the box fan, groaning from the heat.

"What are you doing, Florrie?" Momma's melodious laughter echoed through the fan.

I laid my arm over my forehead. "I'm so hot, I'm going to die."

"Be sure to say hi to Jesus for me."

I bolted to a sitting position. "Can we run through the sprinklers?"

Momma nodded. "I'm going to take lunch out to Daddy. I should be back in an hour."

Norman shrugged. "I'm not too hot."

"Don't you like running through the sprinkler?" Andrew asked.

"I've never done it."

My eyes widened. "You've never run through a sprinkler. What planet do you live on?"

"Earth."

The boys followed me to the side of the house where the hose was laying on the ground.

"We have to hook up the nozzle to the hydrant." I picked up the garden hose and screwed it on the faucet.

"I want to play Red Rover," Andrew said.

"Alright," I nodded, dragging the sprinkler system to the middle of the yard. "You guys stand on that side and I'll stand on this side. We'll take turns running through."

After five minutes, we were cooled off, and Andrew said, "Now Red Rover."

Andrew stood on the other side of the sprinkler. "Red Rover Red Rover send Florence right over."

I made a mad dash through the spray.

Norman ran from the other side. We collided in the middle, our heads smashed. He stumbled back and fell to the ground. Blood gushed from his brow.

"Are you okay?" I asked, getting drenched beneath the spray, I bent next to him.

"I think so." He held his hand to his head, and glanced at it. When he saw the blood, he turned white. "I'm bleeding."

"Yes," I said, scared. His mother wasn't going to like this.

No, she wouldn't like it one bit.

11
August 11, 1984

Florence

During a radio voice test, U.S. President Reagan joked he "Signed legislation that would outlaw Russia forever. We begin bombing in five minutes."

We'd just returned from an auction sale in Galesburg, when Andrew said, "James told Norman you like him."

My face flushed hot, and the earth around me spun. I whirled around and glared at James. "You said what?"

James took a quick step back. "I…he…you."

"He told Norman you like him like him," Andrew said, making kissing noises.

Humiliation swept over me. I never wanted to lay eyes on Norman Miller again. "I'm going to my room. You guys have fun without me."

Ten minutes later, James was banging on my door. "Come on, Flowie. We want to go wide in the boat."

"Then go."

There was a scuffle outside my door.

Then Norman's voice, "Please come out, Florence. Andrew said you guys had a new boat. Please?"

Had he forgotten? What had my brothers actually said? Maybe he wouldn't be any different. Yeah, I would just pretend I knew nothing about it.

I opened the door and passed by them without a word.

"Yay," James said, racing after me.

We arrived at the slough. Norman's eyes lit with the brightness of the sun when he spotted the canoe.

We ran over to it.

"This is so cool," he exclaimed. "Where did you get it?"

"Dad got it at an auction sale in Galesburg," I said, snatching the life jackets off the bottom.

"Can we go out in it?" Norman crouched down next to the boat.

"Do you think your mother will care?" I asked, eyeing the scar still visible across his forehead. The stitches he'd received running into me slashed right through his dark blonde eyebrow.

"We'll be careful," he said.

"Okay." I buckled life jackets around my brothers and got in the back. "Norman you get to be up front since you're the oldest."

"We're the same age." Norman motioned between us.

"You were born in the morning. I wasn't born until five o'clock. Momma told me." I pushed us off.

Norman paddled forward.

Once we were off the bank, I crawled inside.

Gnats hovered in circles above our heads. An occasional dragonfly touched down on the surface of the murky water.

"Okay, we're married," I motioned between me and Norman. "And Andrew, James, and John are our kids."

"We're pirates," Norman said, passing back handkerchiefs. "Florence, as deck maid, you can put these on them."

"Ugh," I said, turning John around to tie the bandana.

"That's 'arr'." Norman reached for the paddle. "Now first mate Andrew, you get to row."

"Okay, second mate Norman."

"It's Captain Norman." Norman thrust his chest out.

Andrew laughed. "Arr, Captain Norman."

"Arr, Captain Norman and Sir Andrew," James and John shouted.

Leaning forward to tie the bandana around James' head, I began counting the minutes until it was time to go in.

"What's the mission?" Andrew asked.

"Well, in Treasure Island, they sailed for pirate's gold," Norman said.

James grabbed a cattail as we passed a patch of reeds. "I got the tweasure." He tore it apart, the seeds floating away in the wind.

"Or how about this," I pulled out my Raggedy Ann lunch pail and popped it open. "Candy bars for everyone."

"Heath!" James exclaimed.

I handed John the bag of peanut M&M's and passed the Mr. Goodbar to Andrew.

"I only like Almond Joy," Norman said, glancing away.

"I know." I passed it forward and I took the Reese's.

"Florence you're the best," Andrew said through a mouthful of chocolate. "Isn't she, Norman?"

He ripped open the candy bar. "Yeah she is."

12
September 12, 1984

Norman

American country singer Barbara Mandrell was badly injured in a car accident, and Florence's dad surprised her Momma for her birthday with a 1981 black cherry Pontiac Trans Am Firebird.

"You got Momma Kit!" James shouted.

"Kit," John said.

"Did you buy it from David Hasselhoff?" Florence asked.

Mr. Solberg set his hands on his hips. "The 1981 Pontiac Trans Am is powered by a 4.9 liter V 8 engine and is backed up by automatic transmission."

It was the prettiest thing I'd ever seen.

I hung on every word as he continued, "Power steering, power disc brakes, power locks, power windows, remote mirror, tilt steering wheel, cruise control, factory tachometer, gauges, clock, factory AM/FM cassette radio, power trunk release…"

"Can we go fow a wide?" James cut in.

"Where was it made?" I asked.

He smiled. "The good old US of A. Andrew, you want to drive?"

"He's too little," Florence gasped.

He glanced over at me. "Norman? How about it? You want your first drive to be in this beauty?"

My heart gave a swift hard kick in my chest. "You aren't serious."

"Of course I am," he glanced over at Inga. "How about it, honey? You mind if Norman takes it for a spin?"

She took John's hand and drew him back. "No. Have fun."

Shaking from head to toe, I got in the sports car behind the wheel.

"You want to go top speed?" Mr. Solberg asked.

"No," I nearly shouted.

"I'm joking, son." He pushed my shoulder. "Top speed is 116 miles per hour. Acceleration....a quarter mile drag time."

"I see," I said, but I didn't. All my attention was focused on the driveway.

"Gets seventeen miles to the gallon on the open road..."

Hopefully there wouldn't be a test at the end.

13
October 26, 1984

Florence

The Terminator directed by James Cameron, starring Arnold Schwarzenegger and Linda Hamilton was released in the U.S.

Friday after school, beneath a canopy of leaves the Millers' gray Chevy arrived in our driveway as we were raking the yard. I heard the car door shut, and Sheriff Casey was talking to Momma.

Norman made his way over. "Hi guys."

"Hi, Nowman," James ran over to him. "Wew raking leaves so we can jump in them."

"There's an extra rake in the shed," I said.

"I'll get it," Andrew shouted and took off on a run.

The air was cool and crisp as we raked the yard together. Dark clouds moved overhead.

"Is your dad home?" Norman asked.

"He's working in the bee shed to get it ready for winter," I told him.

"Oh." Norman sniffed, wiping his nose on his sleeve. "Is your momma's car in the garage?"

The car was all he talked about.

The leaf pile was quite large. "Okay everyone step back. Evel Knievel wants to make a run for it," I glanced at James.

"I get to go first?" James blinked. "Geronimoooo," he hollered, and came barreling through, kicking leaves to both sides as he plowed into the pile.

"That's not how you do it." Andrew raked it back, and then handed me the rake. "Watch me," he leapt into the middle. I wiggled my way to the bottom. Even Norman piled in.

"We better finish cleaning up," I said, moving out from the pile.

"Then we can climb trees." Norman raked around me.

"There's a .22 rifle in the shed," Andrew said. "We can shoot rats."

"Not around John," I said.

A first snowflake whispered from the rolling clouds through the cottonwoods. And another.

"It's snowing!" James shouted.

"Let's have a snowball fight," I said.

"We can belly-slam our sled downhill," Andrew chimed in.

Then, as quickly as it came, the snow stopped, a ray of sunshine peeking through the clouds.

Disappointed, we returned our rakes to the toolshed.

At the door, I paused at the sound of meowing coming from inside.

"Kitties." John ran toward the sound.

We rushed over to the corner and discovered a nest made from grease rags. Three white kittens made their way toward us.

"They look part Siamese," I said, "These must be Chessy's."

John reached for the closest. "Kitty."

After playing with them, I returned mine to the nest.

Norman set his alongside mine.

John clutched the one in his hands. "Mine."

"It's not yours, John," I said. "We have to leave him here or his momma will be looking for him."

John held the kitten closer. "Kitty."

"Alright. You can show him to Momma," I nodded. "Then we'll bring him back.

At the house, Momma had Russian tea ready for us, hot chocolate for Norman.

"Oh, John. What do you have?" she asked.

John held up the kitten. "Kitty. I keep him."

"What's his name?"

"Sam." John stroked the kitten's head.

Momma smiled. "He's pretty. Shall we bring him to the living room? We can sit together and pet him before he needs to go home."

On the living room couch, John held Momma's ear, Momma held the kitten, and we all took turns petting Sam.

Afterward, we returned to the kitchen and our drinks.

"Want to go to the playroom?" I asked.

John said, "I bring Sam."

"You have to ask Momma." I got up from the table.

"Alright, if you're careful," Momma glanced at me. "Florence, will you be sure Sam is returned home when you're done?"

"Yes, I will." I hurried to the playroom and turned on the light.

We worked on puzzles, that is, I worked on a puzzle while Norman, Andrew, and James built a clipper ship with Legos and a Lincoln Log cabin.

John played on the floor with Sam.

"Norman, do you want to take the car for a drive?" Dad called from the top of the stairs.

"Sure." Norman abandoned the Legos and the rest of us, taking the sunshine with him.

I returned my focus to the puzzle.

Andrew and James resumed the wall they had been building.

John held Sam tightly to keep him from escaping.

It wasn't the same without Norman.

I stood. "Let's take Sam back to his momma."

The boys dropped what they were doing.

John stood with the kitten.

Together, we returned the kitten to the shed.

14
November 18, 1984

Florence

The Soviet Union helped deliver American wheat during the Ethiopian famine. At home, it began with a stomachache and spread like wildfire.

Gray skies loomed over a flat, frozen earth.

On the school bus ride home, Andrew sat quietly next to me, staring out the window.

Michael Sharp sang Michael Jackson's hit "Thriller" from the back seat, *"There ain't no second chance against the thing…"*

"Norman Miller has the chickenpox," Momma was telling Dad when we walked into the house.

"Tell them to send him over," Dad said, "Florence and the boys haven't had them yet."

I heard Momma speaking on the phone in the kitchen to Norman's mother in hushed tones. "No, we just think it would be best for them all to get it while they're little. Of course not. Why would we blame you if they get sick? Elizabeth, we want our kids to get them."

Two hours later, Norman arrived while we were on beanbags watching *Seven Brides for Seven Brothers* in the playroom.

"I made cookies," I opened the cupboard above the long table against the wall where I'd stashed them yesterday. "Ginger, your favorite."

"I'm not hungry."

Norman never turned down food, especially cookies. His mother didn't let him eat them at home.

When Mrs. Miller arrived, she placed her hand on his forehead. Norman mumbled a response on his way out the door.

The next day, Norman was at our house again.

We were playing checkers in the playroom when Andrew tugged on my arm. "I don't feel good."

I laid a hand on his forehead like I saw Norman's mother do. "You feel a little warm. Sit here and I'll cover you up." I pulled a beanbag over to him. "*Savanah Smiles* and a bowl of ice cream with chocolate syrup should fix you right up."

Subdued, Norman scratched his chickenpox.

"Here," I grabbed the calamine lotion from the counter his mother left. "We'll put some on for you."

"I'm so itchy."

"Stop that," I ordered, twisting the top off the bottle. "You'll get scars."

"Girls are too fussy." James ran Matchbox cars down racetracks.

"The fussiest," Norman said across from me.

"I'm a girl." I stuck out my tongue.

"You don't count." Norman jumped three of my checkers. "King me."

By the third day, a hot knife of sharp pain stabbed my stomach. When Norman arrived, I was doubled over in pain.

"Pillow fight," he announced, holding the couch pillow over his head. He sure didn't seem sick.

"This pillow has chickenpox," he whacked me on the side of the head.

"Quit it," I said.

Andrew ran and grabbed four pillows from the storeroom across the hall.

Everyone joined in.

On the beanbag, I drifted off as they made a ruckus around me, only to wake in a cold sweat.

"Want to watch a movie?" Norman dug through VHS tapes. "*Little House on the Prairie* is on. It's the one where Mary Ingalls lost her son in a fire and stopped talking."

"No." I mumbled from the beanbag. "I'm so itchy."

"*Seven Brides for Seven Brothers*? Your favorite."

"No."

"*Psycho II* is on."

"We aren't allowed to watch scary movies."

Norman shrugged. "So we won't tell. Unless you're scared."

"I'm not scared." I wrapped my shawl around me.

"The first one, *Psycho*, was an Alfred Hitchcock movie from 1960 with Anthony Perkins."

"So?"

"Bad guy's name is Norman."

"Not today."

Before long, it was quiet. Too quiet. I heard Norman and the boys in the corner, whispering. Before I could ask them what they were up to, Norman said, "Shhh, okay come on."

"What are you guys doing?" I asked, sitting up straight.

"Nothing," Norman said with a grin, and turned to Andrew. "Ready?"

Andrew nodded.

Norman cleared his throat. "Theeere'll be bread in the city tomorrow..."

"...In the city tomorrow there'll be bread," Andrew sang in turn.

"If you say you don't believe..."

"Then the bread you won't receive."

They were wearing paisley bandanas Karate Kid-style, and proceeded to sing the entire song.

"This is the time..." Norman leaned toward Andrew.

"To go back and find..." Andrew leaned in.

"The friends who were hungry..." They sang in unison.

Shoulder to shoulder, they serenaded without skipping a beat. "...If you say you don't believe then the bread you won't receive..."

James popped behind the two of them, wearing my Barbie sunglasses. "But in the city tomowwow thew'll be bread."

"You'll be dead," John finished in G.I. Joe shades.

I was laughing so hard I forgot my stomach hurt.

Afterward, James and John sat next to me.

"My stomach hurts," James said.

"Tummy hurts," said John.

15

December 18, 1984
Spiritwood Lake
Spiritwood, North Dakota

Florence

My brain picked what to forget about that day. Memories at nine were wisps of a dream.

Momma's hair was like autumn sun.

But for what happened, I might not remember it at all.

***

Inside the lake house, plush dark orange carpeted the living area. The fireplace chimney was dark brown, disappearing through the tall ceiling. Large glass windows faced the lakeside.

Momma and Dad were sharing portions of *The Jamestown Sun,* drinking cups of coffee. Momma laughed at something he said, and Dad leaned over, kissing her mouth.

Dad took a family picture with his Polaroid camera.

I stood next to Momma with a dirty face and a short bob of red hair that matched hers. Alongside Dad were Andrew, James, and John, all dark hair and matching brown eyes.

Another photo was taken afterward by the sheriff.

The Ziggledorfs boarded quarter horses.

A favorite hobby was riding around the lake.

The winter moon shone a path over the frozen water.

We rode along the familiar trail behind the property wrapping around the lake.

Deep snow over knots of prairie grass, through the trees, past the fence to the lake house, I rode with Dad on a new gelding named Cinnamon.

Momma was on her usual ride, a mare called Clementine.

Then Clementine and Momma were no longer walking alongside us.

Later, I couldn't recall if it was warm or cold. Momma washed the car earlier that morning, but I couldn't recall the color of her coat.

The grin on my dad's face as he kissed her at the front door was etched in my memory.

The slam of the door when they returned still rang in my ears, but not what Dad said. I remembered like yesterday what I said, *No, Daddy. Maybe she's not dead,* and that he started to cry.

At the funeral home, Momma in the casket, appeared to be sleeping.

Maybe she's not dead.

16
Christmas Eve 1984

Norman

A cold wind blew from the north across the prairie.

At her momma's funeral, Florence wore a green velvet dress and black patent leather shoes. Her red hair, two smooth braids. I'd never seen her in a dress or braided hair, her eyes puffy from crying.

The ride to the Solberg farm afterward was a somber affair where I didn't dare ask questions and Mother fired them at Dad in a loud whisper, "Did Florence see it happen?"

"I'm not sure."

"She fell and hit her head on a rock?"

"Yes."

"I heard Ziggledorfs had a new quarter horse, but I had no idea it was so spirited."

"She rode Clementine. Bruce was on the new gelding."

Silence.

"How will Bruce manage with the kids?"

"Good question."

The first thing I noticed when we arrived at the Solberg house was the girls with pale hair and eyes of gray.

Ghosts or angels, I didn't like the look of them.

The second: Inga Solberg was in the kitchen brewing coffee.

My breath caught. I squeezed my eyes shut. When I opened them, she was still there.

The shocked look on Dad's face said I wasn't dreaming.

Mother appeared stunned.

Dad couldn't stop staring.

In a loose-looking button-down black shirt, Mr. Solberg made his way over to us. "Casey, this is Sophia Dunn, Inga's twin sister. Her daughters, Leah and Lana," he said. "They live in Kent, Washington."

Mother smiled. "I didn't know Inga had a twin."

"Hi Norman." Mr. Solberg forced a smile. I'd never seen him force anything. "Florence is in the living room. She'll be glad to see you."

I removed my boots, wondering what that meant.

"Florence hasn't spoken since it happened," her dad told mine.

"Poor dear," Mother murmured.

There was nothing poor about Florence.

Then I saw her at the table, mouth drawn in a grim line. Her green eyes, tearless.

I held my breath, waiting for her to start humming like Mary Ingalls on *Little House on the Prairie* when she lost her infant son in the fire.

Andrew, James and John were sitting at the table dressed in church clothes. With napkins on their laps, they had the table manners of the Queen of England.

Sophia Dunn served coffee.

Dad sipped his, eyes never wavering from her.

"Sophia and the girls are here until the end of January," Mr. Solberg said, running a hand down the back of his neck. "They're staying in the lake house."

Sophia dabbed tearless eyes with a handkerchief.

The towheaded girl in the blue dress looked bored.

Her twin sister in the red was looking at her as though waiting for her next command.

A shiver ran through me.

17
New Year's Day, 1985

Norman

It was Tuesday, the U.S. president was Ronald Reagan, the UK Prime Minister was Margaret Thatcher, Pope St. John Paul II was leading the Catholic Church, and no one was leading the Solberg boys.

We arrived at noon with taco dip, beanie weenies, chips, and soda pop.

Andrew and James were watching *Lucky Luke* on TV with their twin cousins, Leah and Lana.

John came over to me and held his arms up. I picked him up and he reached for my ear.

"Hi Norman." Mr. Solberg walked in, wearing a red sweater vest and a tired look. He smiled, a distant one that didn't reach his eyes. "Florence will be glad to see you."

Florence sat at the dining room table. Her face was pale. Her empty stare made me want to leave the room and not come back until her cheeks were ruddy and her eyes, sincere.

"Look Florence. Norman's here." Her dad nudged her with his elbow.

"She's been like that since our momma's funeral," Andrew said.

"How are you holding up?" Dad asked Mr. Solberg.

His eyes were watery. "Florence hasn't spoken to anyone."

I sat down next to her, holding John who was holding my ear.

"I brought a snowsuit," I said. "Let's go make a snowman."

When she didn't answer, I looked over at her dad.

He nodded. "It'll be good for you, Florence. Norman, you can leave John here."

"You two coming?" I asked Andrew and James on our way outside.

"Nah," they said in unison, eyes glued to the TV.

I set John next to Andrew. John took hold of his ear.

***

In the backyard next to the cluster of trees, we worked on a snow family. That is, I built a man and wife while she sat on a boulder and watched. I put finishing touches on the wife, setting large pink buttons for her eyes.

"Should I put freckles on her?" I asked Florence.

She didn't answer.

"You better stop me." I dotted Mrs. Snowman's face with raisins.

Then she said, "Maybe she's not dead."

It was my turn to remain silent.

"She's in heaven," she spoke to the air. "People aren't dead in heaven."

Did she imagine her momma trying to claw her way out of the coffin? I couldn't let her think that.

"She died," I said confidently, placing the carrot nose in the center of Mr. Snowman's face. "My dad's the sheriff. He was there and said she was dead, so you..."

"No!" she screamed, flew at me, hitting my chest.

Shocked, I stumbled back and held my hands up, shielding my face. "Hey wait..."

"No! You're mean. You don't know. You're just a stupid boy."

"Florrie, you don't..."

"Maybe she's not dead!" She hit me again, sobbing hysterically. "I want my momma."

"Let's go find your dad." I took her hand, dragging her toward the house. "He'll be glad you're talking."

"I want my momma!" She screamed the entire distance.

Bruce Solberg met us at the door, my mother behind him.

Florence flung herself into her dad's arms. He picked her up, flicking me a glance.

"Norman, what did you do?" Mother asked sharply.

"I'm sorry. I shouldn't have said..." I stammered.

"Thank you." He rubbed his own tears with his free hand.

"Poor Florence," Mother said. "Poor, poor girl."

There's nothing poor about Florence Solberg, I reasoned stubbornly, even while the sound of her sobs echoed in my mind long after I went home.

18

Florence

The moon glistened off rippling water as I strolled along the lakeside path.

Momma walked next to me, silent as the twilight.

I turned to tell her I was glad she wasn't dead.

Hair white and wild, she turned to me, wrinkled, aged in her eighties, and smiled a wide, toothless grin.

I woke, a scream bursting from my lips, heart pounding. John was in his crib next to my bed, sleeping soundly.

I crawled out of bed and crept down the hallway and up the stairs to Momma's room.

In her room standing alongside the bed, I pulled back the covers to see if Momma really looked like an old woman.

"Florence?" Dad mumbled in the darkness.

"I had a bad dream." I sobbed. "Momma was old."

He lifted the corner of the blanket, and I scrambled beneath.

Tears rolled down my cheeks, sobs wracking my body.

"Momma's dead, Dad."

"Yes, sweetheart. Momma's dead."

"I don't want her to be dead."

He wrapped his arms around me. "Me, either."

The next morning, I was up as the sun was a soft pink line on the horizon. Aunt Sophia was at the table, sipping coffee.

Dad was paging through *The Jamestown Sun*.

"Good morning, Florence."

"Good morning."

"No more nightmares?" He looked up from the paper.

"Nope." I popped bread into the toaster.

Aunt Sophia's eyes welled with concern. "You had a bad dream."

"Yeah."

"She must have been sleepwalking," Dad said. "She came into my room thinking her momma was going to be an old woman."

Dad folded the paper. "I'd like to head to Fargo to see about a honey separator. Maybe pick up a few other things."

"Can I come?" I reached for a knife and the butter.

"Not this time," he said. "You got school."

"What are you going to do about James and John?" Sophia took a sip of coffee.

Dad stood. "I'll call Elizabeth Miller. See if I can drop them off on my way."

She pursed her lips. "I could come over for the day."

"Really?" Dad looked skeptical. "I hate to bother you."

"It's no bother," she said. "The girls will be working on schoolwork their teachers assigned. I can watch them until five. Then I was going to run into town myself."

"That would be great. Thanks, Sophia."

19
January 18, 1985

Florence

AIDS charity record "That's What Friends are For" hit Number 11.

Sophia came over right before supper with Leah and Lana.

"Florence, I have something for you." Sophia glanced at Leah, "Give those to Florence."

Leah handed me the pair of teal boots she'd been holding.

"I've always wanted Moon Boots." I pushed my foot inside the right one. They were as warm as they looked.

Sophia held up a Crock-Pot. "I brought chili and all the toppings. Saltine crackers too. Lana, put those on the counter."

Warmth burst through me. "I love chili."

She gave me a tender smile. "Your momma told me a while back. How are you doing, dear?"

My eyes welled with tears, spilling over.

"Oh you poor dear." She set the Crock-Pot on the counter and drew me into her arms. "Leah and Lana brought My Pretty Ponies. Why don't you three go play while I set the table."

I followed the twins into the living room.

"We don't want to play," Lana said. "We want to watch TV."

"Can I play with them by myself?" I asked.

"No," Leah said. "They're ours."

I retreated to the kitchen. "Sophia, they won't play with me. They won't let me play with their toys either."

"How would you like to help me with dinner?" she asked. "Or you can sit on that chair and watch me. Afterward, we'll take the boys and go over to the lake house."

"I'd like that."

The sun twinkled through the naked branches of cottonwoods. I walked into the lake house. Plush cream carpet replaced orange shag. The fireplace mantel was painted white. Light paneled wood cupboards instead of olive green ones.

"What happened here?" I asked, horrified.

"I did a little updating," Sophia said proudly.

"Does Dad know you did a little updating?"

She frowned. "You don't like it?"

"I thought you were going back to Seattle in a few days."

"I am," she pouted, her eyes narrowing. "You act like you want me to leave."

"No, I don't mean that. I just mean, Dad likes to be asked if you're going to do something this big. What about Uncle Mike? Does he know you're staying longer?"

"This conversation is over." She drew a breath. "I'll talk to your father."

At the supper table, she did just that. "I got a job at the clinic as a phlebotomist. The girls can finish the year here. I already called Roosevelt Elementary."

Supper was Sophia's chili, shredded cheese, sour cream, and tortilla chips. For dessert, cream puffs.

"What about Mike?" Dad took a bite of chili.

"That's over. It has been for a while. We've been separated for over a year."

"I thought you said he was on a business trip."

"Yeah, well you were grieving. I didn't think it was right to bring up my problems when you guys had so many." She sprinkled her chili with shredded cheese. "I can help out with the kids in the morning. That way Andrew and Florence can go back to school. You'd like that wouldn't you?"

"Of course."

"Don't say anything. Just think about it. Okay?"

20
January 21, 1985

Norman

Czech tennis star Ivan Lendl defeated Boris Becker of Germany to claim the season-ending Association of Tennis Professionals Masters Grand Prix title for a third time at Madison Square Garden, NYC.

At the Solberg lake house, the ice-skating party was scheduled for early afternoon.

Mother was in the front seat of our Chevy, whispering to Dad about the details on the way.

"It won't be the same without Inga there. I'm surprised Bruce is going through with it," Mother said.

"Sophia Dunn is putting it on."

"Poor Florence."

Dad sighed. "There's nothing poor about Florence. She might have a temper, but she's brave and tough as beef jerky."

"Yes. Perfect little Florence Solberg," Mother muttered.

"What's that?" Dad asked in a loud voice.

I was with Mother on this one. The Solberg farm hadn't been the same since their momma died.

"Stop at the pharmacy," Mother ordered. "My prescription is ready."

Dad stopped, tried the pharmacy door, and returned to the car.

"It's closed?" she asked.

"Yep."

"What will I do?"

"Have to wait until Monday."

When we arrived, made-from-scratch hot cocoa and Chex Mix were served. Bruce Solberg stood outside on the deck in front of the homemade ice cream maker, dumping ice and salt in the sides of the canister.

I did a double take at the sight of Florence's Aunt Sophia. The resemblance between the sisters was uncanny.

Mother rubbed her palms on her jeans, something she did when she was nervous.

There were a bunch of kids playing ping-pong in the playroom with Florence's cousins, Leah and Lana. Among the guests, Alice Wilson, Lily Winters, Marsha Nelson and Leo Nelson.

At the basement entrance, Florence and her brothers were grabbing ice skates.

"Hi guys." I dug in the bin for a pair.

"Hi Norman," Florence said.

The Solberg brothers said nothing.

We were making our way toward the shore before I had the nerve to ask, "What happened to your mother?"

She glanced over at me. "Didn't your dad tell you?"

I shrugged. "They said she fell off her horse and hit her head."

"I was riding with Dad and Momma was next to us. Then she wasn't. Clementine tripped and Momma flew out over her neck, hitting her head on a rock.

"I didn't see it happen," she continued. "But afterward I saw her eyes and I knew."

I didn't want her to stop talking, but had to know. I kept my eyes fixed on the shoreline. "Knew what?"

"That she was dead."

From the corner of my eye, I saw Bruce Solberg talking to Sophia, his eyes registering compassion. Suddenly, she rushed into his arms.

I turned back to Florence. Her eyes, bright and fierce, caught mine. Deep sorrow was etched in their green depths, and I sucked in a breath.

She'd seen it too.

The resemblance between the sisters affected both our fathers. Similarities ended at appearances. Inga Solberg was warm, friendly, inviting. Her sister was…

I considered the skating party, down to homemade apple cider and borrowed skates. Party guests like marionettes, the only thing real was Florence, Andrew, James, and John. The affair was counterfeit. It was missing something. Inga Solberg's touch.

Sophia Dunn was a copycat.

"I sometimes wonder whether you think you have been sent into the world for your own amusement." -Uncle Screwtape

C. S. Lewis, *Screwtape Letters*

21
February 23, 1985

Norman

Goaltender Patrick Roy made his National Hockey League debut for the Montreal Canadians, and Sophia Dunn and her daughters were living at the Solberg lake house.

Florence met me at the door. "Sophia made a salad with walnuts and raisins. Who puts walnuts and raisins in salad?"

"How long is she staying?" I removed my jacket.

"Dad said until school is out." She took my coat. "She applied for a job, but decided to take care of us until they go back to Seattle."

"She makes us clean," Andrew grumbled.

"All the time," James chimed in.

"There's a new rule," Florence said. "If the boys aren't picking up their stuff or haven't made their bed, they don't get dessert. I make dessert every day. Sophia loves baked goods."

"Sounds like my mother," I said. "I have to make my bed every day too."

"We can't go skating until after lunch. Sophia invited the new hockey coach over."

"Who's he coach for?"

"St. John's Academy."

"Norman, this is Ted Orn, the new hockey coach." Mother rushed over to me from the kitchen, sounding giddy.

Ted Orn was tall with broad shoulders, dark brown hair, a butterfly collar and corduroys. "Hello Norman. Do you play hockey?"

I glanced at my mother.

"Norman's in fourth grade."

"You can probably play next fall." He eyed me. "If you practice. Can you skate?"

"Yep."

Before dinner, Mother arranged chairs so I was sitting next to Coach Orn.

Florence sat across from me. "Sophia, can we clean after ice skating? Norman won't be able to stay all day."

"We'll see," she said, but by the look in her eyes, I could tell she didn't appreciate being asked permission in front of guests.

I knew my mother wouldn't.

To lighten the atmosphere, I turned to Coach Orn, and said, "Wayne Gretzky was the top scorer in the 1978 World Junior Ice Hockey Championships."

His brow lifted. "That's true. In June 1978, he signed with the Indianapolis Racers of the World Hockey association. He played for only a short time before being traded to the Oilers."

Excitement rippled through me. The Solbergs knew nothing about hockey. "When the Western Hockey Association folded, the Oilers joined the National Hockey League, Gretzky established many scoring records and led his team to four Stanley Cup championships."

I liked Coach Orn. He liked hockey and wanted me to play. By the stars in Mother's eyes, it was a real possibility.

"We're going skating," I said eagerly. "The Solbergs have extra skates. There might be a pair that fits you." I glanced over at Florence.

She nodded. "I think there is."

"One way to find out." Coach Orn stood, giving Mother an award-winning smile. "If you'll excuse me."

"Of course." Her cheeks flushed.

We grabbed ice skates, and made our way down to the shore.

I flicked a glance at Coach Orn. "At the Solberg farm, we ice skate at the slough, but here we get to ice skate on the lake as long as we stay near the shore and it's cold enough."

"Are you any good?" Florence asked him.

"Me?" he chuckled. "I've been known to hold my own."

We skated with the broom and had a mock hockey game. James and I and the coach played hard and fast. Andrew, Florence, and John backed off.

"You're too rough." Florence's eyes flashed fire.

Coach Orn smiled. "Maybe you should sit this next one out."

"We're going in," she announced, and all her brothers followed.

"Sorry if I got you in trouble with your little friends," he said after they were gone."

"You didn't." I wanted to know what Coach Orn thought of my skating, but didn't want to ask outright. "I'm not as good as you, but before last year I couldn't skate at all."

"You try hard."

Try hard? As in I was good or as in give it up?

I spent the rest of the day, and long into the evening thinking about what he said, wondering what he meant by it.

22
May 28, 1985

Florence

David Jacobsen was taken hostage in Beirut, Lebanon.

Sophia was in the kitchen when I woke up.

Most mornings, Sophia arrived long before anyone was awake, making coffee for Dad. Then she'd talk with him about the day. I didn't like the intimate atmosphere between them.

This morning, she was alone, talking on the phone. By the sound, I guessed it was nosy neighbor, Gloria Waverly.

"It's Bruce's money and land." She fiddled with a fridge magnet. "He can't raise those kids alone. He hired Ted Orn, the hockey coach for the summer. Me? I might have suggested it. Florence? She's only ten."

Nine.

"Besides, she's spoiled. Inga never made her do house chores. What? Oh, I don't know…Gloria? I have to go, I'll call you later." She hung up the phone.

Spoiled?

"Where's my dad?" I asked her.

"You are a bit old to be crawling in bed with Daddy," her tone was dark and cold.

Angry tears sprang to my eyes. "I had a bad dream."

"What would your mother think about you using silence and bad dreams to gain sympathy? Your father works hard providing for you and those boys, and how do you repay him? You manipulate him."

"I…I wasn't. I…" Fury boiled hot inside me. "How dare you judge me? You aren't my momma." I swiped away rebellious tears with the back of my hand.

Her eyes narrowed. "Stuff the tears. They don't work on me."

Before I could respond, Leah walked in. "I just saw a commercial for the new Barbie Bathhouse. I want one."

"Me too," said Lana behind her.

"Okay honey. Florence, you're staying here to watch the boys. I don't want them screwing around."

Relief flowed through me. I would much rather hang out with my brothers than with her.

"They should vacuum their rooms and the hallway. When you finish with that, they should wash walls. They're filthy. If you finish all that before we get back, you can start supper." She turned to leave. "Oh. And keep the laundry going."

James and John wandered into the kitchen.

James sat next to me.

John tugged on my arm. "Can I play with Sam?"

"For a few minutes," I said, "then we have to do house chores."

Sam was waiting by the door in the tool shed.

"Can I bring him inside?" John asked.

Sam proved to be a great cat. Even in the house, he stayed close to John. I nodded. "He can help us clean."

At the house, I grabbed the mop and bucket. James got the duster. He actually liked dusting.

John put Sam down and reached in the clean laundry basket for a dishrag. Sam followed at his heels.

"Get that thing out of here!"

The shout had us frozen in place, except Sam, who bolted.

John ran after him.

Sophia's eyes flashed daggers at me. "What is wrong with you? Cats aren't allowed in the house."

"I thought you left," I said in a small voice.

Her eyes narrowed. "Oh, so that gives you license to bring an animal in here?"

"Dad doesn't care," I said, a tremble in my voice. "Momma always let us."

"Your momma isn't here. I am, and I want that thing out." When we didn't respond right away, she roared, "Now."

We flew down the basement stairs to the playroom. Sure enough, John and Sam were there on the couch.

"I hate her." Tears ran down John's face.

"No hate, John." I hugged him. "After all, you don't want to turn out like her, angry and bitter."

"Or bowed," James said.

"Or bored," I agreed. "Let's take Sam back to the shed. Tell you what. If we get our chores done early, we'll have ice cream."

"Wew not allowed," James said.

"She put me in charge," I said. Like John, I hated Sophia. Unlike John, I knew such emotions were infectious. Just because she was stuck in a state of discontent and boredom, didn't mean we had to be.

It was up to me to make sure we wouldn't be.

After the graveside service for Momma, she would leave and we would be free of her.

At least it's what I told myself.

Truth was, neither she nor Dad had mentioned it in months.

***

At the gravesite on the edge of Valley City next to Grandpa and Grandma, a gravestone marked a freshly dug grave:

Inga Solberg: September 1953 - December 1984.

Wishing Dad talked about her, I clung to every memory. Momma loved me and did not think my hair too red for it matched hers. Dad was different since she'd been gone, almost like he died.

Standing next to Sophia, he even smelled different. Like dried wheat and peppermint rather than sandalwood.

Staring at her gravestone, I tried to retrieve an image of her, and drew a blank.

James stood on the other side of me, picking his nose.

John held the corner of my shirt in his hand.

Andrew reached over and took my hand.

I burst into tears. "I can't remember what she looks like."

A day didn't go by I didn't imagine Momma alive, and the hole Clementine tripped in hadn't been there. Then maybe Momma, five months pregnant, wouldn't be here either.

Against the bright morning sky stood a little girl with fiery hair, three brothers, and no baby sister.

Me, Florence Dawn Solberg.

23
June 14, 1985

Florence

The winners of the 21st Academy of Country Music Awards were Alabama, George Strait, and Reba McEntire.

The Methodist church threw a picnic, volleyball to follow.

Leah said church guys were boring.

I, on the other hand, loved church events and the people. They were all nice and friendly. I imagined heaven being like such a day as this. Only, there I was good at volleyball.

Gloria Waverly's son, Jason stood out. Dark blonde with an athletic build, Jason was good looking for sure, but in a girly sort of way, like Steve Taylor. The kind of guy Leah and Lana drooled over.

And they were.

My cousins stood next to him, giggling at everything he said. Leah and Lana excelled at volleyball. They were only 13 and he'd just graduated high school.

Jason pulled his shirt over his head, and tossed it to the side revealing springy chest hair.

There was something in his eyes that belied his confidence. Not to mention his loud voice.

A plate and tongs in hand for grilling, Reverend Alder strolled past the volleyball net.

"Keep the shirts on, guys," he called.

Jason obviously was the only one shirtless.

His face flushed red, his eyes took on a steely look.

He served the volleyball, remaining shirtless for another ten minutes before retrieving the discarded item of clothing. As he tugged it back on, my heart tugged. Show off or not, no one deserved to be humiliated in front of everyone.

Reverend hadn't returned and no one said anything.

"Reverend can be a bit much sometimes," I told him as people headed toward the food line.

He didn't answer.

"Anyway, good game."

More silence.

I turned to go, and he said, "I've never seen hair that color before."

I halted, glancing back. He was staring at my red bob.

I smiled. "It's one of the things that makes me special."

His brow arched, and then a slow grin worked its way across his face. "A special girl needs a special name."

"I'm Florence," I said proudly. There was no one I knew with my same name.

"That is pretty special." He winked. "I'm Jason."

24
July 28, 1985

Florence

NASA released a transcript from the doomed Challenger, and pilot Michael Smith could be heard saying, "Uh-oh!" as the spacecraft disintegrated.

Dad was sipping coffee at the kitchen table, alone.

"Hi Dad," I said, sitting across from him.

"Hi Pumpkin."

Since Sophia arrived, she made sure coffee was ready by the time he woke, like it was her career.

She bought the coffee.

Dad thought the coffee tasted good and drank it. He added sugar to make it sweeter. She made it stronger if it was too weak. He altered it anyway it suited his needs. I even heard him say once it made him feel good.

John sat next to me and reached for my ear.

"Where's Sophia?" I asked.

"She had to run to Fargo today," he said. "Also, she doesn't like when you call her that."

"It's her name, isn't it?"

He pinned me with a serious look. "That's Aunt Sophia to you."

"Why, did she say something?"

"Yes."

"What?"

He sighed loudly. "She said she doesn't like you kids calling her Sophia. She's auntie."

James wandered in wearing pajamas, his hair sticking straight up on end.

I thought about Sophia making coffee every morning. She enjoyed the taste, the way it made her feel, but she didn't love or care about coffee. Neither did she love Dad. Or us for that matter. It was never about him or us.

It was all about her.

It had always been all about her. That's when it hit me.

Dad was coffee to Sophia.

"Speaking of Sophia...Aunt Sophia, isn't she supposed to be going back to Seattle?" I draped my arm around James.

"Plans changed." He downed the last of his coffee. "She's staying for a while."

"How long is a while?"

"John, Sam is an outside cat. You'd do best to keep it that way." He set his empty cup in the sink. "I've got to run to Valley City."

"How come?"

"For supplies. I'll be back for lunch."

"I want to come. Can we go to the cemetery?"

"Not this time, Florence," he reached over, rubbing my head.

"Why not? Can I help with the bees?"

"Not this time, Florence," he said again on a tired sigh.

"Why not?"

He didn't answer. There was a faraway look in his eyes. Fathers don't cry, but his eyes shimmered in the kitchen light, like tears. We watched him drive out of the yard, taking all the happiness with him.

25
August 28, 1985

Florence

An attack on a synagogue in Istanbul killed 23 people, and we were at Gloria Waverly's for a visit.

Gloria came from *family money* according to Aunt Sophia. Her house was a mansion compared to ours. There was a Jacuzzi tub in the bathroom.

Leah and Lana brought their swimsuits and headed outside to their backyard swimming pool.

I filled a bowl with snacks laid out on the kitchen table.

"Florence, why don't you go outside?"

I didn't bring my suit, but I knew she was trying to get rid of me. Probably to gossip about Dad to Gloria.

Aunt Sophia was a self-absorbed man-hater. She would eat him up and spit him out. She had to go. I wouldn't think of it any other way.

I wandered toward the sound of music, and discovered Jason from the church picnic sitting on a white leather sofa in front of a big screen TV. He wore Bermuda shorts and a white crop top that showed off his tanned muscles.

He glanced over and saw me. "What's up, Red."

"Hi. What are you listening to?"

His eyes were fixed on the screen. "'Jump' by Van Halen."

"I've never heard it before."

He laughed. "Where did you come from?"

"My house."

"No kidding." He shook his head, chuckling.

"How can you watch TV and listen to music at the same time?"

"Easy."

Glancing at the screen, I expected to see *Terminator, Beverly Hills Cop* or even *Police Academy.* All of which I'd seen with Norman and my brothers.

"What are you watching?" I asked.

"*Sixteen Candles.*"

"Seriously? Can I watch too?"

"Sure. Afterward, it's this one," he held up a VHS tape of *Romancing the Stone*. "Maybe *The Karate Kid.*"

"All of them?"

"You bet."

"I guess I can watch until I have to leave." I sat down. "Want to share my snacks?"

"No thanks. I'm sort of a germaphobe."

"Oh. Well, you can just have it."

"No, I couldn't do that."

"I don't mind. Really." I handed him the bowl.

He smiled. "You really are something."

***

The van window had been left open. On our way home, we swatted flies. Sophia took a different road than the one leading to the farmhouse.

"Where are we going?" I asked.

"I thought you might want to visit your mother's grave." Sophia drove through the cemetery, stopping nearby where they put Momma in the ground.

"Can we wait in the car?" Leah asked with a whine.

"Yeah, can we?" Lana chimed in.

"Of course." Aunt Sophia smiled.

The summer sun overhead made everything hot and muggy. I glanced over at Aunt Sophia. It was unsettling how much she looked like Momma.

"My sister was a good woman," she said, her presence, a soothing balm over a sore wound.

"I wish I had flowers." I knelt in front of Momma's grave.

Aunt Sophia was holding a picture, her thumb running over it. "This picture was taken when we were eighteen."

I glanced at it. It was Momma and Aunt Sophia, taken in the sixties. The dresses were both beautiful and smart, just touching their knees.

"I love the dresses."

She gave a laugh. "Inga made them."

My eyes widened. "She did?"

"I gave her a pattern. She was the one who could sew. The perfect one." She tucked the photograph in the back pocket of her jeans. "The dresses weren't right. I told her exactly how I wanted them, but she made them too short and they were the wrong shade of blue."

Unsure what to say, I said nothing.

Aunt Sophia stood alongside the gravestone. "Do you think she'd be okay with her only daughter acting like a little flirt?"

My head came up. "What?"

Her gaze caught mine, darkness replacing the sunshine in her eyes.

They reminded me there was no reality where Momma wasn't dead.

26
December 28, 1985

Norman

Ted Hughes was appointed British Poet Laureate by Queen Elizabeth II, and Ted Orn, the hockey coach, was coming for dinner.

It had been snowing all night. Outside my bedroom window was a glistening sheen of winter wonderland.

Dad was on call for the Sheriff's Department.

Mother had gotten the *TV Guide* in the mail the day before. On the paisley olive-green sofa, she clicked through three channels.

In the kitchen at the breakfast table, I clicked through reels on my View-Master.

Dad got called out.

Ted Orn arrived a half hour early for lunch in a black suit and tie. Every day this week, he'd brought me to the indoor rink so we could hit the puck around.

Coach Orn flashed a smile. "Hey Norman. You going to try out for the team?"

"Maybe."

"You better. You're becoming the guy to beat."

My face grew warm. "Yeah."

"Seriously, Mrs. M. You should have seen him yesterday." Coach Orn gave a loud laugh. "He skates circles around me."

"He's a natural," Mother beamed. "Are the other kids doing as well as he is?"

"Of course not." Coach Orn winked at me.

I shifted uncomfortably in my chair. Truth was, I was the only one Coach Orn had brought to the rink. He said the players with the most promise got the opportunity.

He told me not to mention it to Mother because she'd spill the beans to the other mothers. There would be an uproar likely to put a kibosh on the whole thing.

Plus, he assured me Leo Nelson was next on the list.

I didn't like keeping it from my mother, but I also didn't like the idea of not getting to skate.

Mother handed us a bowel of dip and a bag of chips. "I made an appetizer if you two want to watch the game while I put the finishing touches on dinner."

"Sounds great." Coach Orn turned to me. "How about it?"

"Okay." I didn't really like watching hockey, only playing it, but he'd done so much to help me. I was reluctant to sound ungrateful. Plus, Mother would give me the raspberries if she thought I was being rude.

I grabbed the clicker and the blue screen flickered on.

"What channel?" I clicked through the four including Prairie Public Broadcasting.

The game came on. Coach Orn was a pretty animated fan, leaping from the couch when a player got checked or scored.

I sat on the other side rather stiffly, attempting to relax.

"I meant what I said about your improvement yesterday," he said, his suddenly loud voice was quiet, intimate.

"Thanks." Suddenly, our living room sofa seemed like a loveseat.

"Makes a difference when you train like a professional rather than with little girls."

Irritated, I said, "The Solbergs are my friends."

"During hockey season there are no friends."

"If it hadn't been for them, I wouldn't even be able to skate."

"Norman, you were born to play hockey."

"You think so?" A spark of excitement lit in my belly.

"I know so."

Basking in the knowledge of my skill, I didn't remember much of the game after that. Coach Orn was a little gung ho, but I was confident he was the one to help me become one of the greats.

27
October 21, 1986

Norman

A 55-year-old American writer Edward Tracy, was abducted in Beirut, Lebanon. "Israeli-American spy" a revolutionary group called him, bringing to seven the number of Americans missing in Muslim, West Beirut.

The early evening sky was heavy with dark wet clouds. In the west, the setting sun, a strip of yellow orange.

Coach Orn pulled up in his '56 Chevy. "Hey Norman. Heading home?"

"Yeah."

"Need a ride?"

"Nah. I'm good." The past few weeks, I'd intentionally put space between me and Coach Orn. He was demanding and critical, and I was to the point where I didn't even want to join the team.

"You sure? I was just on my way over to your place to give your mother the schedule."

"I hate to bother you." I felt uncomfortable in my mistrust of him when everyone thought he was the greatest thing since Pat Burns.

Well almost everyone.

Dad didn't have much time for him. Partly being the sheriff, and partly because of my mother's starry eyes.

"I get it," he said easily. "Have a good one."

"Well, if it's not a problem for you, I guess it's okay." If I refused, Mother would never let me hear the end of it.

"I'm headed that way anyway. Hop in."

"All right."

"You can put that in the back." He pointed to my backpack.

I tossed it in the back seat and got in the passenger side. He shifted in reverse.

Suddenly, I was keenly aware of the scent of tobacco and whisky.

"Is it all right with you if I stop by my cabin? I rented a couple of movies and forgot to return them."

"That's fine." I glanced over.

He smiled.

It wasn't until much later I realized the mistake I'd made getting in his car.

***

Ten minutes later, he pulled up in front of a hunting cabin north of town, and shifted into park.

"Want to come in for a soda? See the place?"

"I don't know. I should be getting home. Florence and Andrew will wonder where I am. We were supposed to carve pumpkins."

"It'll just take a second. Brian is a coach for North Dakota State University. He's a recruiter for the Bison hockey team."

"I don't know…"

"Come on, you worry too much."

Inside the cabin, man cave was written all over it. The walls were adorned with hunting trophies and a light-up Miller Lite sign.

There was a bar with a man dumping chips into a bowl. He was balding and thin. Another man with black hair and dark eyes was on the couch watching a TV with rabbit ears.

The bald man made his way over to me and handed me a glass of beer.

"I'm too young."

Coach Orn gave him a hard look. "Come on, Brian. He's a kid, you degenerate."

Brian laughed. "Sorry. Looks like a man to me. I've got Mountain Dew, Pepsi…"

"Pepsi is fine," I said.

He poured a glass and handed it to me. "So Orn tells me you're the best center he's coached."

My face flushed hot. "I don't know about that." I took a sip of Pepsi. It was cold and refreshing.

When I asked if I could have more, even while knowing to do so was impolite, he filled my glass.

"I should probably head home." I jerked a thumb toward the door.

"No problem," Coach Orn said, fading from focus.

I blinked hard, making the edges come together.

He gave me a curious glance. "You alright?"

"I'm fine." I reached my hand toward the table for leverage. A cold ball dropped in my stomach.

"It's not poison," a low voice was not at all reassuring. "Just a little something to help you relax."

Relax for what?

Panic was a dreamy wave of warmth. "What…" Looking down at the cup, and then up at the blurry figure, I whispered, "This place is magical," before slipping into the blackness that waited.

28

Florence

Ask five different people what happened, you get five different answers. Everyone was talking about it except Norman. Hearing how it happened through the grapevine and ultimately Sophia, personal and intimate, made me feel like an outsider.

Each version like a play watched from the side or the front. Like colors of a sunset being both gold and pink. Or a bite of a fresh fall apple from the tree.

Aunt Sophia heard it from Gloria who heard it from Uncle Don at lunch who mowed Mrs. Henke's lawn that Coach Orn and two of his friends got Norman drunk and sexually assaulted him.

Elizabeth Miller had been drinking for two days straight afterward, and had gone a little mad according to Uncle Don.

Who could blame her? *We all go a little mad sometimes.*

I figured it was the closest to what actually happened.

The school loved Coach Ted Orn. The superintendent loved him. The girls loved him. Why he singled out Norman rather than the enamored girls, no one knew.

His mother claimed it was because Norman was extremely gifted, took to hockey like Wayne Gretzky, and Coach Orn was jealous.

In hindsight, everyone agreed Coach Orn took Norman under his wing and gave him special treatment.

His mother was glad to see Norman had potential, and Sheriff Casey was always working.

After an exceptionally promising summer, Orn took the team to Dairy Queen after practice. Norman was the last one dropped off. Only he wasn't dropped off at his home.

The doctor's report showed traces of sexual assault and traces of drugs in Norman's system.

Coach Orn claimed he got Norman's consent which Norman neither confirmed nor denied.

With no prior record and the school not wanting press, the Superintendent demanded Coach Orn's resignation.

Afterward, Sheriff Casey flipped out and wanted him charged. Without an eyewitness and Norman remaining silent, the judge was reluctant to charge him with assault.

Coach Orn was originally from Portland, Oregon. His past employment record was clean of prior felonies.

He resigned.

Norman ended up transferring schools to Jamestown Middle School.

Richard Denton and Brian Locke, the other two men involved, cut a deal to get out of a drug charge.

Rumor had it Sheriff Casey didn't take it well at all, and threatened to murder the three of them.

Even when the truth came out, Norman's classmates avoided Norman like the plague. To keep from getting dirty? To avoid that stain of sin?

To make Norman out to be weird or strange.

That way, parents could say it was a fluke, and such a thing couldn't, wouldn't happen to just anyone.

Only Norman because he was odd and a little bit gay anyway.

I wasn't sure how anyone could be just a little bit gay, but my heart ached for Norman. And the story changed each time it was told. It was as though they were talking about a complete stranger. Not our Norman.

Not the Norman Miller who was our friend.

29
November 22, 1986

Norman

Edmonton Oiler Wayne Gretzky became the 13th National Hockey Leaguer to score 500 goals, while my mother seemed concerned about my own lack of interest in hockey.

"Just because you quit the team, you won't shirk your responsibilities at home, I hope," Mother said. "I can't keep up this home by myself. There's the cooking, and cleaning, garbage..."

"I can make meals on weekends and put them in the freezer." She avoided talking about what happened. I worked it to my advantage. I could feel her pity, and had no problem using it to do what I wanted.

"For the whole week?" she asked. "There's no freezer room."

"There's the deep freeze in the garage," I said with growing excitement as the ideas came to me. "Saturdays I'll clean bathrooms. First Saturday of the month I'll clean windows."

"And don't forget Mass." She clicked through prime time TV between *The Cosby Show, Night Court,* and *Miami Vice*. "If you're going to Jamestown Middle School, I don't want you abandoning religion all together."

I'd transferred to Jamestown Middle School after Coach Orn resigned. It was a big enough school where news traveled on a hushed wavelength.

"I'll finish in plenty of time for Mass," I said with confidence.

"I appreciate your thoughtfulness," she sighed. "Your dad is never around."

I'd seen Dad talking to Sophia Dunn at church, and by the look in his eyes, I had a suspicion he was spending time out at the lake house.

I didn't care.

He freaked out about Coach Orn, demanding to know exactly what had happened so he could lock him away forever. I couldn't talk to him about it. To anyone about it.

Because it wasn't clear in my own memory.

"When he is home, your father is too tired to help around the house," Mother was saying. "I have a job too."

That job changed weekly. This week it was selling jewelry over the phone.

"I know you do, Mother."

"Yesterday was so hard. Mrs. Henke ordered fifty dollars' worth, and then called to tell me she couldn't pick them up. I had to drive them over there. Then there was garbage behind the car in the garage. I had to move it before I could leave."

"Gotta go," I said, "I'm going to the library to study for the math test."

"You're such a good boy."

I rode my bike to Leo Nelson's house. Pulling up to his front door, I could hear the music from the street.

When Leo answered the door, I gave him a high five.

"Hey buddy." I grinned.

"Come on in." He held the door open.

Leo wasn't anybody's buddy and I didn't really like him.

I did, however, like his father's whisky.

30
Christmas Eve, 1986

Norman

The spirit of Christmas swept across the frosted windows, over the doorways, and on the fake evergreen in the living room. A nativity scene sat on the window sill.

Mother invited the Solbergs over for supper. She had never invited them over to our house before. It had always been Dad welcoming them. I knew the reason. Damage control.

I was a bundle of nerves.

If they ignored me, I'd want to curl up and die. If they didn't, I'd want to curl up and die.

Dad left for work.

I helped my mother clean, excusing myself around the time of their arrival.

Mother's eyes filled with pity but she said nothing.

The doorbell rang downstairs. I curled up on my bed, wishing them away.

My mother's voice drifted up the stairs. "Come in. I'm sorry Norman won't be able to join us. He isn't feeling well."

I knew the minute they were outside my bedroom door.

I was both thrilled and furious they never listened.

"Go away."

***

Florence

Norman's legs curled to his butt in the fetal position on his bed.

Hand in hand, of one mind, we entered the room, closing the door behind us.

No one spoke.

The hockey stick hanging on the wall gave me courage to ask, "Want to go sledding?"

He grunted.

"What?"

"No."

"Why not?" I asked.

"How about a snowball fight?" Andrew asked.

He rolled off the bed and stood.

"Hooray," I clapped my hands. "You're coming with us."

He didn't answer.

We followed him down the stairs. We dressed in winter clothes for the park in silence.

A hush was firmly in place the time it took to get to Klaus Park, during the snowball fight when Norman sat on a snowy bench, and all the rest of the evening until right after supper when he retreated to his bedroom.

Silence: a weapon Norman wielded well.

31
January 23, 1987

Florence

We emerged from the school bus, steam billowing as warm air married with the frigid January evening.

Thin crystalline slices of hard snow tipped in a wave next to the shed.

Frozen air bit through my gloves and coat, burning my cheeks and the tip of my nose. Hard tufts of snow crunched beneath our feet as Andrew and I headed toward the house.

Matching rings cradled the sun hanging low in the sky as the afternoon stretched.

Andrew pointed to the winter sun. "Sundogs."

"I hate those," I said, knowing they promised a far colder tomorrow than even the ten below today.

The tips of my fingers started to ache, and I slapped my gloved hands against my thighs. "What do you think really happened to Norman?"

"They forced him."

"Into their car?"

"Yes."

I blew a long sigh, letting my head fall back toward heaven. "Thank the stars. For a dreadful minute, I thought it was..." I swallowed hard. "Never mind what I thought."

"And in other ways," Andrew added in a low voice.

Those four words took my breath away, and my heart cracked. "I suppose that's what all the drastic changes are about. Switching schools, quitting hockey, not hanging out with us anymore."

"I just…don't know." Andrew pushed his hat back, scratching his head with four impatient fingers.

"The worst is the way he won't even look at me at school. If he sees me in the hall, he turns the other way." I tugged my coat tighter.

"You love him." Andrew's eyes searched my face.

"Yes."

"Still?"

"Always." We reached the house and I voiced what my mind insisted to be the case, "Norman is tough. He'll get through this. You'll see."

"I hope so," he said, casting a last glance at the sundogs touching the earth in the far west.

A shiver rolled through me as I stepped inside the house.

No matter how bitterly cold today, tomorrow would be worse. Far worse.

An inevitable frosty promise.

32
April 3, 1987

Florence

The Duchess of Windsor's jewels were auctioned for £31,380,197.

Jason was in our kitchen wearing a sports jersey and stonewashed jeans. His thick dark hair was feathered back.

"Hey Red." He winked.

And like that, all the days of silence and sadness washed away. I sailed toward him, throwing my arms around his neck.

He laughed, unhooking my fingers. "Hey now. Mom could walk in any minute."

"I don't care," I said, even as I flushed crimson.

He strolled over and flipped the stereo on. He was the only person I knew who watched TV and listened to music at the same time.

He drew the lights dim and returned to the couch, sitting close to me.

My heart thumped in my ears. Between Norman's continued silence and my own nerves, I told him, "I'm having trouble getting along with my Aunt Sophia."

"Oh yeah?"

"Yeah. I suppose I like being around her because she looks like my momma did, but she acts nothing like her. I don't even know if she likes me."

"Her loss."

I smiled and prattled on, "School is way harder than it was last year. Elementary school had been so great. I hate middle school. Norman avoids me. All the girls ignore me."

"Did the girls talk to you before?"

My cheeks reddened. "No. I guess that doesn't bother me so much, but Norman used to be my friend. Although I suppose after what happened, he's embarrassed. Plus, everyone knows Sheriff Casey's at our lake house all the time." I pressed my lips together, wondering why I had said so much, wishing I hadn't. "I suppose you heard about what happened to Norman."

"I suppose everyone has."

I relaxed a little.

His eyes told me he adored me. He wasn't like anyone else. I could tell him anything.

His lips met mine briefly, then he pulled away, and said, "Can I teach you how to kiss?"

"Isn't that what we just did?" I asked, heart thundering.

"In the grown-up way."

"But…"

His face drew close to mine. "Don't worry, I'll take good care of you."

Then he was kissing me and his hands were everywhere.

He thought I was irresistible!

"…Why can't this be love…?" Van Halen sang in the background.

I felt like I was on fire, and pulled away, gasping for breath.

"When you grow up, you are going to be mine." He tugged at the edge of my shirt. My body responded to his intimate touch. My heart thumped wildly in my chest.

"I like sex hot and heavy," he whispered, sliding his hand up my shirt and beneath my bra.

Suddenly terrified, I pulled away.

Just then, Leah appeared in the doorway. I glanced back at Jason who didn't seem at all flustered.

"I was just leaving," I stammered, and flew from the room.

Alone in my room, I dragged in deep breaths, struggling to sort out my wild emotions. What had Leah seen?

He was in college!

I didn't know exactly what happened next, but I was sure we'd gone far beyond friendship. Could we be together? Did he want to?

The ache flooding my body was unfamiliar and terrifying.

When you grow up, you are going to be mine. When did he consider a girl to be grown up? When I was sixteen? Would he find someone else by then? Maybe we could be friends first.

I was supposed to marry Norman.

At the thought, a dark gray cloud filled my entire being. Depression rolled in, and I lay, staring up at the ceiling.

Norman hadn't been to our house since it happened. Even if he worked the bees in the spring, I had a feeling I wouldn't see him around. He was different now. Older.

Broken.

I lay, listening to Dolly Parton and Kenny Rogers sing "Islands in the Stream" on the clock radio.

33
June 12, 1987

Florence

U.S. President Ronald Reagan challenged Mikhail Gorbachev to "tear down" the Berlin Wall.

"You could have a big dipper going up and down, all around the bends…" I flipped the radio off at the sight of a white Chevy in the kitchen window. I didn't want Peter Gabriel singing "Sledgehammer" when Jason was around.

I hadn't seen him since that afternoon we'd made out on the couch. It took me until evening to realize I'd made a mistake in letting him kiss me. In me kissing him back, even for just a moment. Would he expect to pick up where we left off?

"Hey Red," Jason entered without knocking.

"You live here now?"

He laughed. "Nope."

His mom and Sophia were always talking jewelry or going shopping, but Jason was in college. Even if it was Saturday, shouldn't he be studying or something?

"Looks like someone changed over the winter." He grinned, his eyes dipping to my chest briefly.

He wandered over to the pantry, searching the shelves. He gave my braid a tug, pointing at the cereal box on the shelf. "I was wondering if you wouldn't mind grabbing that for me."

Fear crept up the back of my neck. "What?"

"Do it," he said, his voice teasing.

"Why can't you?"

"Because I asked you to."

Just give him the box of Wheaties so he leaves you alone. I reached for the cereal on the shelf closest to me.

"Nice," his voice drummed. "But I wanted the Cheerios."

"I can't reach those."

"I bet you can. Try. For me." Something in his voice sent a shudder through me.

I reached up, way up. Feeling the edge of the box with the tips of my fingers, I grabbed it, and caught his gaze on my breasts.

Embarrassed, I folded my arms across my chest.

Just then, Leah entered the kitchen.

I wanted to be anywhere other than there.

"Who's the weirdo that comes around here all the time?" Jason asked, pouring himself the cereal.

"You mean Norman Miller?" Leah giggled.

"Looks like someone who would keep stuffed trophies in his house." He snickered.

"Norman?" I asked, incredulous.

"He sure is a grouch." He took a bite of Cheerios.

"He's the kid Coach Orn and his buddies supposedly raped at some cabin somewhere." Leah's eyes were heavy, "Ted Orn looks like a movie star. He could take me to a cabin in the woods anytime he wanted to."

"Leah," I said, "Ew. Anyway, the whole thing is horrible. You can't blame Norman for getting a little mad sometimes."

Leah laughed. "We all go a little mad sometimes."

"What?"

"Inside joke," Jason mumbled through a mouthful.

Anger swept through me. "I hate inside jokes."

"It's not an inside joke. It's a movie reference." Jason lifted the bowl to his lips, downing the last of the milk.

"But you said..."

"It's a movie reference." He wiped his face with the back of his hand. "Lighten up."

"Oh."

"Anyway, you should know it. If you didn't live under a rock, you would." He winked at Leah.

She beamed.

His eyes reverted to our TV with bunny ears in the corner of the kitchen counter. *Family Ties* was on.

Retreating to my room, jealousy wormed its way in my chest until it reached my heart. Hatred like I'd never known ran hot.

I wished my cousin was dead.

34
July 9, 1987

Florence

Colonel Oliver North admitted to shredding Iran-Contra evidence. I was at the Jamestown public swimming pool.

In the changing room, I admired my reflection in the mirror. The swimsuit was a hand-me-down yellow bikini from Sophia. The top fit nicely, rounding my breasts. The bottoms were full, rising to the tops of my thighs just below my belly button.

I'd slipped past Dad's radar by donning an oversize t-shirt and shorts on my way out of the house.

"You look so old-fashioned," Leah said, adjusting the strings on her black bikini. Her hair, sun streaked, her figure, perfect and tan from laying out and not working with bees.

"Why don't you make like a tree and leave?"

She gave an incredulous snort. "What did you say to me?"

"You heard me. Your mother's not here, so buzz off and go find someone else's life to ruin."

"Whatever." Her nose came up and she turned, rounding the sunlit corner to the pool area.

I grabbed my towel, took a deep breath, and did the same.

Music from the loud speaker next to the snack bar got my heart thumping. *"'Who's Johnny' she said and tried to look the other way her eyes gave her away…"*

In my yellow polka dot bikini, I was that girl, intriguing and elusive.

Beautiful.

Leah was talking to a muscular guy with his back to me. He turned around. It was Jason. Eyes the color of the pool water caught mine, and he winked.

My heart thumped wildly. I blushed, glancing away. When I looked back, his attention had reverted to Leah.

The pool was empty, clear blue water sparkling like diamonds beneath the hot summer sun. I dipped my toe in. It was cool.

Andrew and Norman lined up for the diving board.

Moving away from the water's edge, I got behind them. "I like this song," I said. "Who sings it? El something?"

"El DeBarge," Andrew said.

Norman's eyes faced forward. He made no mention about my new suit or even looked at me.

The song switched and it was now Robert Palmer's voice floating across the pool, *"When I took you out I knew what you were all about…"*

"I love this song too," I exclaimed. "I even know who sings it. Robert Palmer."

"Since when did you and Andrew Culverwell break up?" Norman asked.

"Since…" I trailed off.

Stacey appeared, sidling up to Norman. Stacey Clark was at least five inches shorter than him, and gazed up at him adoringly. I wondered if Norman missed being able to look a girl straight in the eye.

Probably not as cool as having one bat her eyelashes at him.

He said something to her I couldn't hear and she laughed, laying her hand on his arm. Her swimming suit was one piece and lipstick red, a striking contrast against her brown waves and blonde highlights.

Suddenly, I didn't feel like diving in and wandered over to the ladder marked *6 FT*. I sank down on the cement. *"...You can feel the cushions but you can't have a seat, you can dip your foot in the pool..."*

Thank you Howard Jones, I believe I will.

"...but you can't have a swim..."

I sighed, pushing to my feet. I didn't much feel like swimming anyway. Wandering over to my towel, I scanned the area and saw Jason suntanning on a lounge chair. He was alone. His blue eyes caught mine.

My cheeks colored. I grew warm, waiting for him to come over and talk to me. He didn't.

Leah strolled over with a pile of nachos and a can of Pepsi. He sat up and took both from her.

***

That night at the youth group bonfire, Jason was there. "Hey Florence. Was that you I saw at the pool?"

"Maybe." I blushed beneath my sunburn.

"Why didn't you come over and say hi?"

"Why didn't you?" I caught his eyes.

"I didn't know if I should have."

"You should have."

His grin was easy. "It was really rather unfair, you know."

"What was?"

"Seeing you in that bikini," he said, fanning the front of his polo shirt. "Let's just say some guys like the dainty little girls they can look down on. But what I saw was a woman who knows what she wants, and is not afraid to get it."

Unsure if it was a compliment, I mumbled, "Thanks."

"No, thank you. Although, next time you might want to shave." He smirked, running a finger down my nose.

"I've been shaving my legs since I was eleven."

He eyed me through heavy lids. "You're only eleven now. Or is it twelve?"

"Almost twelve." I straightened my shoulders.

"Your momma never told you." His smile turned sad.

"Told me what?"

He leaned toward me, his gaze dipping along with his voice, "You need to shave down there. Suit was totally see-through."

My heart stopped and the atmosphere around me was swallowed up in a flash of shame. I wished the floor would open up a trapdoor.

"Not that I noticed," he said quickly, lifting his eyes. "They were talking about it and I overheard."

Don't ask. Don't… "Who's they?"

"You know." His finger ran over my lips. "Your brother and his friends."

Norman? He wouldn't. Jason was lying. Andrew and Norman wouldn't really be talking like that about me. And Stacey…I wanted to die. They most certainly wouldn't talk that way around her.

My chin came up. "I looked in the mirror before I left the locker room."

"Did you shower first?"

"What?"

"My point," he whispered. "Was it wet?"

"No." My stomach rolled. Was it? What difference did that make?

See-through.

Embarrassed, I justified my thoughts with more racing ones. It couldn't have been. Someone would have said something. Lana would have or Leah for sure. Or Norman. That one had me dashing to my room, flying on my bed beneath the coverlet.

Someone did say something. You just couldn't handle the truth.

I stayed like that for a long time, wishing the world away.

35
October 19, 1987

Florence

The stock market crashed, marking today Black Monday and Leah and I were getting ready for skate night with the church youth group at Skateland.

I donned my favorite brown and white-striped sweater and corduroys, and stood in front of the mirror. My reflection reminded me I was tall, my waist, slender. Maybe Norman would ask me to skate. My cheeks flushed at the thought of my hand in his, our fingers entwined.

"You're so thin." Leah eyed me from the mirror where she was applying mascara.

I flicked her a glance. "I thought we weren't allowed to wear makeup."

Leah shrugged. "My mom lets me. She said if the barn needs painting, paint it."

Confused, I said, "Doesn't that mean…"

Leah cut in, "You should you know. Mascara would really bring out your eyes." She held out the tube.

Your eyelashes are so long and thick. You have beautiful eyes, Florence, Momma's words rang in my memory.

"No thanks," I told her. Instead, I pinned the sides of my hair back with barrettes braided with pink and white dangly ribbons, rehearsing my response if Norman asked me to skate.

When we arrived, Norman was already there, skating with Stacey. I watched them skate away with my evening plans.

So what? I would have a good time anyway. I didn't need Norman to have fun.

By the time I got my roller skates laced up, everyone had paired off. All that was left were Andrew, James, John and me. Not wanting to appear a loser, I was careful to keep space between them and me.

Disco lights lit up the floor. Couples held hands, skating in a circle while Tiffany sang "I think we're alone now."

"In your part of the country, pussy is bad," Leo Nelson rolled up alongside me.

Leo's dad worked as a janitor at the school. It was his second time at youth group. He was loud, obnoxious, and I made it my mission to avoid him. Not to mention, he was at least three inches shorter than me.

Glancing over at him, his pizza face and wild hair, I figured it might count as Christian service to skate with him.

"Kyrie" by Mr. Mister began to play, fueling my determination.

"I love skating, don't you?" I said to him, thinking how to steer the conversation toward skating with me.

He had to look up at me. "In your part of the country, pussy is bad."

My ears got hot. What did that mean? "I don't understand."

"In your part of the country, pussy is bad," he repeated, this time with more secretive force.

Andrew appeared, giving Leo a hard push. "Stay away from my sister."

"Hey," he held up both hands. "I didn't mean any harm."

After Leo skated off, Andrew turned to me. "Why didn't you get rid of him yourself?"

"I was about to," I said, picking up the pace.

The trouble with brothers and rescuing, they asked a lot of questions and saw through the answers. I was glad I hadn't brought the matter up to Andrew.

Jason. I would ask him the next time I saw him.

I didn't have long to wait. Gloria Waverly was talking to Aunt Sophia in our kitchen when we got home.

I found Jason watching TV in our living room, hurried over to him, and blurted, "What's a pussy?"

Dragging his eyes from the TV, he gave an incredulous laugh. "What did you ask me?"

My face grew hot. "I heard…"

"What do you think it is?" he cut in, his suggestive tone stopping me short.

"A cat. Right?"

"You've got a lot to learn, little girl." He shook his head, chuckling.

"It must be something bad or you would tell me."

"It's your…" his gaze dipped between my legs.

The truth was a hard slap in the face. Mortified, I turned, dashing from the room.

His laughter chased me down the stairs.

36
December 12, 1988

Florence

Palestine Liberation Organization leader Yasi Arafat accepted Israel's right to exist. I woke with a toothache that pounded through my head.

Digging around the wooden shelf mounted on the wall next to the tub, I caught a glimpse of my reflection in the mirror above the sink.

My cheek was swollen to an unrecognizable size. There was Tylenol in the cupboard above the fridge.

On my way to the kitchen, I saw Gloria Waverly's Cadillac Fleetwood in the yard from the kitchen window. A closer look revealed Jason was with her.

I dashed down to the playroom. Andrew, James and John were playing Sorry next to the couch.

I rushed over, and shut the lamp off and a spark flew out.

"The lamp's bowken," James said.

"Broken," echoed John.

"It's from Momma. I can't throw it away. We'll fix it."

"Flowie locked the doow cuz thews a bad guy," James told John.

"Shhh," I hissed.

Leaning against the back of the playroom door, I hid behind it, praying he'd go away.

"You push and pull," Jason said in a low voice on the other side of the door. "Kiss me then push me away."

"Did not." I put my hands over my ears. "I don't want to anymore. Please go away." My heart hammered like a builder on a rooftop.

"I only want to talk. You're too much of a tomboy for anything else," there was harsh laughter in his voice.

"My brothers are in here."

"Make it easy on yourself and let me in. If you do it now, I'll forget the trouble you're giving me."

What did he want?

To pretend.

"Come on," he urged. "You can't hide forever."

It would be bad if I opened the door, and bad if I didn't.

"I'm not hiding," I unlocked the bolt and pushed the door open.

Jason stood with empty eyes. There was no mercy, no reason. What had I gotten myself into?

I stepped out into the hallway and shut the playroom door, leaning back against it. Whatever else he had to say, I didn't want my brothers hearing it.

He laughed. "What happened to your face?"

"My tooth hurts."

"You even sound stupid." He continued to chuckle.

Furious, I said, "I'm telling my dad."

"Loose lips sink ships." His eyes went black. "It would be a shame if Norman found out what you told me."

Fear coursed through me. "He won't believe you."

"Maybe he won't," he nodded thoughtfully, grabbing my arm. "Then again, maybe he will. And maybe, just maybe, he'll hate you forever."

Like you deserve.

Panic, real as the nightmares, clawed my belly.

Would I even get a chance to talk to Dad without Sophia breathing down my neck? *Do you think she'd be okay with her only daughter acting like a little flirt?*

"What are you two doing here alone?" Aunt Sophia descended the stairs.

Jason's hand was gone from my arm and he took a step back. "Nothing," he said, the glint in his eye promised punishment, and he stomped away.

"I was making coffee when I heard the two of you all the way from the kitchen," she said.

Weird how Aunt Sophia still made coffee every morning here when pretty much everyone knew what she was doing at the lake house with Sheriff Casey.

She gave me a hard look. "What happened to you?"

"I've got a toothache."

"Why didn't you say anything?"

"I thought it would go away."

"What if it's an abscess? You'll die, and everyone will blame me." A look of horror crossed her face. "An abscess can kill you."

"Cannot." My heart kicked up.

She's trying to scare you.

"My boss in Seattle, Barney, had a tooth abscess. It went into his jaw and made its way to his brain. He died."

I shivered.

"Get your coat." Aunt Sophia sighed. "I'm taking you to the dentist before your father sees it."

It was an abscess. Aunt Sophia was right. The dentist pulled my tooth and gave me a prescription for antibiotics.

On the way home, a snowflake fell, and another. By the time we reached the house, the wind had picked up.

***

A blizzard swept through the prairie while Jason Waverly was on his way back to Valley City State University.

Sheriff Casey found him three days later, his white Chevy car buried beneath the snow. He was badly frostbitten but still alive. In the end, Jason lost his right arm from the elbow down and all his fingers on his left.

There were pictures of his car, arm, and recovery set up in the foyer of the church.

He got up behind the pulpit to give his testimony.

"I thought I was dead for sure," Jason told the congregation. "I jumped from the front seat, to the back, and then the front again. I had a candy bar and took tiny bites of it. If it hadn't been for The Lord, I'd be dead. Now I realize He has a special plan for my life."

After the service, I stopped to talk to him.

His eyes met mine, and my heart plummeted. He looked lost. His eyes watered.

"You told your dad," he accused in a low, secretive tone. "But when you reached for the cereal, kissed me, wanted it, how was I supposed to control these urges I get?"

My face went hot. How was this my fault?

Then Mrs. Henke made her way over. "You brave, brave boy," she said, draping her arms around him.

When we arrived home, Dad gave me a hug. I couldn't remember the last time he had. "I spoke with Jason after church. He said he apologized."

Apologized?

Later, I lay on my bed, staring up at the ceiling, pondering his apology while Roxette sang, "Listen to your Heart", Chicago told me to "Look Away", and most fitting, Alice Cooper warned about lips of venomous "Poison".

37
October 14, 1989

Norman

Looking back, there were warning signs before the crash of 1987. Economic growth had slowed while inflation was increasing. The strong dollar was putting pressure on U.S. exports. Then, the stock market and economy were diverging for the first time in the bull market, and as a result, valuations climbed to excessive levels.

I'd seen the warning signs, grabbed a pack of Dad's cigarettes, a bottle of Mother's wine, and headed for the door anyway.

"Where are you going?" Mother asked, swaying slightly. She'd been drinking all morning.

"Out."

"What do you mean out? I didn't give you permission to go anywhere."

"I'll be back." I walked out the door.

Driving down Main, windows rolled down, I lost track of time. Ideas of normalcy seemed a mere dream now.

My stomach groaned loudly.

Drive to the lake house and talk to your dad.

Instead, I pulled up to Lily Winters' house.

I knocked on the front door and regretted it almost immediately. What was I thinking? What if her dad was home?

"Hey." Lily answered in Bermuda shorts and a white Guess t-shirt. Her curly brown hair was half-up half-down. Bangs ratted high, she wore dangly feather earrings.

"What's up?" I said.

"Not much."

Her smile gave me confidence to ask, "Where are your parents?"

"In Fargo." She eyed the bottle of wine in my hand. "Did you want to watch TV?"

"Nope." The self-loathing in my voice reached my ears. I struggled to hold onto aloofness, instead, eager to ease my pain. Powerless for nonchalance, I was unable to play whatever game required to keep my heart intact.

"Do you want me to leave?" I asked.

"No."

"What do you want to do?"

"You want to come to my room?"

My eyes widened. "Sure."

In her bedroom, she turned the tape in the player over. Belinda Carlisle's "I get weak" began to play. She stood close. The buzz I had going gave me confidence to kiss her. She stiffened, and then kissed me back. Her kisses were open mouth.

I pulled away slightly. "You've been kissed before."

"Does that bother you?"

"No." My mouth met hers once more.

Stacey drew back and pulled her shirt over her head.

I reached in my pocket for a condom.

Her eyes widened at the sight.

"You don't want to be a mother, do you?" My body followed hers to the bed, covering her.

***

Afterward, I retreated to the bathroom. Self-loathing swept through me. In the mirror, my own reflection accused me. Feeling used, I leaned against the wall and slid all the way down. Banging my head against the wall, tears streamed down my cheeks.

I wasn't crying. It was allergies.

On the way home, I reached for the pack of cigarettes and pulled into the mall parking lot.

My stubborn thoughts reverted to another day and the smell of nicotine.

***

Someone set a cup in front of me. "It's hot," a voice warned.

I blinked the face into focus. It was the bald man with the horn-rimmed glasses and ugly clothes.

"One will make him pliant, and he won't fight you." I recognized the voice. Coach Orn.

"What did you bring him here for?"

"His dad's the sheriff."

"Even worse."

"You know you want to."

"We'll get caught."

"It will be fun."

I would never forget the room with the window.

The dirty mattress.

The worst and best moment when the door burst open.

Dad stood, his wild-eyed gaze reached the mattress, and then mine. The horror therein, seared my brain. The humiliation.

Afterward, he fired questions at me, "Did they touch your privates? Did they make you suck them?"

And the lie out of my mouth, "No. You came just in time."

Tears of relief flooded his eyes. "Thank Jesus, Mary, and Joseph."

That look, that relief, convinced me. I remembered it wrong. It hadn't really happened. I was saved before the unthinkable. Before having to pleasure those three perverts.

Whatever helps you sleep at night.

But I wasn't sleeping at night. I was going mad.

We all go a little mad sometimes.

38

Norman

After the crash of '87, exchanges implemented circuit breaker rules and other precautions to slow down the impact of irregularities, hoping markets would have more time to correct similar problems in the future.

The next night in my parents' Chevy car, Lily climbed on my lap as soon as I put it in park. It was over in fifteen minutes. I avoided the bathroom mirror afterward, wetting my pillow with a few tears.

The time after that, I lay staring up at the ceiling, a smile on my face.

By the fourth time, no tears leaked from my eyes.

I must be getting the hang of this.

***

In church, I half listened to the sermon, which was something about Jesus and Him wanting me to be happy.

I didn't want to be happy, I wanted to be normal.

Afterward, Leo Nelson came up to me and held up his hand for a high five.

I ignored it.

He walked closely next to me. "Hey man, I heard about you and Lily."

My eyes narrowed on him. "I don't know what you're talking about."

"Sure you don't," he grinned.

I kept walking.

Dana Johnson, the hottest girl in ninth grade, caught my eye. She had an hourglass figure and long blonde hair.

"Dude, she's coming over," Leo said in an urgent whisper.

She strolled up to me. "Hey."

"Hey."

"Want to come over to my house after church?" before I could respond, she leaned closely and whispered, "My parents are out of town."

Was she serious? "Sure."

Afterward, at home, Dad was in front of the TV.

Mother met me at the door. "Where were you?"

"Church."

"Church was over an hour ago." Her eyes were wild.

"I wasn't kidnapped again, if that's what you're asking."

Pain scorched her eyes. "It wasn't."

"Don't worry about me, Mother. I'm fine." And I was, for the first time since that weekend, I felt desired and wanted by girls.

I felt normal.

"The more often he feels without acting, the less he will be able ever to act, and, in the long run, the less he will be able to feel." -Uncle Screwtape

C. S. Lewis, *Screwtape Letters*

39
December 26, 1989

Norman

TV soap opera Search for Tomorrow ended a 35-year run.

At least that's what my mother told me.

The Solbergs stopped over with Christmas gifts, and I saw my chance. "Can Andrew and I head over to the mall? We could stop by Walgreens on the way home, and return gifts for you." I caught Florence's pained expression, and added, "Florence too. I can even bring them home afterward."

"Thanks, I appreciate it. Let me get them ready for you."

Energy on that crisp December afternoon sizzled. The early winter sun twinkled over department stores.

Andrew, Florence, and I made our way around scattered icy patches of snow along the sidewalk.

Christmas lights lit up the tree at the front of Walgreens.

We made our way inside. A group of girls were at the end of the aisle, Alice Wilson, Lily Winters, Marsha Nelson, and one I hadn't seen before with long, blonde hair and a lilting laugh.

"I Saw Red" began playing over the loud speakers. *"Oo it must be magic how inside your eyes I see my destiny..."*

"That's Darla Mackey," Andrew said in a low voice.

"Does she have a boyfriend?"

Andrew shook his head. "Don't know. She's from Oregon. James said he saw her in church."

"So they're staying?" I stomped blood back into my toes.

"Not they, she." Andrew rammed his hands into his pockets. "Gonna live with her dad."

"She's a cheerleader," Florence's voice was quiet.

"Huh." I had trouble dragging my eyes away.

Andrew jabbed me in the side with his elbow. "Pay attention."

"I think I'll say hi," I said, rubbing my side absently.

"...my heart just spilled onto the floor..." Warrant continued its lament.

Florence squeezed my hand. "No."

"What are you doing?" I attempted to shake free, glancing over at the new girl. Sure enough, she was watching us, her eyes on Florence, then me.

I turned and glared at Florence. "Thanks a lot."

"Norman, my beef isn't with you." She caught my eyes, and the look in hers was somehow intimate. Like I belonged to her. I didn't like the feeling in my gut. I wanted space.

I watched the new girl walk out.

Furious at Florence for interfering, it was out before I could stop it, "No," I agreed. "Looks like it's with a pretty girl who's shorter than you."

Florence's cheeks turned red as her hair. She released my hand in a violent push.

Passing us on her way out, Marsha slowed. "Norman Miller?" Her eyes slid down my chest, lower, and back up again. "You sure grew up."

I smiled. "I..."

Andrew laid a hand on my arm. "Let's go."

Clenching my fists, I headed for the truck. "Get in," I gritted and cranked the engine.

Andrew got in the passenger seat and Florence in the back. As soon as she shut the door, my tongue flew on its own, "Why did you do that? Pretend that we-we're… act like you're my girlfriend."

Her eyes were focused on her lap. "I'm sorry."

"Dude," Andrew admonished next to me.

"This isn't my fault," I grumbled, staring straight ahead. "You, are not my fault."

The interior of the cab fell silent.

In that same silence, I stewed about my harsh words and angry reaction. In the rearview mirror, I saw her downcast face, a tear slide down her cheek. I hurt her.

She knew I wanted to ask the girl out. She knew it and ruined everything.

Those eyes of hers saw me for who I was. No one did that. Not even my own mother, and I hated her for it. Hated her more for being a woman. Suddenly, I couldn't wait to get rid of her, and laid my foot on the accelerator.

At last, we came to the road leading to their farmhouse.

Florence yelled, "Stop!"

My foot came down, the truck, to a sliding halt.

"I'm going to walk from here." She exited the truck, her voice was low when she said, "Goodbye, Norman." Then she shut the door, turned and made her way home.

"Like I'm the bad guy," I shouted, reaching for the handle.

"Don't," Andrew's voice held a warning.

I glanced over at him.

"I'm sorry she made you mad," he said.

"I'm not mad. People change, Drew. Grow up. Evolve." I shifted into gear. "I have."

40
May 21, 1994

Florence

South Yemen seceded from Yemen, and with shaky hands, I fastened pearl earrings in the entryway mirror.

"Where are you going?" Andrew eyed me.

"Dairy Queen."

Andrew watched me for a moment. "He's changed, Flor." Sorrow shadowed his eyes. "You don't have what he wants in a woman."

"Who?"

"Norman." His eyes met mine in the mirror. "He's seeing Lily Winters."

"He 'sees'…" I made quotations, swallowing jealousy, pride, and hope in one big gulp, "…everyone."

Andrew shifted from one foot to the other. "I'm sorry, Flor."

Norman had always been out of reach. Just beyond my grasp. We grew up together, and there was nothing new about me to discover. I wasn't mysterious or unexpected.

But I would be.

***

The back porch view of the setting sun was a deep orange flame against the earth.

As the day faded into a cream periwinkle behind a skeletal tree, Norman mounted the stairs.

My heart stopped, then pounded in my ears at breakneck speed until I was lightheaded.

"Hi Solberg."

"Hey." Why did he have to call me that today of all days?

I studied the man before me. In a light blue t-shirt and faded blue jeans, he was formidable.

Silence ensued.

"Andrew tells me you're going to school in Alexandria." I folded my arms across my chest.

"Yeah."

"I'm thinking of Bible College in the fall."

"Oh yeah?" He ran a hand through his tousled hair.

More silence.

"Is it true you're living in Mrs. Henke's basement apartment?"

"Yeah."

"I'd stop by, but Mrs. Henke is a lady." I lifted my voice, quoting the wealthy widow, "'Ladies know their place.' According to her, I don't."

"You're Methodist. Sue Ellen Henke might look past the non-Catholic part, but everyone knows where Methodists go when they..." he straightened. "...wait, you'd come to my apartment?"

My face grew warm. "Not with her watching, but yes, I would visit any friend."

"Alone?"

"I'm eighteen." I squared my shoulders. "It's 1994. Last I checked, there's no crime against visiting a friend." What would it be like to be kissed by him? My heart thundered in my ears.

"I don't think that's such a good idea."

I took a step toward him, close enough to see the brown flecks in his eyes. "Why not? We're friends, aren't we?"

"Of-of course. I said…" Norman took a step back.

He obviously wanted to get away from me. Like he had for the past four years. He'd been with a ton of girls, not one of them good enough for him.

"You're mine," I said, grabbing the front of his shirt. "In my dreams you are, anyway, and no one touches you!"

Whatever he was about to say was cut off when I reached up and pulled his head down to mine, his lips on mine.

He stiffened, grabbed both my arms to push me back, and I held on, kissing him like it was the last time, knowing it was.

He pulled away, visibly shaken. "What do you think you're doing?"

"I thought…"

Anger flared in his icy gray gaze. "You didn't think at all."

"What's wrong with me?" I set my hands on my hips. There's no way he knew about Jason. Was there?

He doesn't have to know to see the stain of filth on you.

"Nothing," he bit out.

"There must be something. You've dated everything that moves since we've been fifteen years old." His rejection stung like a salt lick in a gaping wound. I drew a deep breath. "Except me."

"We're," he waved a wild hand between us, "not like that. We've never been like that."

"I'd like to be."

Shock registered in his face, he said, "I've never…Your brother is my best friend."

"I thought I was too." Each word, a flaming arrow to my heart.

"Yes, a friend!" he shouted.

Humiliation made me shrink back. "I'm sorry, I didn't know." My voice sounded small, agony tearing me up inside. "You mean, all that I felt, that I hoped…I didn't see at all?" The anguish must have been in my eyes.

He winced. "I didn't come here for this."

"What did you come here for?" I demanded, hurt turning to swift anger.

He ran a shaky hand down the back of his head. "I came to say goodbye."

My heart was a lump in my throat. "What?"

"I'm leaving Friday. I'm going to work in Alexandria for the summer. If you were my friend, you'd be happy for me."

"Why would I be happy for you?" I clenched both fists at my sides.

"Do me a favor until then, Florence." He pulled his cap down. "Don't pay me a visit at my apartment. Not after the way you kiss." He turned and made his way down the stairs.

"Wait a minute," I called. Hopping on one foot, I peeled my boot off and threw it at his head.

It hit its mark with a thud.

"What the..." He turned around, his eyes widened in surprise as he rubbed the spot. "Mature, Florrie. Real mature."

Now it's Florrie. "Goodbye, Norman," I turned away.

"I'll see you Christmas break," he called after me.

"Don't bother." I retreated into the house, with every step my heart cracked until I was sure it had broken to pieces on the kitchen floor.

"They are the kind who worm their way into homes and gain control over gullible women, who are loaded down with sins and are swayed by all kinds of evil desires, always learning but never able to come to a knowledge of the truth. Just as Jannes and Jambres opposed Moses, so also these teachers oppose the truth. They are men of depraved minds, who, as far as the faith is concerned, are rejected. But they will not get very far because, as in the case of those men, their folly will be clear to everyone."

2 Timothy 3:6-9

Part II

41
September 2, 1996

Norman

Jerry Lewis' 31st Muscular Dystrophy telethon raised $49,200,000.

Freshman in blue gym uniforms, inscribed in yellow, *Alexandria Technical College*, filled the gym. I hauled a practice dummy across the gym floor, sweat dripping down my back.

"I was at West Acres mall in Fargo, North Dakota, and saw one of you there, your girlfriend wearing the Alex Tec jacket," Coach Richard announced, his voice echoing across the gym.

Oh boy.

The woman I'd been seeing, Marissa Potter, wanted to go to the mall and had forgotten her jacket. I let her wear mine, the one the school issued law enforcement students. The coach made a big deal about only cops in the program were to be seen in the community wearing the gear. What were the odds Coach would see us?

"Who was it?" his voice boomed.

Apparently, pretty good. I kept my head down, waiting for him to lecture us all.

"No volunteers?" he scrubbed his jaw. "Tell you what, I was going to have the guilty party do a hundred pushups, but I guess the whole class can do them."

My hand came up. "She was cold."

"She should have worn a jacket. It's wintertime in the Midwest." He stared me down.

I stared back.

"I'll let it slide this time." He reverted his attention to the class. "Okay, all of you get back to work. Those dummies aren't going to drag themselves."

A collective groan emerged from the group.

I stooped to grab my dummy.

"Marissa Potter. Nice." Coach Richard held up his hand.

I gave him a high five. What was I supposed to do?

The guy next to me said, "That's it? You're just gonna let him walk?"

"Did you say something?" The coach cupped his ear with his hand.

"I said…"

"Change of plans." Coach Richard waved his hand over the room. "All ya'all do two hundred pushups."

***

The early winter sky was layered in gray and blue clouds with a strip of yellow and pale pink in the distance.

A red Audi pulled alongside me in the school parking lot.

"Norman," Andrew called, rolling down the window. Seal's "Kiss from a Rose" boomed through the car stereo.

"Man, you are a sight for sore eyes."

"You asking me out?"

I laughed. "What are you doing in town?"

"I'm on my way to see Florence. What are your plans for dinner?"

I shrugged. "Not much. They involve the Student Center and watching *Star Trek*."

"Perkins okay with you?" Andrew asked.

"That'll work."

42

Norman

At Perkins restaurant, the table between us was crowded with pancakes, dishes of whipped butter, eggs, syrup, strawberries, muffins, hash browns, sausages, bacon, coffee, ice water, and orange juice.

"How's school?" Andrew asked.

"Eh," I said, having lost my sense of humor as the day wore on. "Looking forward to spring. Classes are driving me nuts."

"You do realize it's only September."

"Sadly."

Andrew took to his pancakes with a butter knife and fork. "I see they're hiring cops in Jamestown."

"You should apply."

"Funny, since you're the guy in law enforcement academy." He took a bite of pancake.

"I don't intend to work for the same place as Dad."

"Different department." He arched his brow. "You sure you aren't stalling?"

"Why would I do that?"

"Because you don't really want to be a cop. You want to be in the bee business," he stabbed his egg. "I would give anything to be in your shoes. Even my sister."

"You're offering me Florence? You know it's 1996, right?" I said, "She's the kind of woman you marry."

"Then marry her." Andrew dug into his hash browns. "We've been friends all of our lives. Why not brothers?"

"Yeah, well she isn't speaking to me." I downed my orange juice.

He glanced up. "What did you do?"

"Just before I left for school, I stopped by to say goodbye and she kissed me." I cut my egg with a fork.

"And?"

"And then she threw her boot at my head."

Andrew laughed. "Awesome."

"She's your sister. Kind of my sister too," I felt my face flush at the admission, the memory of her lips brought a sudden surge of warmth. "This isn't *Empire Strikes Back*."

He grinned. "Find out you have more than sisterly feelings, did you?"

"I can't go back even if I wanted to," I skated my glass around clockwise, realizing I did. More than the air in my lungs.

"Probably for the best." Andrew wiped his mouth with a napkin, tossing it on his plate. "You two were always like gasoline and a flame."

***

We stepped in line at the checkout counter. Andrew opened his wallet. Tucked alongside the bills was a photograph of Andrew, James and John, Florence in the middle.

The air left my lungs. Her jeans were high and fitted. A white t-shirt showed the smooth skin of her flat belly. Red hair flowed like cascades around her shoulders. Her full lips, painted coral, a warm contrast against her cheeks.

Peaches 'n cream.

Andrew's eyes were on me. "You want me to put in a good word? Afterwards, I'll go home and talk to dad. He might throw in a colony or two to sweeten the deal?"

"I'm with her." I pulled out my own picture of Marissa to show him the knockout I was dating.

His eyes widened. "Nice."

We walked outside, a gust of wind hit my face, taking my breath away.

"Sweet," I whistled low, passing a 1995 black Jaguar XJS in the parking lot.

"Wait!" someone called behind us. I turned around. A man in a sweatshirt, hood pulled over the baseball cap he wore, trotted toward us. He held up something in his hand.

"You dropped this." A closer look revealed the photograph from Andrew's wallet.

Andrew took it from his grasp. "Thanks man. I owe you one."

He smiled, quick and easy, and headed toward the Jaguar.

Andrew withdrew his wallet, tucking the photo back inside.

"Did you see that guy get into the Jaguar?" he asked, returning his wallet to his back pocket.

I nodded. "Looked like a kid."

"Where would a guy like that have money for such a sweet ride?"

"Wealthy parents?" I watched the Jaguar until it disappeared into the distant twilight.

"Indeed, the safest road to Hell is the gradual one—the gentle slope, soft underfoot, without sudden turnings, without milestones, without signposts…Your affectionate uncle, Screwtape."

C. S. Lewis, *Screwtape Letters*

43

Florence

From my desktop stereo, Switchfoot dared me to move with their latest song.

"What if I don't want to pick myself up off the floor, Jon Foreman?" I lay, staring up at the ceiling of my dorm room at Bethany College of Missions.

"How about a study break?" Karla Mitchell was my roommate and strict as the nuns at Norman's school growing up. She never had fun, or study breaks for that matter.

"Karla. The test is tomorrow."

"Just a muffin from Perkins down the road."

When we reached her car, Jamie Nagen approached. "Hey," he said, his gaze fixed on Karla. Jamie was a first-year student and just as stuffy as Karla. I waited for her to tell Jamie she'd meet up with him later.

Instead she said, "You don't mind if he comes with us."

"No, that's fine." I'd been duped. I was just here in case they got caught by the dean. Dating wasn't allowed between first-year students.

At the table, they pulled out their books in front of their coffee.

"I thought we were just coming for a muffin," I frowned.

"We'll quiz each other," Karla said.

I took a sip of coffee and sat the mug down.

The hairs on my head prickled. I felt like I was being watched. Scanning the room, my eyes met with a pair of vivid blue ones. His eyes held mine for what seemed forever. I let my gaze drop to the western shirt he wore. He was handsome and appeared to be in fine shape.

I flicked a glance at Karla. She was sitting so close to Jamie she was practically on his lap.

Throughout the study break, Mr. Blue Eyes frequently looked at me. Sometimes he only glanced quickly in my direction, but other times his eyes grazed over my body, down my legs, making me feel both uneasy and excited.

His gaze came back up again and met mine in an intoxicating dance.

I turned back to Karla who was giggling at something Jamie said. Turns out even the goodiest of two shoes could be persuaded to break the rules given the right guy.

***

I drove to Cub Foods for grapes and cereal in the red Audi. Andrew had bought a new Chevy car and I was awarded his old one.

Afterward, I got in the driver's seat, checked the rearview mirror and shifted into reverse. I came to an abrupt halt at the crunch of metal.

Glancing back, I saw I'd hit a black Jaguar. Of all the luck! Where had it come from? I drew a breath, braced myself for rage, and got out. "I didn't…"

"I'm so sorry. This was all my fault."

It was the man from Perkins.

He wore a dark blue sports coat, white sweater beneath, and faded blue jeans. A lock of dark hair fell across his forehead. He had boyish good looks and a baby face.

He ran a hand through his hair. The scent of coconut oil wafted toward me, flooding my nostrils. I thought of the beach and nostalgia swept over me.

"What? I…"

He reached into his back pocket. "Let me get my card. My insurance should cover this."

"Shouldn't we call the police?"

He bent down, touching the fender. "I don't think we need to. My brother owns a garage and will have it fixed up in no time."

"I don't know…"

He straightened, squinting at me. "Don't I know you?"

Heat crept up my neck. "I-I saw you at Perkins the other night."

His full lips curved into a slow enigmatic smile, revealing strong white teeth against his tanned face.

I inhaled sharply, air lodging oddly in my lungs.

He smiled. "Alex Diestrum."

"Florence Solberg. I'm a freshman at Bethany College of Missions."

His eyes widened. "You gonna be a missionary?"

"I've always wanted to go to Japan." My face burned, this time with embarrassment. For the first time, I felt like a fuddy duddy.

"Really? I'm partial to Greenland myself."

"You travel?" I realize it was a long conversation to have in the parking lot over a fender bender, but I found myself reluctant to leave.

"A bit." He flashed another warm grin, checking his watch, he got into his car. "Say, I've got to get going. I'll be in touch."

"Wait! Don't you want my number?" my voice trailed off as he drove away.

44

Florence

In the girls' dorm on the third floor, there were two wall phones in the center of the hall next to the lounge. One for the north end, the other, south. Down the north hall was our room.

The phone rang.

"I'll get it," Karla called. "Hello? Yeah, just a second. Florence, it's for you."

Andrew was on his way home. Probably forgot something in the Audi. I took the receiver from her grasp. "Hi Andrew. What's up?"

"Who's Andrew?" said a deep voice.

A shiver rolled up my arm. "My brother."

"This is Alex Diestrum."

He didn't need to tell me. I would have recognized his voice anywhere.

"How did you know my phone number?" I twirled the phone cord around my finger.

"You gave it to me." There was a smile in his answer. "Want to take a study break? I know this little Italian place."

"But I don't remember giving you…"

"That is, if your boyfriend doesn't mind."

I giggled. "I don't have a boyfriend."

"Good," the word rolled off his tongue. "You hungry?"

"Starving."

"I'll pick you up at six." A pause. "Wear something nice."

***

A black Jaguar pulled up in the parking space outside the girls' dormitory. Alex stepped out. He wore a white shirt, bolo tie, and khaki pants. Another man emerged from the passenger side. He was shorter, with a trimmed beard and slicked back dark hair.

Alex's eyes roved over my green sweater and black stretch pants. "You look beautiful."

"Should I have worn a dress?"

"Nope. You can't improve on perfection."

The man next to him cleared his throat.

Alex turned toward him. "Florence this is my brother Earl."

I smiled at him. "Nice to meet you."

He nodded. "Alex said you have a vehicle for me to look at."

I led him over to my parking space and red Audi. He ran a hand along the bumper.

"What do you think?" I asked.

"Doesn't look too bad." He straightened. "I can have it fixed by Friday."

"Really? How much is it going to cost me?"

Alex reached for my arm. "I told you I've got this." He led me over to the sleek automobile he arrived in. I sank down in the passenger seat. The interior smelled like Old Spice and cigars. Both foreign and dangerous.

Odd.

Alex smelled like coconut, reminding me of the days at the Jamestown Public Pool.

We arrived at Uno restaurant. It was nice but nothing fancy. I wasn't out of place in my green sweater and black stretch pants.

Both handsome and sophisticated, Alex drew the attention of the room when he walked in.

Our waitress, a pretty woman with a black ponytail and strawberry lipstick, took our drink orders. I thought about the money in my pocket and ordered water.

Alex leaned toward me. "So tell me, why Japan?"

"It's a beautiful culture and country. Andrew says…"

"Right. Your brother." His friendly demeanor, engaging and charming. "Any sisters?"

I shook my head. "No sisters, but two brothers besides Andrew, James and John."

"Your parents are Catholic?"

"You sure are curious."

He sat back. "Star struck is more accurate a description."

"My momma…"

The waitress returned with a water for me and a whisky sour for Alex.

He took a sip. "Gentleman Jack next time, but this is good too." He winked at the waitress.

She blushed, took our dinner order and moved to the next table.

"Sorry about that," he said, turning back to me. "What were you saying? Something about your mom."

"She died when I was eight. My Aunt Sophia and cousins, Leah and Lana moved into our lake house afterward."

"Is that sadness I hear in your voice?" His handsome face flickered with concern. "Put on the garment of praise for the spirit of heaviness."

My mouth dropped open. "How did you…?"

The waitress brought our food.

I'd ordered cheese ravioli and hid my disappointment at the four sauceless pieces on my plate.

"Looks good," Alex told the waitress, eyeing his chef salad.

She set another drink in front of him. "This one's on me because of the first one."

"Oh, you didn't have to do that," he said in a tone that was clear she did.

After she left, he turned, gazing at me beneath heavy lids. "You know what I do about unhappiness? I buy it off."

"You can't fix unhappiness with stuff." Something was off. One minute, he seemed nervous, unsure. Polite. The next he awarded me a winning smile that was hot enough to curl my toes. It was both unsettling and exciting.

Familiar.

"This is good," I said, taking a bite of the buttery French bread.

"It's delicious."

"I love it." I took another bite.

"If you love it so much, why don't you marry it?" He grinned, a silly boyish one.

"Funny." I took a sip of water. "So what do you do for a living?"

"I'm an interior decorator."

"Seriously? I'll bet there's good money in that."

"Depends on the client but I do alright. I survey the home and then quote an estimate according to needs and budget."

"Did you have to go to school for that?"

"Yeah. I went to Wahpeton. They have a two year technical school there. Then I had to pass a licensing exam required by the National Council."

"You make good money then?" I took a bite of ravioli.

"Upwards of six figures."

I arched a brow. "Six figures?"

He smiled. "Maybe."

"Do you work for a corporation?"

"No, I'm independent."

I checked my watch. "I'd better get back or Karla will call the security guard."

He chuckled. "I thought she was the security guard."

"Yeah." He noticed! What else had he seen?

He pulled up behind the girl's dorm and put the Jaguar in park.

"I had a good time," I glanced out the window at the crescent moon. "Look at the moon. The heavens really do declare God's glory. Did you know the moon moves one to two inches away from the earth per year? A couple billion years ago, it would have been too close to the earth and past the Roche limit."

He gazed into my eyes and I thought he might kiss me. He didn't, and I reached for the door handle. "I'd better head inside."

In the entrance of the freshman dorm, he said, "Saturday's supposed to be a clear night for stargazing."

"They have forty acres in the back of the campus. It's a pretty walk."

"Will Saturday work for you?"

"Saturday's perfect."

After he left, I walked on air all the way up the staircase to the third floor.

A flatterer never seems absurd; the flattered always takes his word.

-Benjamin Franklin

45
September 5, 1996

Florence

Following U.S. cruise missile strikes on Iraq, crude oil prices rose as the market speculated when Iraq would begin exporting oil under UN Resolution 986.

Charlie Peacock's "Kiss Me Like a Woman" created a scandal on the third floor in the girl's dormitory, and I was thrilled to see Alex waiting outside the dorm at nine on my way to the student center.

He wore a brushed corduroy jacket lined with fleece, worn faded blue jeans, and a ski hat. A few dark locks poked from beneath.

Delighted, I asked, "Is it Saturday already?"

"Couldn't wait," he said, reaching for my hand.

I smiled. "I'm ready if you are."

The night sky twinkled with stars. "Did you know the Northern Hemisphere is always pointing in a different direction than the Southern Hemisphere?" I said. "Take Australia. Stargazers get a slightly different view of the sky and can see different constellations than those in the United States."

He pulled me over to the shadows of stairs alongside the gymnasium.

"You're a Christian, aren't you," I said.

He glanced over at me.

"I mean, what you said the other day about the garment of praise."

"That's my favorite verse," he said. "And freckles are my favorite too. And your hair is like a flame. And your eyes…" his tone, husky. "Like emeralds."

Unaccustomed to such bold praise, I said, "During the year, our view into space through the night sky changes as we orbit. It looks slightly different each night because Earth is in a different spot in its orbit."

Then, I felt his fingers slip beneath my shirt, resting just beneath my breasts.

"Th-The stars appear each night to move slightly west of where they were the night before."

His hands came up, closing over my breasts. He leaned in and whispered, "My little stargazer."

"I thought you were interested in astronomy," I whispered back. Any protest I had to his illicit touch scattered into the night.

"I'm more interested in you." His eyes dipped to my mouth. "I had no idea you knew so much about astronomy."

My heart thumped in my ears. "You won't see them. Not with a full moon."

"I don't know any constellations."

"Don't you want to kiss me?"

"I just wanted to take you someplace that wasn't out to dinner so you couldn't order the most expensive thing on the menu."

"What?" I pulled away from him, heat rushing my neck, flooding my ears.

I'd ordered ravioli and hadn't looked at the price. I'd been thinking more about the calories. He couldn't have worried about the cost.

"I offered to pay," I said.

"Did you know I'm part werewolf?"

I laughed. *Was he serious?*

"In the 1500s, three men were brought to trial for murder, torture and other heinous crimes. One of these men was Michel Verdun, self-proclaimed werewolf.

"During Verdun's trial, he named two accomplices to his horrific deeds–Philibert Montot and Pierre Bourgot. Pierre also claimed to be a werewolf."

I should have paid for supper.

"…A man came upon a vicious wolf, but managed to escape the attack, severely wounding the beast. The man followed the bloody trail…and at its end was wounded Michel Verdun."

How long had what I'd ordered bother him? Who had he told?

"The man became convinced that Verdun was able to transform himself from human to wolf, and something in between. The story spread, and Verdun was charged with lycanthropy—the ability to change from human to wolf—and was burned at the stake."

It was a weird tale that didn't seem like something he'd made up. But why tell it at all?

"I'm a werewolf," he stated, rather matter-of-fact.

"You are not." I glared at him.

"Am too," he said, his eyes serious. "I'll prove it. Feel your chin."

"Okaaay." I felt along my jaw.

"Now feel mine. You'll feel the crack in it."

I reached over and touched his chin. He brought his face up to mine and screamed. I yanked my hand back, punching his arm. "You scared me."

"I had you going," his eyes twinkled in the moonlight. "Admit it."

I rolled my eyes. "I know there's no such thing as werewolves."

We reached the girls dorm and stepped inside the entrance. Abruptly, his eyes changed from teasing to desire. "I've never met a woman as beautiful or as sexy as you." He ran a finger down my cheek. "The stars light up the sky, but you light up a room."

I licked my lips, hoping he would take the hint and kiss me. "Want to come up? Karla is gone."

"I can't do that, Florence. It would be wrong."

Like a blast of cold water, I bolted back to reality. "I was teasing."

"You didn't tell her about us, did you?"

"No." My cheeks burst into flames. "Good night, then."

"Good night, my little stargazer."

Later, lying in bed, I thought about the evening, the way it ended. I'd been too bold. Next time, I'd play it cool.

If there was a next time.

A lie stands on one leg, truth on two.
-Benjamin Franklin

46

Florence

Next time was the very next evening. Alex met me on the way to the dorm after supper.

"Hey," he grinned.

"Hi." Heat crept into my cheeks at the sight of him in a black button-down shirt, two buttons undone, and faded blue jeans.

"I didn't expect to see you." I pushed an unruly lock of hair away from my eyes.

"I thought maybe we could head over to my place and hang out."

His place! "That sounds nice."

The ride in his Jaguar was scented with coconut. His townhouse was in Eden Prairie. The carpet was cream and plush. White and clean, there were blue lava lamps on the living room end tables.

Sterile.

I removed my shoes by the door and found myself holding my breath. "It's very nice," I said.

"Can I get you something to drink?" His eyes shifted, and was there a tremble in his voice?

Could it be he was nervous?

The thought made me smile. "No thank you."

"Have a seat." He set his sunglasses on the glass coffee table. They landed with a clank in the quiet room.

I sat down carefully on the leather couch. "How long have you lived here?"

"Not long," he said from the kitchen. "What will you have to drink?"

"I'm good," I said.

He moved about while I scanned the living room. There was one picture of the ocean, and a picture window opposite. There were shades on all the windows. I didn't see any family pictures.

He returned with two glasses. "I know you said you didn't want anything, but I wanted you to try this drink I made you," he said with a smile.

"What is it?" I took it from his grasp.

"A grasshopper. Nonalcoholic."

I set it on the end table, patting the cushion next to me.

He sat stiffly, looking like he wanted to be anywhere but next to me.

I smiled, leaning toward him.

He leaned back.

I sat back, frowning. "Do you want me to leave?"

"No! No, of course not." He pulled me roughly against his chest. "You make my heart pound," he whispered, then I felt his hands on the edge of my shirt. He pulled it from its tuck, his fingers making their way up.

Like last time. Not very original, and I felt my cheeks flush at the uncharitable thought.

His face was in my neck and his hands were up my shirt. Soon, clothes were discarded.

This is it, I thought on my back on the floor. This is the moment. And then…nothing.

"Alex?" I asked tentatively.

He sighed, pushing off me. "I'm sorry, I've got a lot on my mind."

"Like what?"

"Nothing," he zipped up his jeans.

I reached for my shirt. "I'm a good listener."

He sighed. "I hate to bother you."

I reached over, laying a hand on his arm. "Tell me."

"Remember Earl?"

"Your brother that fixed the car? He did a great job."

"Yeah, well now he's saying I owe him. That he never agreed to do the work for free. He wants his money."

I frowned. "I thought you said…"

"I know what I said," he snapped, and then blew out a breath. "Sorry. He said it was a gift, but now he's doing a takeback."

"How much was it?"

"A lot, but he'll settle for half."

"Which is…?"

"Nine hundred bucks."

"Nine hundred…holy moly Rocky."

"I'm sorry to have even brought it up to you. It's not your problem. I'll figure something out."

"No, I'll call Andrew."

Brief anger flickered in his eyes. "Your brother?"

I blinked, taking a step back. "I won't tell him you said you'd take care of it. Anyway, it was my fault to begin with."

He scrubbed his jaw. "What would you say?"

"That I was too scared to say anything. It's his car. Don't worry about it."

"You don't have to run it through your insurance if it's under a thousand."

"There you go."

Relief flooded his features. "I owe you one."

"No problem."

"I've got tomorrow evening off. Want to come over again?"

"I don't have to."

"I want you to."

***

The next evening, Alex picked me up in his Jaguar. By the time he pulled up in front of his townhouse, I was a bundle of nerves. How far would we go? How far did I want to?

Inside the entrance, I kicked off my shoes on the small linoleum space, feeling no more at home than yesterday.

"Make yourself comfortable. I'm going to shower." He winked.

Heart thundering, I stepped into the plush living room. There was a tape on the VCR. It looked like a home movie. His family? I flicked a glance around, put it in, and pressed play. Images flashed across the screen. Hypnotized, I stared, wave after wave of lust slammed into my lower belly.

The shower shut off, and I jumped, pressing eject with shaky fingers. I set the tape back on the VCR, making sure to line it up exactly as it had been before.

Alex strolled in wearing nothing but lounge pants and a devastating smile. Damp hair curled at the base of his neck. He had a glass in each hand, one with amber liquid, the other was pale red.

He handed me the pale red one. "You'll insult me if you don't take it," he said. "Besides, it's virgin. I know your favorite is 7 Up. I put in a splash of grenadine for color."

I took it from his hand and sank to the couch.

He sat next to me, his eyes held mine over the rim of the glass as he took a sip.

I took a sip and winced. "How much grenadine did you put in this?"

He chuckled low in his throat. "So tell me about Jason Waverly."

My face went hot. "There's nothing to tell."

"There's got to be something. You mentioned him that first day."

Had I? "He was the son of my aunt's friend."

His brow arched. "A friend of a friend?"

"Something like that." I took another long swallow, feeling relaxed, and sat back. "Did I tell you he was easy on the eyes?"

"Really?" His fingers played with the edge of my shirt.

Feeling warm and tranquil, I continued, "He was muscular and older. I was a kid, too tall, too awkward, too out of touch with the way things were." I found myself telling him about the pool and the boys, and my swimming suit.

"I'd like to have it out with them." A dark look flashed across his handsome features.

"That was a long time ago. I'm over it."

He set his drink on the end table next to him, and shifted closer. His hand came up my shirt, and the room began to buzz. Was the TV on in the background, or were images merely playing over and over in my head?

"Is there anything wrong?" Alex sounded far away.

"No," my own voice sounding funny in my ears.

As my lids grew heavy, my last thought was we hadn't even kissed.

47
November 22, 1996

Florence

O.J. Simpson took the stand as a hostile witness in the wrongful death lawsuit filed against him, saying it is "absolutely not true."

All the clothes I owned were laid out on the bed: three pairs of pleated stretch pants, four blouses, and two cardigans.

Karla sat on her bed, watching me.

"I can't believe Alex is coming to chapel." She eyed the pile of clothes. "Don't you have a dress to wear?"

"One." It was plain and pale blue, wrinkled and ugly. I looked ugly in it. For the first time, I wished for a pretty dress. Something in red.

"I'd wear the pegging Skidz and pink shirt."

I fingered the pants from Merry Go Round. In the end, I chose the pleated teal pants, teal blouse, and matching sweater with lavender piping.

Alex pulled up in his Jaguar and got out. He wore white sunglasses that matched his white sports jacket, a light blue sweater beneath. His blue jeans were dark and snug.

His eyes switched from warm to cool in an instant. "I thought you were going to wear a dress."

I smoothed my hand down my leggings. "What's wrong?"

"Nothing."

"You don't seem too happy to see me."

"Of course I'm glad to see you. I always am."

"Thanks for coming to chapel," I told him, entering the sanctuary. "I think you're really going to like this guy."

"Whoa," he whispered, halting at the back row. "Let's sit here."

The speaker stepped up to the microphone. "Good afternoon, students and guests."

"Who's this guy again?" Alex asked.

"Dale Rolland." I tapped his bulletin. "He survived a bad car accident, and now goes around telling people about how Jesus saved him."

"Imagine you're seventeen and on your way to…" the speaker continued.

"You look nice," Alex said in a loud whisper.

I smiled, hoping he would take the hint.

The speaker continued, "It was raining and I'd been drinking. When I hit the curb I knew was there…"

"Drinking and driving?" Alex's whisper was loud.

I glanced around. Jamie and Karla sat in the pew ahead of us. Jamie turned and scowled.

Alex fell silent, and I breathed a sigh of relief.

Rolland continued, coming to the part about laying one's life down, and I glanced over at Alex.

He checked his watch. "Want to come over to my place afterward?"

"Sure," I said, willing to say anything to get him to be quiet.

After the service, Alex was talking to Derek Winkler, a sophomore and his girlfriend, Rebecca Darling. Derek was a good-looking guy with blonde hair, and didn't seem interested in Bible school."

"Hey Florence," Andrew called, waving his hand as he made his way over.

"Andrew," I rushed him. "What are you doing here?"

"I heard about the speaker and wanted to hear his testimony."

Alex thrust out his hand. "Name's Alex Diestrum. I'm with Florence."

Andrew shook it. "Andrew Solberg, Florence's younger brother."

"Cool." Alex flashed a grin.

"Hey, have you two eaten?" Andrew asked.

Alex and I exchanged glances.

I answered, "Not yet."

"What about Texas Roadhouse?" Alex rolled his bulletin against his palm.

Andrew's eyes lit. "I wanted to try that place."

"Meet you there?" Alex said, drawing me against himself.

Andrew looked disappointed. "I was hoping Florence wanted to come with me so we could catch up."

"No problem." Alex released me.

Andrew reached into his pocket for his keys. "There's room enough for all of us if you want to ride along."

Alex arched a brow. "You don't mind?"

"Nope."

"I have to look out for Florence," Alex said, next to me as Andrew pulled up to the front of the restaurant. "She likes to order the most expensive thing on the menu."

Fuming, I said, "I can't believe you just said that."

"Hey, babe," he winked. "Lighten up."

48

"What do you think?" Andrew asked when we were seated.

"I like the peanuts." I took a few from the silver bucket in front of me. "I can't believe everyone just drops the shells on the floor."

"I hear they have good steak here," Andrew said, taking a drink of his Roy Rogers. "Norman's college girlfriend moved to Jamestown with him."

"Oh?" My mouth went dry. Last I'd heard from Aunt Sophia he'd gotten a job at the police department.

Andrew set his glass down. "Not sure what Aunt Sophia told you about Marissa, but he's been dating her since fall of his senior year at Alex Tech."

"They're engaged?"

"Nope, but my guess it's only a matter of time before he proposes."

"I'm happy for him." Suddenly, the peanut in my mouth tasted like cardboard.

"Dad would never have let you marry him anyway," Andrew shook his head. "He's Catholic. A bunch of Mary worshipers, am I right?"

"Andrew." What had gotten into him? I'd never heard him disrespect Norman, or anyone for that matter.

"Did you know the pope is called His Holiness?" Alex cut in.

"Yeah," I said, ready to change subjects. Priests were called Father, something Jesus said only God in heaven should be called, but talking about it seemed disloyal to the Millers.

But Alex wasn't finished, "The Pope is called 'Vicar of Christ' and is infallible. The congregation is full of do-gooders who don't want to go to hell."

"Who is the Pope anyway?" I asked.

"John Paul II," Andrew answered.

I enjoyed talking to Norman about Catholics, finding common faith and mission. Now, the discussion made me uneasy.

After supper, Andrew dropped us off at Alex's car parked next to the girls' dorm. "See you at Christmas, Florence," he said, and flicked a glance at Alex. "Nice to meet you."

"You too."

Watching Andrew drive away, I mulled over their conversation, preparing a rebuttal. "You know that cure for happiness you were talking about is in a set of beliefs," I told Alex.

"Unless that set of beliefs is garbage," Alex said, his skeptical look apparent beneath the campus outdoor lighting. "Want to come to my house?"

I frowned. "I don't know, it's pretty late and I have a test tomorrow."

"We won't be long. An hour," he said.

"Well I…"

"Hey," Derek Winkler called. Emerging from the administration building, he jogged over to us. "What are you guys up to?"

Alex scratched the back of his head with four quick fingers. "I was just trying to talk Florence into a movie. I rented *The Dead of Winter*."

"I've wanted to see that," Derek said.

"Why don't you join us?" Alex reached into his pocket, pulling out his car keys.

"I'd like to but Rebecca hit the hay super early."

Alex grinned. "Doesn't mean you have to."

When we arrived at his townhouse, Alex made his way to the kitchen and began fixing drinks.

Locating the rental, I popped the tape into the VCR and sat down on the couch, hoping Alex wouldn't bring up the Catholics or their church.

To my surprise, Derek sat next to me. A heady scent of aftershave wafted toward me. His arm brushed mine.

"Here you are, Florence." Alex handed me a ginger beer, and then turned to Derek. "Jim Beam on the rocks for you."

Derek took the drink and caught my eyes. The look in his was lustful and scorching.

Familiar.

I sipped my spicy drink. "Aren't you dating Rebecca Darling?"

"Depends on what you call dating," his hand was high on my thigh.

I shot a glance at Alex. His eyes were heavy as he sat in the chair, watching us.

"I mean, will she be mad?"

Derek chuckled low in his throat. "About what?"

"I don't know," I said, trying to remember what we were talking about.

In a dreamlike state, I watched Alex pull the blinds.

Was Derek tugging at my shirt? I tried to stand, lost my balance, and fell back down to the couch.

49

Florence

"Dehydration," the school nurse, Frieda announced. "You have two options. You can sit in here during your lunch hour and drink juice …or you can go to the clinic in Shakopee for an IV."

"I'll drink the juice."

I woke up this morning in my bed, but couldn't remember how I'd gotten back to the dorm. Searching my brain, the last thing I remembered was saying goodbye to Andrew.

Feeling like death warmed over, the room spun. A wave of nausea swept over me, and I made a mad dash to the bathroom. I barely made it to the toilet before throwing up.

Karla announced she was taking me to the school nurse.

Now in her office, Nurse Frieda gave me a long look. "Were you out drinking last night?"

"No, of course not."

"Uh huh."

"I'm serious, Frieda. I don't drink."

The door opened, and the campus security guard Steve walked in. "Afternoon, Florence."

"Hi," I said in a small voice.

Campus police were hired by the college to make sure we didn't skip curfew or do anything crazy, like sneak in through the dorm windows. Steve was a nice guy who felt like the students needed to live a little.

Steve pulled a chair over and sat across from me. "Do you have anything you need to report? Anything done against your wishes?"

The tips of my ears went hot. "No."

Frieda excused herself. The door shut with a soft click.

He pinned me with a serious look. "Have you been hallucinating, had trouble breathing, problems with vision…?"

"No, no, and no."

"Are you sure? You wouldn't be in trouble if you did."

"No. I think it's just the stomach flu."

His eyes searched my face.

I dug into my purse for my compact, glancing in the small mirror and saw my lips were swollen and red with kissing.

Give it up or be good at it.

"Florence?"

I blinked. "I'm sorry, what did you say?"

"If you become unusually tired after having a drink, you may have been drugged."

Fear swept cold through me. "It was nothing like that."

He appeared unconvinced.

I sipped my apple juice.

He sighed. "You'll call me if you remember anything?"

"Of course."

After he left, I drank three more cans of apple juice and returned to my room. I called in sick for both classes and my housekeeping job, and crawled beneath the covers, falling asleep.

It was dusk when I woke. The soft light from the lamp on Karla's desk illuminated the darkness.

"Feeling better?" Karla asked, sitting at the desk in front of her textbooks.

"What time is it?"

"Nine."

Nine! "Did Alex call?"

"No. But I didn't get back until seven thirty."

I bolted from bed, hurried to the hall phone and dialed Alex's number. After the third ring, the answering machine picked up, "Hey, this is Alex. You know what to do." *Beep.*

"Alex, it's Florence. I just woke up. I mean, I slept all day because I wasn't feeling well. That is, I'm sorry I missed you when you tried to call. If you tried to call. Anyway, call me back." I hung up and returned to the room.

"Landon Albert wants to see you in his office tomorrow morning before your class."

The dean? "What does he want?"

"I don't know."

Was it something to do with Alex? I didn't know of any rule I'd broken, but I'd been with him nearly every night since September.

"Maybe I'm on the dean's list."

Karla looked up. "Wouldn't they send you a letter?"

I laid back down in bed, dreading the impending visit to Mr. Albert's office.

50
December 10, 1996

Florence

Rwandan Genocide: Maurice Baril military advisor to the UN Secretary-General and head of the UN Military Division of the Department of Peacekeeping Operations, recommended the UN multinational forces in Zaire stand down.

The dean gave me a warning: get your grades up or go home. Imagining Aunt Sophia's delight at my failure, I was in front of my textbooks, attempting to study.

Except I couldn't get Alex Diestrum out of my head. He made me feel like I could walk on water. Where was he? Why hadn't he called?

My stomach rumbled. I glanced at the clock. Nine. They would be serving nachos in The Oasis tonight. A study break wouldn't hurt.

On the way to the student center, I thought about Christmas break. Being done with school after that wouldn't be so bad. Maybe I could get a job in Jamestown.

"Florence," a low voice behind me called.

I came to a halt, rubbing my palms with my thumbs. Without turning around, I continued toward The Oasis.

"Hey! Florence," he said again, louder as he caught up to me, reaching for my arm.

I yanked it away, whirling around. "What?"

His eyes sparkled and his face was flushed. He looked handsome and really, really good. "I wrote you a poem," he said, handing me a piece of paper.

I unfolded it. "Soldier Boy"? What kind of poem was this?

You were my first love
And you'll be my last love
I will never make you blue
I'll be true to you

I looked up. The twinkle in his eye and his boyish grin told me he was happy about the poem, serious even, and I didn't have the heart to hurt him.

"Where have you been?" I asked.

He grinned. "Did you miss me?"

"It's been over two weeks since that night at Texas Roadhouse."

"Who's counting? I had a job in Wisconsin. I just got back."

"And you couldn't call?"

"Should I have?" He arched his brow.

Irritation crept up the back of my neck, mostly for myself. I'd blown the whole thing up in my head. "Sorry. I didn't mean to act like an obsessive freak."

"Hey, it's okay. You're my obsessive freak."

"I've got to go." I pulled away.

He reached for me once more. "Why so glum, chum?"

Annoyed, I sighed. "I'm failing college."

He gave a laugh. "I guess you can't be both gorgeous and smart at the same time."

I frowned. "Is that supposed to be funny?"

"No. I just am surprised." He gazed at me through lowered lids.

"What am I gonna do? Dad will probably wonder what happened. Then there's Sophia. She'll look at me and I'll see triumph in her eyes. And don't get me started on Leah and Lana."

His eyes dropped. "The day I turned thirteen, Dad left us."

I stilled. "You and your mother?"

"Yes. We were out in the garden. Mom and I were planting baby potatoes. We couldn't wait for fall. I was good at meal planning, and they would go perfect for Dad's favorite meal, baby potatoes, peas, and roast beef."

"You were thirteen?"

He gave a sheepish smile. "I liked to help her."

My heart clenched at the thought of him at thirteen gardening with his mother.

"I've never felt connected," Alex said, locking his eyes on mine. "Somehow you found me when no one else could. I know you see me. Know me, although I don't know how.

"You are never gonna believe what I did."

"What?"

"Check this out." He held up two plane tickets marked Las Vegas.

"What are these for?"

"Duh. We're going to Vegas."

"I can't go on a trip! My grades suck. That means I can't come back to school. I have to figure out what I'm going to do next year. Not go on vacation."

"You can do that in a hotel room in Vegas," he urged. "You were going home for two weeks anyway, right?"

"Well yeah."

"So, come to Vegas with me. Ten days is all I ask. If you come back and still want to go home, tell your family you decided to quit."

"Lie?"

"Okay, tell them the truth. Then get a job so you don't have to listen to their lectures. Or…" he paused, his eyes held mine. "You can come live with me."

"Live with you." I shook my head. "I don't think so."

"Then let's get married."

"In Las Vegas?"

"I missed you. I went away, hoping to get you out of my head, but I can't stop thinking about you. You're sweet, like sugar," he murmured, lowering his mouth to mine, and kissed me.

Ravenously.

It was passionate and forceful. Stunned, I stood frozen before my arms found their way around his shoulders. I tentatively slid my tongue against his. He mimicked the action. My fingers went up his jaw and through his hair. He cupped his hands around my face, sliding his hands in my hair.

I remembered his kisses being soft. Had I merely dreamt tenderness? Imagined a gentle embrace? The lips that kissed me were hard. The arms holding me were rough…almost mechanical.

He withdrew slightly. "I want you too much," he murmured, his tone ardent before his mouth took mine once more.

Fervor.

Las Vegas sounded exciting. Perhaps a chance to gather my thoughts and form a battle plan.

51
December 21, 1996

Florence

Taiwanese-American AIDS researcher David Ho was named *Time Magazine's* Man of the Year and the lobby of the Golden Nugget bustled about with tourists. A couple at a booth motioned me over.

"How long are you staying in Vegas?" the woman asked.

"Ten days."

"Are you planning to do any gambling?"

I shook my head. "I don't gamble."

They shared a laugh.

She said, "That's good because this city isn't built on winners."

Alex reached for my arm. "Come on. They're salesmen trying to sell you a tour."

When we reached the hotel room, there were rose petals leading to the bed. The rose petals and balloons were over the top. I felt both uncomfortable and flattered.

He was trying to make things right.

"You are the sun, moon, and stars to me," he said. "I knew from the moment I laid eyes on you there would never be anyone else that could make me feel this way."

I turned to him and he got down on one knee. "I've never felt this way about anyone. Marry me?" He popped open a black ring box and a diamond sparkled.

"Alex," I breathed.

He took the ring and slipped it on my finger.

"It fits." I glanced at him, an overwhelming feeling of love swept over me. It was too soon. How could I be certain? *I knew the moment Case introduced us. There was no one else for me,* my dad's words came rushing back.

We were married at The Wedding Chapel by Elvis Presley.

In the hotel room afterward, Alex said, "Get dressed up. I want to walk Fremont Street."

I flashed my warmest smile. "I thought maybe we could spend our wedding night in the room."

"I don't want to just sit around."

"Oh, I don't think we'd be sitting around." I drew my arms around his neck. Every tilt of my head or murmur in my throat, he copied. Was none of it real?

Was he real?

"It's like I'm kissing myself," I said, and as soon as the words left my mouth, I wished to drag them back.

His eyes went dark and he took a step back. "What does that mean?"

"Nothing."

"Too late now. What did you mean by that comment?"

"Do you like kissing me?"

He laughed. "What?"

"Do. You. Like. Kissing me."

"You're crazy. You know, on second thought, I'd rather not spend the evening with a miserable crank." He stormed out the door. "I'm leaving."

"No, wait! I didn't mean it," I called, but he was gone.

I hurried after him, halting in midstride. Two housekeepers in the hallway stared at me. Couples leaving their rooms glanced back.

Afraid to make a scene, I returned to the room and plopped down on the bed.

What happened?

One minute, I was on my honeymoon being kissed by my devastatingly handsome husband, and the next, I was alone. Why did I have to say anything? Everything had been going fine until I opened my big mouth.

Where had he gone? He'll come back. He just needed to blow off steam.

***

I watched *Happy Gilmore* and was finishing *Romeo and Juliet* when the door opened and there stood Alex.

I sprang from the bed and rushed him. "Where have you been?"

"Relax," He chuckled. "I went for a walk on Fremont."

Kissing his neck and mouth, I murmured, "I'm so sorry," over and over.

"Okay, okay." He set me away from him. "Get dressed."

"Why?" I reached for him once more.

He pulled back quickly.

I frowned. "I said I was sorry."

"We'll come back and do this later. Let's go to Fremont, baby."

We ended up at a strip club, Glitter Gulch.

The atmosphere was dark. I was more conscious of couples around me staring than I was of half-naked women on stage.

Fear waned, and I started to relax even as my ears began to ring.

Alex's eyes were on me.

That was good at least.

"Want me to pay for a lap dance?" he asked.

"You can have one," I said. Then I could drink my water and clear my head.

His lids lowered. "What if I want you to have one?"

If I said no, would he get angry and storm off again? Then I would be alone in a strip club. A shiver rolled through me. It didn't matter, I couldn't do it.

My face went hot and I glanced away. "No thanks."

Much to my relief, he didn't push it.

Back in the hotel room, I got on the bed and reached for his shirt, pulling him toward me. "Come here."

He sat down on the edge and picked up the phone. "I wanted to check out Red Rooster."

"What's that?" Straddling his lap, I kissed his neck.

"A club."

"We can do that tomorrow."

"Too late. Taxi's on its way." He stood, and I tumbled back onto the bed. He crossed over to the bathroom, and grabbed deodorant, applying it under each arm.

"I'll stay here," I said stubbornly. "You can go alone."

"Fine." He whipped the stick of deodorant at me.

It struck my cheek. "Ow," I shrieked, more terrified by the act than the pain.

"I'm sorry, baby." He rushed over, gathering me into his arms. "I didn't mean to hurt you. I had too much to drink."

Holding my eye, I said, "It's okay." *It has to be.*

Sorrow shadowed his eyes. "I couldn't get it out of my head that you don't like kissing me."

"I'm sorry," I said, unbidden tears spilling over, sliding down my cheeks. "I didn't mean it. I don't know why I said it."

"It's okay," he said softly. "If you stop crying, I'll let you make it up to me." The look in his eyes was endearing.

"I don't want to do anything with anyone but you," I sobbed.

"I know. I've just heard about the club and wanted to see what it was all about. I also know you want to be good." A pause. "By the way, I got something for you."

I frowned. "What is it?"

His smile was cagey. "Just a little something to give you energy."

"Can't we go tomorrow? Say, earlier in the day?"

"Tell you what. We'll go, and the second you say done, we'll leave."

"Done."

He grinned, tweaking my nose. "You're so funny."

***

I woke to late sunshine peeking through the window. My right forearm felt like it was on fire. I glanced down and saw it wrapped with tape and gauze.

My thoughts in a fog, I blinked, *Where am I?* Better yet, what happened? I searched my brain. A vague memory of sitting in a tattoo artist chair with the sound of a tattoo gun buzzing in the background returned. Feeling along his side of the bed, I discovered it was empty.

I sat up. Where was Alex?

The last thing I remembered was him backing me up against the wall, kissing me. After that…nothing.

I didn't even have anything to drink other than the required two at Glitter Gulch.

I stood, and the room swayed around me.

I've never felt like this about any girl.

I stumbled to the bathroom, flipped on the faucet, and caught a glimpse of my reflection in the mirror. My hands stilled beneath the running water. I had a black eye.

A vision of Alex throwing the deodorant at me came rushing back. Taking hold of the edge of the tape on my forearm, I took a deep breath and began to pull. Hopefully I hadn't gotten something stupid like a skull or a voodoo doll.

The mirror reflected an outline of the most intricate of roses. Really quite pretty. Exhaling, I flipped the faucet off and grabbed a hand towel, strolling into the hotel room.

Where had he gone? I checked the digital clock on the desk next to the bed.

Six a.m.

I picked up the remote and turned on the TV.

Flipping through channels, I stared unseeing at the screen. What if something happened to him? What if he never came back?

I could call Andrew. My face burned thinking of how I would explain myself. I hadn't even told him I was dating Alex. He would think I was crazy.

Thinking back on the past month, I seemed less than lucid. But what was to be done? I could go back and pick up my things at Bethany. Telling my family college wasn't for me suddenly didn't seem so bad.

A vision of Elvis Presley slammed into my brain, and my memory highlighted one detail.

I was married.

52
December 27, 1996

Florence

Taliban forces reclaimed the strategic Bagram air base, solidifying their buffer zone around Kabul.

On the flight home, I sat next to Alex in silence. Washed out and emotionally drained, I didn't feel like talking.

Images flashed through my mind. There was one of a house and palm trees around it. Inside, dark seventies-style carpet covered the floor. Mattresses, a hot tub. A handsome bartender and a Korean couple.

"Here comes the stewardess. You want anything?" Alex asked.

I shook my head.

"Did you have a good time?"

"Between strip clubs and you disappearing?" I hissed. "Yeah, it was a blast."

"I left once." His eyes narrowed. "And you know why."

"Twice. And you gave me a black eye." I bought sunglasses at a boutique to avoid questions.

"It's not my fault you can't handle your liquor. You tripped, remember?"

"What?" My ears popped. "Of course I remember you threw deodorant. By the way, a tattoo isn't something I planned on, but now that it's started I'd like it finished."

"I know a guy in Inver Grove Heights. By the way, I forgive you for what happened."

"You forgive me?" I echoed.

Alex cleared his throat.

The stewardess stood in the aisle.

Alex watched her pour a whisky. There was something new in his eyes. Disdain? Interest? He drew a sharp breath, nostrils flared.

Attraction.

There was a look in his eyes I hadn't seen before.

He wants to do it, just not with you.

"We're just talking," Alex assured me, catching my eyes. "Did I tell you my sister is meeting us at the airport?"

"Yes." I smoothed my hair down with a shaky hand. "What is she like?"

"She's terrific." He studied my face. "I don't want you acting miserable when you see her."

Feeling small, I said, "I wouldn't."

"I know you don't enjoy being with me, but let's keep that between us."

"That's not true, I..."

Alex leaned his head back against the seat and let his eyes fall shut.

I had been miserable. Truth was, I hadn't taken a vacation or gone anywhere special since my momma died. And here I'd made my new husband miserable too.

Well no more.

Getting married might have been a hasty decision, but I would be an excellent wife.

When we reached the terminal, a boy in a dirty jacket and jeans with riotous copper curls, rushed Alex.

"Eddy be a good boy," a beautiful woman with dark hair ordered. "You better listen if you know…" Her eyes landed on me.

"Carmen, this is Florence," Alex said, his gaze shifting from me to her and back again. "Florence, this is my sister Carmen and her son Eddy."

Carmen wore a black button-down blouse and black slacks. Her hair was pulled up in a banana clip.

"She's tall, but awful pretty," she said like it was a crime. Funny how she used "awful" and "pretty" in the same description.

"I…"

Her expression changed, and she gave a lilting laugh, laying a hand on my arm. "Nice to meet you. I hope you know how to clean." She flicked a glance at Alex. "My brother has no idea."

"Funny. The place has always been clean when I've been there."

"To impress you." Her smile held a secret. "I'm sure now that you're married he'll let it all hang out."

"I suppose." I gave a weak laugh.

She turned to Alex. "I like her."

My heart kicked up. I didn't have any women friends. She had dry humor and a warm smile.

I liked her too.

"There are things for humans to do all day long without His minding in the least - sleeping, washing, eating, drinking, making love, playing, praying, working. Everything has to be twisted before it's any use to us." –Uncle Screwtape

C. S. Lewis, *Screwtape Letters*

53

Florence

"Good morning." I yawned, padding into the kitchen.

Alex glanced up from *The Washington Post*, his gaze traveled over me, narrowing in on my tank top, pajama bottoms, and bare feet.

He pulled a pen from the center console. "I'll make a list for you of things that need to get done."

"A list?"

His hand flew over a sheet of notebook paper. "Yeah. I've got a new client today. I won't be home until supper. I thought you might need to know where things are."

Groggy, I stifled a yawn. Was it possible to get jet lag from a three-hour flight?

He looked at me expectantly.

I wiped my hands down the sides of my pants. "I'm sorry, what did you say?"

"I asked if you wanted something to eat. Wouldn't take much to whip up a mess of eggs."

"Just tired is all." I yawned.

He tossed back the last of his coffee and stood. "Gotta run."

After he left, I wandered toward the coffee pot.

It was empty.

Now I had a mission. I opened a cupboard. Rolled oats. I wrinkled my nose. Oatmeal was the worst.

Checking each cupboard, I came across coffee at last.

There was a knock on the door.

My heart kicked up. Alex hadn't mentioned company.

I answered the door.

Carmen stood with a warm smile, holding a bag and two coffees. Her son hid behind her legs.

"Carmen," I held the door wide. "Alex didn't tell me you were coming."

"I brought coffee and scones from the bakery down the street," she said, glancing behind me. "Is this a bad time?"

"Not at all. Come on in."

She crossed over and set the scones on the counter next to the stereo. "You're listening to R.E.M.? I love this song."

"It's the radio." I took a coffee from her.

"…It could depend on your take. You, me, we used to be on fire. If keys are all that stand between can I throw in the ring? No gasoline, just…"

Carmen's eyes were on me. "Everything okay?"

"Yes. Why shouldn't it be?"

"I don't know. You were acting strange last night."

"How so?" I tucked an auburn curl behind my ear. Truth was, arriving home was like bits and pieces of a dream.

"Nothing I guess." She shrugged.

"Would you like to sit down?"

"I can't." She shook her head. "Actually, that's why I'm here. I've got a board meeting today and my sitter canceled."

"You need me to babysit?" I glanced down at Edward.

"Would you?" she asked, her eyes lit. "I wouldn't ask if I wasn't in a pinch."

"It's cool. I used to watch my brothers."

"Okay. He won't eat scones, so I might as well take these with me." She grabbed the bakery bag from the counter, and thrust his diaper bag at me. "He wears pullups. And Alex turned the spare room downstairs into his room for when he's here."

"But I…"

"Gotta run. Thanks again," and she was out the door.

Okay, then. He could play while I worked on Alex's list. I turned to Edward. "What would you like to do today?"

He didn't answer.

"I'll make eggs," I announced. "Would you like that?"

Edward pinned me with his silent gaze.

"I'll take that as a yes." I heated the frying pan, and recalled a loaf of bread I saw on the counter. I cracked eggs and popped slices of bread into the toaster.

Soon, smoke filled the room. I snatched the frying pan off the heat, and beat the flames with a dishtowel.

Staring at the soggy mess, I thought of my brothers growing up, and doubted Edward would complain.

"I know they're a little overdone." I pushed the plate in front of him.

"They don't look like Mommy's eggs." He took a handful and let them fly.

Rubbery remnants hit my face. Okay more than a little overdone. I grabbed his arm. "Now listen here…"

"No," he shouted, and flew down the stairs, slamming his bedroom door.

"You can starve for all I care." Fighting tears of frustration, I wiped the mess off my face.

Breakfast turned into lunch.

At suppertime, Alex sat down at the table, his eyes scanning the steak and baked potatoes on our plates. Then the peanut butter and jelly sandwiches, carrot sticks, and Jell-O on Eddy's plate.

"It was the only thing I could get him to eat," I said.

"I don't like her," Edward scowled at me. "She slams cupboard doors and said a bad word."

"So you do talk." I glared at him. "And you're a tattletale."

Edward stuck out his tongue.

"What did I tell you, Edward?" Alex sighed.

"She's not my mommy." His face screwed up in rage. "I hate her."

The feeling was mutual.

Alex reached for the basket of bread and took a piece before passing it. "I told Carmen we'd watch Eddy for her tomorrow."

"I'm supposed to babysit?"

He buttered his bread. "I never told you, but Carmen has a lot of contacts. She knows influential people."

"What does she do?"

"She's a marketing consultant." He wiped his hands on his napkin. "She hooks me up with her clients who pay me well."

"That's nice."

"It's more than nice. It's what pays for this pretty pad you live in. This steak you served for supper."

"But..."

He picked up his steak knife. "Edward just turned two and can be a handful. Once you get settled, things will get better."

Heart thumping in my ears, I didn't want to watch Edward. I didn't want to get settled, either. I didn't want his food. I wanted to go home. Not to the dorm, but home to North Dakota.

I caught Edward's stare. He met my eyes and smiled slyly.

The little beast.

54

Florence

The next morning, I was up before Alex and tiptoed to the kitchen to start coffee.

Just like Aunt Sophia.

Ignoring the thought, I pulled two mugs from the cupboards. Soon, the rich aroma filled the early morning atmosphere.

In a black silk shirt and gray slacks, Alex strolled in.

"I made coffee." I poured a cup and handed it to him.

He took a sip and winced.

"What's wrong with it?" I frowned.

"A little weak." He set his cup on the counter. "Don't worry about it. I'll grab Starbuck's on the way."

"I had a nightmare last night."

"Hmm."

"We were at a house with palm trees and I was with another man while you were watching."

He gave me a heady look. "You are quite the little pervert."

"Me? What? I…"

Carmen entered, Edward in tow.

Didn't she believe in knocking?

"I better be going," Alex said, brushed past her and out the door.

"There's snacks and pullups in Eddy's backpack." She pulled a small Tupperware container from her purse. "Oh, and here's a piece of apple pie for you."

After she left, Chumbawamba "Tubthumping" began to play on the stereo. I turned up the volume.

Maybe today wouldn't be so bad.

My belly rumbled. I put the slice of pie on a plate and put the Tupperware in the sink. When was the last time I ate apple pie? I reached for it at the same time as Edward.

His grubby little paws were faster, and he shoved the dessert in his mouth, wolfing it down. Then, he turned and smiled at me through full cheeks.

"That's it," I shouted, pointing toward the basement stairs. "Naptime."

"I don't wanna."

I took a step toward him and he ran, thundering down the stairs, and slammed his bedroom door.

"Who's the one slamming doors around here?" I shouted, taking a deep breath. What was I doing? Arguing with a two-year-old.

And losing.

After twenty minutes, he was silent. I tiptoed down the stairs, peeking inside his room. He was sleeping, rosy cheeks, he looked like an angel.

Satan started out an angel.

Early morning, I located the cleaning supplies and started with dusting. It was a tedious task. Suddenly, I missed James.

Midmorning I made a grocery list: sugar, flour, and butter.

In the basement next to Edward's room was a small walk-in pantry. Cans of vegetables, including carrots and turnips filled the shelves. There was a bottle of wine and behind that, a jar of auburn liquid. I unscrewed the lid and took a sip.

Homemade apple pie. Perfect.

Three stolen sips later I was giddy.

There was a knock on the door. I replaced the lid with trembling fingers, and dashed up the stairs to answer it.

Andrew stood with my sphinx lamp and a grin.

Shocked, I opened my mouth but no words came out.

He chuckled. "Aren't you going to invite me in?"

At once, a wave of emotion swept over me, and I threw my arms around his neck.

He patted my back awkwardly.

I held fast. "I missed you so much!"

"What's going on?" he held me at arm's length, searching my eyes. "When you called and said you left school, that was bad enough, but what's this I hear about you getting married?"

I took the lamp from him. "This needs to be fixed."

"I brought it to Uncle Don."

"Thank you," I said, plugging it in by the coffee pot. I turned the switch. It came on without a spark.

"Can I get you something to drink? Coffee?"

"Yes, please."

"What are you doing here?" I set Andrew's coffee at the kitchen table across from mine and sat down. "How are things at home?"

"I came to meet James' girlfriend. He met her at Best Buy." Andrew sat down in front of his coffee.

"Sounds serious."

"Yeah. Dad said you called."

"Sophia answered." I took a sip.

"Dad sold the lake house." A pause. "He didn't say why, but I got the feeling it was about needing cash."

Aunt Sophia.

"I see." I searched for a way to explain what he didn't ask. "We didn't plan to rush anything, but we were married in Vegas."

He arched a brow. "First I heard of it was from Sophia."

"I'm sorry about that," I said, shame churning in my belly.

He nodded. "She does have a way of getting information no one else has."

Edward ascended the stairs.

"Cute kid." Andrew smiled.

"This is Alex's nephew, Edward." I led him toward the table. He hung back behind me.

"Carmen, Alex's sister is...."

Alex burst in the front door. "Look who I ran into."

James at his arm along with a pretty woman with dark hair and pixie features.

"Hey Florrie," James said. "This is my girlfriend, Renee." He glanced over at Andrew. "Hey bro."

"How did you two meet?" I motioned between Alex and James.

"He was looking for a refrigerator," James said. "We got to talking, and I realized he's married to my sister." He arched a brow. "Invite must be in the mail?"

I folded and unfolded my hands. "It was sort of rushed, and I..."

"Alex. Long time no see." Andrew stood and thrust out his hand.

Alex shook it, flicking me a glance. "Florence didn't tell me you were coming or I would have taken time off."

"I didn't tell her. I had to check out a honey separator, and thought I'd stop in and see how the two of you are getting along."

Alex flashed a devilish grin. "Perfect. You know what I happen to have?" He reached into the cupboard above the stove, and pulled out a humidor box. "Cuban."

"These are illegal," Andrew said even as he took one.

"Only if you're caught." Alex winked at me. "How about you, James? Want one?"

"Of course."

"Renee?"

She shook her head. "Do you have Pepsi?"

"Yes," I said, pulling drinks from the fridge.

"What do you say we head out to the deck and light these up?" Alex bumped Andrew's shoulder. "I can make you a Roy Rogers, Andrew. You downed quite a few at Texas Roadhouse."

"You coming Florence?" Andrew glanced back.

I shook my head. "Edward doesn't like the smoke."

After they made their way out on the deck, Edward reached for my hand.

I smiled down at him.

Today was a good day.

55
July 1, 1997

Florence

Thatcher and Chinese Premier Zhao Ziyang signed the Sino-British Joint Declaration, agreeing to return Hong Kong, a British colony since 1842, to China. The parties involved stuck to the agreement and, at midnight, Hong Kong became part of China.

Edward ran around swiping walls with the feather duster.

I'd never liked the little man more.

Another night sharing a bed with Alex, and he faced the wall. His only comment last night was when I had turned out the lamp and it flickered. "Get rid of that thing. It's older than my grandma."

Thanks a lot, Uncle Don. "I can't. It was my momma's." A vision of Momma flickered in my mind like the lamp.

His response was a grunt.

A sudden image of our hotel room in Vegas flashed through my mind. There were drinks in the back of the limo, and we arrived at the house with the palm trees and seventies carpet.

To get my mind off the images, I retreated to our bedroom and grabbed the blanket, laying it out across the basement floor. "Get on, Edward. Your turn first."

Edward eyed the blanket. "Nuh uh."

"I'm the grown-up, you have to do what I say." I tilted my head toward the comforter. "Come on. It'll be fun."

"Okay." He plopped down on the edge of the blanket.

"You're a lot heavier than you look." I dragged him around the floor.

"This is fun." He giggled.

"It sure is, Edward."

A shy smile worked its way across his cherub cheeks. "I'm Eddy."

Around and around we went, I pulled him around on the floor until we were both in stitches.

Eddy said, "Faster."

"Oh, I can go faster," I panted, flinging him across the floor, and directly into Alex.

Alex glared us down with an icy-blue gaze. "What's for lunch?"

Rats. I forgot the chicken in the fridge.

Eddy jumped off the quilt, wearing a guilty look.

Alex stood there, hatred oozing from his pores.

I wiped my hands down the sides of my pajama pants. "I didn't hear you come in."

"So you're keeping secrets from me," he said in a cold voice.

My heart stopped, then kicked up, hammering in my ears. "What do you mean?"

"The telephone bill came today." He waved it in front of my face. "Four hours of long distance charges?"

I took it from his grasp, scanning it. "You know about this. I called my dad. You were there when I hung up."

"Your dad. Right." His eyes, murderous. "Not some Jason or Norman."

"I swear. There's no one else back home."

"I forgave you for Vegas, but I haven't forgotten you broke your marriage vows."

What was he talking about? But somehow, I knew. *The house with the palm trees.* "I'm..."

He threw me a look of disgust. "Get dressed."

I rushed to the bedroom. With shaky hands, I changed clothes. What had I done? I drew a deep breath and returned to the kitchen.

John Popper sang on the kitchen stereo, *"...Because the Hook brings you back, on that you can rely..."*

Eddy set the table while I made fried egg sandwiches.

"We need to talk." He sat down and reached for a fork.

My heart kicked up, thumping in my ears. "What about?"

"The apple pie."

Relief flooded me. "I'm sorry I forgot about it. When your sister was here, I was busy doing laundry. I'll do better next time."

"Not that apple pie." He shook his head. "The drinking."

I swallowed hard. "Drinking?"

"Oh yes. I know all about it." A lofty look came over his eyes. "I'm not the only one with secrets."

I didn't know what to say. So I said nothing, sat down and dug in.

"We must picture hell as a state where everyone is perpetually concerned about his own dignity and advancement, where everyone has a grievance, and where everyone lives with the deadly serious passions of envy, self-importance, and resentment." —Uncle Screwtape

C. S. Lewis, *Screwtape Letters*

56

Florence

"Alex told me you like lists so I made one," Carmen announced on her arrival with Eddy. "Oh, and not so much TV for Edward today. He's only allowed to watch one *Pepper Ann*."

Anger bubbled up in my stomach, leaving a sour taste in my mouth.

After she left, I turned to Eddy. "Finish your breakfast. After we do dishes and clean up the kitchen. Then it's your room."

He screwed his face in hot anger. "No!"

Before I could get another word out, he dashed from the table and headed for the basement, laughing like the devil himself.

Looking down at the remains of breakfast, cold dry toast and hard eggs, I wasn't quite so hungry myself.

I scanned her list:

Clean windows, inside and out.

Scrub tile floor on hands and knees. Mop only works between thorough cleanings. This includes the kitchen and the bathroom.

Dust.

Vacuum the window sills. Striped flies are disgusting.

Shower needs scrubbing. Use Soft Scrub (whatever you've been using doesn't work).

Clean

Wait. How would she know if the shower was clean? *She inspects it when she uses the bathroom.* I could see her doing just that. Fury swept through me, right down to my bones.

I stood and stacked the plates.

Eddy pounded up the stairs and grabbed my hand. "Come."

I stopped. "What?"

"Come." Eddy tugged on my hand.

"Okay, hold on." I wiped my hands on a towel, and followed him down the stairs.

He halted at the bottom.

The basement was full of water. At least an inch covered the entire floor.

"Oh boy." Looked like a job for a plumber.

The plumber arrived a half hour later and was hotter than a toaster. His muscles rippled beneath the tight black shirt he wore, the emblem *Damian* on his left pocket. His faded work jeans revealed muscular thighs, the stuff of romantic novels. He smelled of outdoors, pipe tobacco and nothing of coconut. Funny how that scent began to prickle my nerves.

He jerked his thumb toward the back door. "I'm going to go see what we got."

I reached in the fridge for a Coke and stepped outside.

He held up dripping black remains. "That's one less rodent in your walls looking for heat and food."

"What's that?"

"A skunk." He grinned. "Skunks don't recognize suburbia. I saw several mounds in the backyard. They dig for grubs and earthworms and damage foundations by burrowing beneath."

"Are they aggressive?"

"They're fight or flight animals. The stench is most notable, but they'll stomp the ground, slap their tail, and will even stand on their hind paws to better display their rear end before they'll spray."

"How much do I owe you?"

"I'll send your husband the bill."

That's when I worried Alex might not like me calling a plumber without asking him. Not my fault he didn't have a phone or way to reach him during work.

Still.

I decided I'd wait to tell him until the bill came in the mail. Maybe he wouldn't even notice and pay it without question.

Not likely.

I'd find out soon enough.

57
August 31, 1997

Florence

Diana, Princess of Wales, died in a car crash in a road tunnel in Paris, and Alex pulled into the drive in a 1985 Corvette.

"Can we go for a ride?" I hurried down the front steps, admiring the red sports car, its shiny exterior, suddenly thankful for a wealthy husband.

"After I'm done polishing it," he made his way around to the front of the car. "It needs a wax job."

"Looks good to me. May I?" I popped the hood without waiting for a response and made my way to the front. "This has a new Tuned Port Injection fuel delivery system. Essentially the German Bosch, featuring a revised intake manifold. Provides an individual fuel injector for each cylinder."

He gave me a blank stare.

"Tuned runners and a new mass air flow sensor, all of which aids in the improved performance." I shut the hood, and stooped, tracing a finger across a front wheel. "Looks like it's riding on a nice set of snowflake wheels, with RWL tires."

Eddy strolled out, drawing alongside me.

"Keep that kid away from it," Alex barked.

"We'll probably just go in now," I said, drawing Eddy along behind me."

"I'll take a beer while you're at it."

***

After putting Eddy down for a nap, Alex was going through mail at the kitchen table as I made my way up the stairs.

"Florence," he called.

"Yes?" I crept in quietly.

He continued to rip open bills, not acknowledging my presence. Beneath a trace of coconut, he smelled of sweat, cheap whisky, and cigarette smoke. Odd. He only smoked cigars.

"The sewer backed up," I spoke through the silence.

He didn't answer.

"I found the tile drain and tried to plunge it."

He looked up, letting out an incredulous laugh. "You should have called the rotor rooter. Neighbor's tree roots plug the line."

I waited for him to get to the point.

A dark look flashed through his eyes. "Do you know how much a plumber costs?"

"No."

"Of course you don't." He sighed, and then like a ray of sunshine, his expression lifted. "Who came?"

"I beg your pardon?"

"Was it Damian? The plumber I mean."

"Yes," I managed a casual tone.

"One time he told me about this really hot chick he hooked up with." Alex leaned back in his chair. "He mentioned she was shaved down there."

"What did he think of that?" I swallowed hard.

"What every man thinks." He waited until I lifted my eyes to his. "That she'll shave it if she really loves her man."

I scowled. "I have a long grocery list for you." Let's see how he liked grocery lists.

He didn't blink. "You're way better at that than I am."

My eyes widened. "You don't mind if I go shopping?"

He stood, made his way around the table, and draped his arm around me. "Of course not. I'll get you the credit card."

"Thank you! I'll make sure I check for the sale items."

He smiled. "Don't worry about it."

Thrilled, I dashed to the bedroom, put on my cutest white Guess shirt and faded blue jeans.

When I emerged, Alex was leaning against the kitchen counter, sipping coffee. He strolled over and handed me a Mastercard. "I pulled the car out of the garage for you. Have fun."

Cranking the Corvette's engine, I was suddenly glad for the man I married. Shifting into reverse, I checked the rearview mirror, and backed up. The crunching of metal stopped me short.

I got out and saw I sideswiped the Audi.

Alex emerged from the house. "What did you do?"

"It's not my fault. What was the Audi doing there? I always park it…"

"I should have known better than to let you drive." He sighed loudly. "I'll call Earl. See if he can get it in today."

"What about the groceries?"

"I guess I'll have to get them on my way home from work."

Following him into the house, the skunk came to mind. I couldn't help but notice similarities between them.

58
June 10, 1997

Florence

"Khmer Rouge leader Pol Pot ordered the killing of his defense chief Son Sen and 11 of Sen's family members before fleeing..." I flipped off the radio and searched the nightstand for a peppermint candy, and sighed. I must have eaten the last piece.

I started to close the drawer and stopped.

There was a picture in the bottom.

I picked it up. It was me on a chair in nothing but lingerie. The background was unfamiliar. Was this taken in Vegas? I fingered the matted surface before turning it over. *Daisy Richards*. The date was smudged and illegible. The cursive handwriting was Alex's.

My heart leapt to my throat. Who had seen this? I would ask Alex at suppertime.

Alex didn't come home for supper.

In the dark of our bedroom, I waited up for him, more alone and afraid with each passing moment.

My eyes grew heavy.

Ribbons of sleep followed where I weaved in and out of consciousness. I was in the house with palm trees. Damian was there and I realized I was naked. Then Damian turned to me, and said, *"Surprise ambushes make skunk spray especially effective."*

I woke sharply, dragging in gasps before I realized I was in my own bed.

The blue light from the living room TV seeped beneath the bedroom door. I glanced at the clock on the nightstand.

1:59.

Didn't he ever sleep?

Sitting up, I grabbed the photograph from the drawer and headed to the living room.

Alex sat in front of the TV. An infomercial was on.

"I found this." I handed him the photograph.

"Whatcha got?" He glanced at it, whistling low. "You are so hot."

"When was it taken?"

"Because you were beautiful." He glanced up. "I was going to tell you and completely forgot."

"I asked when not why. Speaking of why, it has the name *Daisy Richards* on the back."

"It's in the past." He put it on the end table next to him and stood, pulling me into his arms.

Irritated, I remained stiff. "I'd rather you get rid of it. I don't want photos like that laying around."

"Okay." He laid an open mouth kiss on my neck.

I pulled away. "I don't want anyone to see it."

"I heard you." He frowned. "Quit nagging."

Immediately, I relented, "I didn't mean to."

"Whatever. I better hit the hay. Got to be at work early in the morning." He made his way to the bedroom, stopping as he reached the door. "By the way, I sold the Corvette."

"What?"

"Yeah, figuring the cost of damage and a new paint job, I decided it wasn't worth it."

Was he punishing me? "All I do is cook and clean and watch your nephew. I feel like a housekeeper or a governess rather than your wife."

"That's because you don't have a job."

"It sure seems like a job to me."

"Fine. I'll tell Carmen."

"Thank you." I gave him my most sultry smile. "Maybe then I can come and help you at your job."

He scowled. "I work alone."

I crossed over to the bed, turning on the lamp. It fizzled and I glanced at Alex, but he didn't seem to notice.

Imagining the house without Eddy, sadness crept inside my chest. I'd have nothing to look forward to. Day after day, I'd clean his house and cook meals for…no one. At least with Eddy I had someone to watch TV with and read to.

"I'll watch Eddy," I sighed. "But you can't come home late every night. I can't even remember the last time we had sex."

He grinned. "Well come over here and we'll change that."

I strolled over, expecting to be drawn into his arms.

Instead, he held up a gift bag. "I got something for you."

A feeling of love swept over me. "I'm sorry for complaining. I guess I didn't get enough sleep last night."

"I went to the Love Shack." He withdrew a sex toy from the bag.

Horrified, I made no move to take it. "What is it?" I asked, flushing.

His grin was wicked. "I'll show you."

"No thank you." I took a step back.

His brow lifted and his mouth twitched.

"I'd rather just do it the normal way."

"Okay, my little missionary." He reached for the whisky on the bedside table. "Probably best anyway, since you refuse to do any trimming down there."

Weary, I sighed, "Do you have to drink?" even while knowing the answer.

Alex loved his whisky, its power.

"No." He poured a glass. "But I want to."

"Better make it two." It was going to be a long night.

□

59
February 4, 1998

Florence

O.J. Simpson was found liable in the deaths of Ron Goldman and Nicole Simpson in a civil court action.

Waiting for Alex to come home, I drifted to a dreamless sleep.

I woke with a start.

The bedroom was dark. I lay staring up at the ceiling, when I heard voices in the kitchen. Listening for a few minutes, I realized it was Carmen and Alex.

Their voices sounded angry. Then, stopped all together. I tipped over to the door, opening it a crack, and peered through.

Alex kissed his sister.

Voraciously.

Horrified, I stepped back. My mind in a whirl, I peered at them once more. She was in his arms, her hips wrapped around his waist. His mouth devoured hers.

I stumbled back on to the bed.

Their relationship had been incestuous this whole time. Thinking back, I was furious. They'd used me to take care of Eddy. Swiping angry tears away with the back of my arm, I crawled beneath the covers.

By the time Alex entered the bedroom, I pretended to be sleeping, sensing every movement from his side.

At the rumble of snoring, I got out of bed, tiptoed into the kitchen and picked up the phone receiver from its cradle.

It rang three times and Aunt Sophia answered. "Hello."

"Hello, is my dad there?"

"Florence? Why are you calling this late? It's almost eleven o'clock."

"I need to speak to my dad," my voice wavered.

"Hello honey," Dad sounded sleepy. "What can I do for you?"

At the sound of his voice, the tears began to flow. "I want to come home."

"What's wrong? Is it Alex?"

"It's sort of a long story. I'd rather not talk about it over the phone."

"Does she need money?" said Aunt Sophia in the background.

"Wait. Why is Aunt Sophia there?"

"You sound tired." He yawned loudly. "Why don't you get a good night's sleep? Things will look better in the morning."

"I suppose so." What could it hurt? Morning was just a few hours away and wouldn't change anything.

I hung up and made my way back to bed, Blues Traveler "Hook" playing softly on my clock radio, *"It doesn't matter what I say so long as I sing with inflection…"*

By the time the sun began to peek through the window, I was up making coffee. Playing the scene over again in my mind, I wanted to kill them both. I drew deep breaths. Losing my mind would only make me look crazy.

Alex strolled into the kitchen. A five o'clock shadow gave him a sensual look.

If he could play it cool, so could I.

"I know about you and Carmen. Saw the whole thing," I nearly shouted. "How could you? It's so awful."

So much for subtlety.

"You don't know what you're talking about."

"Oh, so I didn't really see you French kissing your sister in here last night?"

His face reddened. "It wasn't what you think."

"It never is. I'm leaving," I said. "I can't stand living in the same house with you and your sister and…what about Eddy?"

He grabbed both my arms. "Listen to me."

I pulled away. "Don't touch me."

"She's not my sister."

60

Alex ran a shaky hand through his hair. "She's no relation to me."

"Why would you say she was?" My thoughts were in a whirl.

"Because I didn't want more drama."

"Drama?" I shouted, beyond caring if I sounded a raving lunatic. "Why would I create drama?"

"Calm down." He took a step back, holding up both hands. "You were miserable in Vegas. Carmen's an old girlfriend. She needed help. I thought if I told you the truth, you'd freak."

"But if she's not your sister…you're having an affair!"

"Look, Carmen's messed up. What else could I do? She's no mother. Not like you. She isn't quite right."

"The whole thing is disgusting." I paced back and forth. "You could have told me the truth."

"No one wants the truth."

"I do."

He arched a brow. "Her name is Carmen Richter. I dated her for five years. I asked her to marry me, but her parents said no."

"So Eddy is…"

"Mine." His eyes took on a gleam.

"I suppose she's shaved down there," the angry words tore from my lips before I could call them back.

"Nah. A landing strip."

A landing strip? "Do you think she's prettier than me?"

"Not necessarily. Although, she doesn't wear those," he said, eyeing my sweatpants. "Do you want to be ugly?"

"That's it. I want to be ugly." I rolled my eyes.

"I'm sure it's not the reason Norman didn't want you." He ran his hands down my arms, pulling my body against his.

"No, he said I was like his sister," each word from my mouth sliced my chest, resistance slowly draining from my body.

"You poor, pitiful woman," he stroked my hair.

Desperate was a better word.

***

Carmen dropped Eddy off. She didn't mention that I knew and I didn't tell her. It seemed to be business as usual.

She prepared to leave, and reached into her purse, pulling out a skinning knife with a leather sheath. "I wanted to give you this."

"What's this?" I withdrew the shiv, scanning the inscription Buffalo Hunter.

"Never know when it will come in handy." Her eyes darted toward the door. "Being married to Alex, you will likely need it one day."

Okay, Ms. Doom and Gloom.

Carmen leaned toward me and whispered, "Also, I wouldn't tell anyone."

"About what?" My heart kicked up.

"Take care of Eddy." She headed for the door.

"What time are you picking him up?"

"Six of course."

At supper, Alex sat across from me at the dining room table.

"Isn't there anything you find more attractive about me than her?" I finally voiced what had been haunting me all day."

"I like your hair."

"Thanks." My subconscious must have known, because I found myself styling my hair like hers and copying her sultry walk.

"One more question and I'll let it go forever." *Don't make promises you can't keep. Let your yes be yes and your no be no.*

"What do you want to know?" Alex's expression was indifferent. He didn't seem angry or embarrassed, rather his eyes searched mine as if discovering something new about me. Something he hadn't known before.

"Does she have a job? I mean, all those days you went to work and she went to work…that is you were both working. Weren't you?"

He pinned me with a serious look. "You don't really want to know."

"Please?"

"She worked with me. We're coworkers for the same corporation."

"I thought you said you didn't work for a corporation."

"Yeah, well, I hope to change that."

You're in love with his potential.

"Did you guys have sex when you were at work?"

"That's two questions." He picked up his fork. "Besides, does it matter?"

"I'll take that as a yes." Wave after wave of sorrow pulled me under an ocean of grief.

"No one thinks of anyone before himself," he said as though asking to pass the salt and pepper. "The only difference between me and everyone else is I don't pretend otherwise."

Also, I wouldn't tell anyone.

And I wouldn't tell him about the knife even as a part of me knew it wasn't what Carmen meant. A small voice inside whispered the truth and it sounded a lot like R.E.M. "Star Me Kitten".

"...I've changed the locks, and you can have one....What is there for me inside? This love is tired...have I misplaced you? Have we lost our minds...?"

Either way, I never saw Carmen again.

61
December 11, 1998

Norman

The night was faint. Falling snow reflected off the winter moon, lighting up the midnight sky.

I filled the squad car with gas at Mini Mart, and stopped in to grab a cup of coffee.

Jill Pederson was working. She was wearing a red sweater with a V-neck low enough to tease but modest enough to get her on Santa's nice list.

She giggled when she saw me. "Hello, Officer Miller. I've been a bad girl."

"Isn't that Santa Claus' problem?" I smiled.

She giggled some more.

Mr. Orson, mopping the floor dutifully, began mopping his way over to us.

Oh boy. I raised my cup and turned to leave.

"How's the beat going?" he called. "Got any stories?"

Mr. Orson was a kindly old man who told everyone who walked through the door that Jesus loved them. He also liked to hear cop tales. The town was small, and small talk got cops into a lot of trouble.

"Eighty-one people were killed north of Tadjena by armed groups in Algeria," I told him.

"That was last week." He dunked the mop.

"One hundred and one people were killed when Thai Airways Airbus A310-200 crashed near Surat Thani Airport."

"The news is pretty depressing." He squinted at me with knowing, piercing eyes. "Things are going to get a lot worse unless you repent."

A series of images flashed through my mind from all the nights I'd spent in the arms of beautiful women. Yet, I felt as empty as the apartment I returned to each morning.

Back in the squad car, I flipped up the computer and checked my messages.

A brown station wagon careened out of control, heading straight for me. My heart slammed hard in my chest. It came to a screeching halt, the bumper, mere inches from the squad car. The entire vehicle pounded, thrumming from the bass radio.

Marissa Potter, the mother of my children, was behind the wheel. Her watery eyes were bloodshot.

Shawn Vitense was sitting in the backseat, stoned.

"Shawn is with me," she announced, jerking her thumb in his direction. "He's in no condition to drive."

"Turn the music off." I pointed down.

Her bleary-eyed gaze widened. "You were right. I'm the one that doesn't know thafe from unthafe."

"Thafe?" I questioned.

"She means safe," Shawn hollered from the back seat.

"If either one of you has a driver's license and isn't boasting about being the Prince of Egypt, I'll hand over the keys," her voice slurred.

"Where are you headed?" I asked.

"I was going to go home, but I'll go anywhere you want to take me," she giggled.

"Step out of the car," I told her.

"I've been drinking." Marissa stepped out, grabbed me by my collar, pulling my face to her level. "It's true. For a while now. Not only today, but for a while," she admitted, released me, and patted my shirt front.

"How much have you had to drink?"

"Tonight?"

"Yes, tonight."

"Three beers."

"Right."

I opened the back seat of the squad car. "Get in."

"Where are you taking me?" she asked.

"To the police station," I answered. The chief was going to have a cow when he found out the woman I'd been seeing was partying with Shawn Vitense.

Things are going to get a lot worse unless you repent.

62
December 13, 2000

Florence

"Surprise!" Andrew handed me a large red box wrapped with a silver bow. "Happy birthday, sis."

I tore it open. It was a down-filled periwinkle parka. "It's so soft." I stroked the jacket, and then threw my arms around Andrew. "Thank you."

He patted my back. "Don't be so much of a stranger. Alex isn't going anywhere. I think it's safe to introduce him to Aunt Sophia."

Standing alongside my brother, Alex beamed. "Were you surprised?"

"Shocked is a better word." I released Andrew taking a step back. No one had ever thrown me a surprise birthday party.

"I had everyone park their cars down the street so you wouldn't suspect anything." Alex drew his arm around me.

Things had been a lot better since Alex's confession. We grew closer. Carmen hadn't returned since that morning she gave me the knife. Alex had become a wonderful husband, attentive, coming home every night for supper.

When Andrew showed up earlier today and offered to take me shopping, I had no idea guests were arriving to celebrate my birthday.

When I returned, I flipped on the lights to a room full of people. Most of which I didn't know, but I was thrilled by Alex's thoughtfulness all the same.

After Andrew left, I slipped away from party guests and down to the basement.

Eddy was watching *Chitty Chitty Bang Bang*. *"You cannot see, how much I long to be free. Turning around on this music box wound by a key."*

I made my way back upstairs where most party guests had left. Three men loomed in the living room.

The Big Three I heard Alex call them.

Roger had a black mustache matching his feathered dark hair and a slight belly. Darrell was with a timid-looking girl. Patterson, the biggest of the three, had horn-rimmed glasses resting on his large nose.

All the blinds were drawn, the music lulled, R.E.M. sang at a soft, easy level, *"Can I throw in the ring? No gasoline, just..."*

The atmosphere buzzed.

Patterson's eyes ran over my body from top to bottom.

I tugged down the brief hem of my dress, Alex's birthday present.

Alex made his way over, a glass of whisky in hand.

"Everything okay?" He wore a shy, adoring expression. A mixture of hope and fear of rejection was etched in his eyes.

Against the tightness in my throat, I croaked, "Thirsty."

Alex handed me a glass of wine. "Something to help you relax."

I stuck my tongue out. "Make me."

He chuckled, reaching for a bottle of water instead.

I took a drink, eyeing him over the top.

Mustache Man's predatory gaze raked over my body. "Daisy?" he repeated, the name rolling from his lips. "I like her."

Alex chuckled. "I told you."

The room whirled, darkness I'd been fighting swirled under me, pulling me beneath. Rubbing my neck, I coughed, trying to speak but no sound came out.

"How are you feeling?" His voice was odd.

Was water oozing from his pores?

It's the water. I glanced down at the bottle in my hand.

The room dimmed.

And went black.

63

Florence

The late afternoon sun poured in our bedroom window when I awoke. Searching my brain for last night's events, I came up empty. I must have drank too much and passed out.

I had to pee.

Really really badly.

I rolled out of bed, weaving my way to the bathroom.

Voices echoed down the hallway.

"…saw what you two are capable of. I can't say I'm not a little more than impressed. But I want my share before you do…whatever it is you do."

The voice was clear. It was the man with the black moustache.

I could barely make out Alex's low tones.

Mustache Man responded, "She's higher than a kite! You see her eyes? Whatever you gave her, she's not going anywhere."

A pause.

"Cute kid you got. I would like to play with him."

This time, I heard Alex clearly, "She'll go to the police. Do you want to end up in prison? Do you have any idea how inmates treat pedophiles?"

And then Mustache Man: "She's stoned."

"This is my house, I invited you in and fed you. If the cops get wind, I'm playing innocent.

Did Mustache Man have a gun? Fear gripped my stomach. I fought back tears and screams clawing at my throat, and slipped down to the basement.

The sound of voices escalating in the kitchen got me moving. The clatter of pots and pans echoed through the darkness. Struggling against the heavy blanket covering my body, voices dimmed as footsteps retreated down the hallway.

Edges of fog clearing from my vision, I turned around.

Eddy stood watching me, a concerned look on his face. "You were seepin'."

I struggled to recall what happened.

Above us, footsteps against linoleum.

They would finish in the kitchen and then come down here. When they did, there would be no stopping them.

"Eddy, you want to play a game?"

His eyes lit. "Yes."

"You have to do exactly what I tell you to."

He nodded. "I will."

"You know hide-and-seek?"

He nodded again, his eyes full of innocence.

"We're going to play that, only we're going to hide together."

His eyes lit with sunshine. "Goody."

My breathing quieted. "You have to be real quiet, though. 'Kay?"

He nodded again. "Who's it?"

"Daddy."

64
December 15, 2000

Florence

I pried open my eyes.

The peaceful ticking of a clock mocked the storm inside me. I searched the cramped pantry space behind the shelves until my eyes landed on the furnace.

Eddy was on my lap. Brief images of the night before came floating back. I listened for the sound of people upstairs.

Silence answered.

Gently, I disengaged from Eddy and crept out of the secret pantry space. I tiptoed up the stairs, glancing at the Mickey Mouse clock on the wall next to the pantry.

Four o'clock.

The silence was disconcerting.

The living room was a disaster. Garbage and empty bottles were strewn about. I peered into our bedroom.

Where was Alex?

That's one less rodent in your walls looking for heat and food.

***

December 22, 2000

Andrew showed up at my door appearing haggard.

"I forgot my coat," he said. "I called you after I arrived home from your birthday party. When you didn't answer, I left a message, figuring you were busy and would get back to me.

"When you didn't, I called again, *This number has been changed, disconnected, or is no longer in service. Please hang up and try your call again.*"

"So you did."

"I did. Same message. Then I started to worry." He set Eddy's diaper bag and suitcase in the trunk of his car. "You seemed pretty disoriented at your birthday party."

"I had too much wine."

"I thought back to the time I showed up and smoked cigars with Alex. I was pretty sure you were drunk then too. And other times you've sounded funny on the phone. You've been drinking too much."

"I suppose."

"You need help."

"I need sleep."

"You've been in the house the whole time he's been gone?"

"I didn't have any place to go," I said. "He sold the Corvette and took my Audi."

Andrew gave me an incredulous look.

"We've managed. There's been enough food for me and Eddy. I've cleaned every day as I always have. Taken care of Eddy just like before."

"Your husband disconnected your phone, left over a week ago, and hasn't called or been back since. And you continue on like normal." He shook his head. "Who does that?"

"Me?"

"A crazy person." He set Eddy in his booster seat.

I handed him the sphinx lamp.

Andrew set it in the empty seat next to Eddy. "You sure you don't need to grab anything else? A bag, backpack, or purse?"

I pulled on my periwinkle parka over my pink t-shirt. "I'll be back. I'm sure there's a logical explanation. When Alex gets back and finds us gone, he'll come for us."

Andrew frowned. "Have any cops showed up?"

"No." I chewed my lip. "There were…some men at my birthday party."

Andrew appeared shocked. "What?"

"I'm scared something bad might have happened to him." I sank down in the passenger seat.

"All the more reason to get you out of here." He shut the door, made his way around to the driver's side, and got in. "What about Eddy's mother?"

"It's a long story," I sighed.

"It's a long drive."

I drew a breath, and began to tell my brother how I met my husband.

65
December 23, 2000

Florence

New Zealand defeated Australia by four runs for Cricket Women's World Cup. Edward wandered out of the guest bedroom Aunt Sophia put us in, rubbing his eyes with his fists. He sat down at the table next to me.

"Hey, fella. What's your name?" Leah asked. Leah was dating Jared Thompson and worked at Gate City Bank as a teller. She'd stopped by to show her mother the $300 leather coat she bought Jared for Christmas.

"How old are you?" Aunt Sophia handed Eddy a roll of lefse.

Leah crouched, flashing her best smile. "Do you like lefse?"

"Can you talk?"

"Are you in school?"

Back and forth they fired questions. Eddy said nothing, his brown eyes moving from one to the other.

Leah's pity-filled gaze fixed on me. "You got your work cut out for you. Poor dear. What's wrong with him?"

"Nothing is wrong with him." I slammed the lefse roll on the plate. "He doesn't talk much. You firing questions loaded like a baked potato doesn't help."

"I'm sorry." Leah's eyes softened. "I didn't mean to make him feel bad."

"Don't say sorry to me." I glared at her. "He's right there."

Silence fell.

Leah stood. "I better be going. I told Jared I'd bring him McDonald's."

"Good to see you." I shifted in my chair, wishing with everything in me I'd held my temper.

She smiled and was out the door.

"It really is good to have you home, Florence." Aunt Sophia took a sip of coffee.

"Thank you." I could tell she meant it. Aunt Sophia had been wonderful since we returned home. It was like the last four years had never happened.

"I have something for you," she pushed away from the table.

An early Christmas present? "Really?"

She returned with a tablet. "You always liked lists when you were little," she said, ripping the top sheet from the book.

My heart dropped into my belly. I put a flat hand over the list and a forced smile on my face.

"Your father and I are so excited to have you home," she said. "Especially your father. I don't have to tell you I'm not the best cook."

No she didn't.

I perused the list. It wasn't so bad really.

I poured myself a cup of coffee and sipped it, wandering over to the living room window. My heart kicked up at the familiar figure in the yard.

Mustache Man.

Returning to the kitchen, I opened a cupboard door. "Who's that in the yard?"

"Marvin Baker. Temporary bee help. He used to work for Merle Anderson."

Not Roger. "Where's he from?" I opened the same cupboard again. "Don't you have sugar?"

Sophia handed me the container. "Chetek, Wisconsin," Sophia supplied. "Then a position opened up in Spiritwood for a kindergarten teacher, and he applied."

"Does he have a wife and kids?" I scooped a spoonful of sugar, dumped it in my coffee and stirred.

"A wife Josephine and daughter around eight? Irmgard." A pause. "Rumor has it, his wife was just released from the State Hospital."

My hand slowed on the spoon. "Did they hire him?"

"Conditional basis. Clara Ziggledorf put in a good word for him with the school board."

"Do you suppose he'll accept it?"

"I hear the school board offered Mr. Baker more than what they paid the last teacher, Ms. Schroeder." Sophia stood. "I've got to run into town for a few last minute Christmas items. Can I get you anything?"

"No thanks."

After she left, I set Edward up with Legos in the living room, and retreated to the basement storeroom at the end of the hall. The shelves were filled with canned food, vegetables, and meat. There were boxes of instant dinners and pasta noodles.

I reached for a box of linguini and a can of Alfredo sauce. There was a bottle of Gentleman Jack whisky behind that.

The lid was tight, but I managed to get it open, glanced around, and took a sip.

After three more, I made my way back up the stairs.

I'd make French bread to go with the chicken Alfredo on Aunt Sophia's list. I wouldn't feel guilty about being here. And Alex would come for me.

Dinner turned out nicely.

Marvin Baker joined us. He had a refined manner. He was polite and quiet with black hair and a large handlebar moustache. A scar slashed his thick left brow.

He didn't act like he knew me.

It wasn't him.

Stupid. Of course it's him. Or he had an identical twin. I could ask Alex about it when he came for me.

Please Alex, come for me.

66

Norman

Andrew sat across from me at Perkins. "Florence is looking for a job."

"Good." I poured syrup over my stack of pancakes. "How is she doing?"

"Seems to be alright now that she's not drinking. Dad says she's been helping around the house and making meals."

"She's an alcoholic?"

"Worse. The whole time she was a Bible School student, she was living a double life. Spending most nights with Alex Diestrum doing God knows what. It's what got her kicked out of Bible College."

"At least she's got a kid now," I said, my chest swelling at the thought of my own girls. "Someone else to look out for besides herself."

"*He* does. Said it was his nephew." Andrew took a sip of coffee. "Get this: he told her she was his sister and then Florrie saw them kissing."

"Ouch." I ripped open sugar packages, pouring sugar into my coffee.

"I can't understand what she saw in that tool."

"She doesn't know he's dodgy." I took a sip and winced. Too sweet. And then it occurred to me, "Diestrum's not going to get over her. My guess is it's something that never occurred to him."

"Right."

Ignoring his sarcasm, I continued, "He married her. He'd told the lie about him being Eddy's uncle to make him seem more credible. A more convincing story."

"Then he disappeared."

"He might be trying to reach her." *Or spy on her.* "Doesn't take a psychic to see he's obsessed."

"If he's so obsessed, where's he now?"

"Biding his time. It's his way of control. To get her panicked without him."

"She is that." Andrew took a sip of coffee. "She can't stop talking about him. She's worried he doesn't know where she is."

"He might even know you managed to snag her away from him. But Alex Diestrum can't let that happen. Not a man like that."

Andrew wiped his mouth on a napkin. "Don't suppose there's anything you can do."

"Unless she reports abuse or has a restraining order against him, there's no keeping him away from her." He wanted Florence. He'd gotten her and he was going to keep her until he didn't want her anymore.

"She's not going to go for that. She's waiting for him to walk through the door and save her and Eddy."

67

Florence

Breakfast was a quiet affair with Dad and Andrew where conversation consisted of passing the butter, salt, or pepper.

Dad paged through the paper.

"Good morning," Sophia entered the room, sucking out all the peace from the atmosphere with two words.

"Good morning," I mumbled into my cup.

She sat down, and began talking incessantly about the news.

I considered mornings past with Eddy and meals waiting for Alex to show. At the image of his handsome face, his low voice, suddenly I couldn't breathe. I would even welcome the scent of coconut.

Dad stood, downing the last of his coffee. "I'm going to head into Jamestown. I gotta get a new thermostat for the shed. Hardware store closes at noon."

I excused myself, and headed to the kitchen to do dishes.

Sophia hurried over. "Florence, I switched the top thing on the list to the bottom. Windows should be washed first."

"It's Christmas Eve."

"It's a short list." She gave an easy smile. "I suppose you could be off today. Hopefully, Reverend Alder won't show up until after Christmas."

"No, it's fine. I'll do it."

She arched a fine brow. "You sure?"

"Yes but…" I trailed off as she trailed away.

I turned back to the dishes.

Andrew entered the kitchen, drawing alongside me. "I'll wash, you dry." He grabbed the sink plug. "You okay?"

I gave him a tremulous smile. "Yeah."

"What's up?" He reached for the dish soap.

"Not much."

Silence.

"I've enrolled in the law enforcement program in Dickinson," he said.

"Congratulations. Does Dad know?"

"Not yet."

"I'm happy for you." I wondered if Andrew would follow through, or if law enforcement was one of those unattainable dreams. "Are you going to move back here?"

"It's a ten-month program." He dipped a plate beneath the suds. "We'll see. Might stick around, who knows?"

"Norman would like that." I dried a coffee mug.

"He's doing right by those girls."

"As he should."

"He's made a lot of steps in the right direction these last few years."

"What choice did he have?"

"We all have choices."

"Why are you telling me this?" I set a stack of plates in the cupboard.

"I'm reminding you he was your friend once." A pause. "He did a background check on Alex."

Fury swept through me like a hot flame. "What?"

"Calm down. You know cops. They're suspicious of everyone."

"And?" My heart thumped in my throat.

"He's married."

"Yeah, I know." I gave a weak laugh.

"To someone else. A woman named Nicole, maiden name Brown." He glanced over, searching my eyes. "You know what that means?"

I didn't answer.

"No regrets? About Alex, I mean."

"Yes," I said with a half-smile. "I have regrets. He made me feel beautiful in one moment. In the next…" *like I didn't exist.* I'd feel like I was his whole world, then like I was alone. "I keep thinking, 'What if he comes back, and we're not there'?"

"He knows where you are. I left a note."

"Thank you." I sighed. "I couldn't even call him or Carmen for that matter."

"Reason enough to leave. He'll come if he cares about Eddy at all."

"And if he doesn't?" I held my hand up. "Don't answer that."

"Wait and see."

"The scariest part is knowing I won't feel that way again. Life has become a mundane cloud of mediocrity. Deep down, knowing if I could go back to him, I would. In a second."

"Not going to happen."

"You're such a good brother."

He smiled. "Can I count on you two for the Christmas Cantata?"

At the hopeful look on his face, I found myself asking, "What time?"

"Four thirty."

"We'll be ready." After he left, I got Eddy dressed and together we worked on Sophia's list.

That's when I realized I didn't have anything to wear.

68

Norman

At the end of my shift, Marissa Potter was sitting on my living room couch in a short red dress, a glass of wine in hand. Her legs were smooth and I knew from experience, soft.

She was a beautiful woman.

Even after the twins were born, her body went back to her hourglass figure. Sadly, her habits had as well. Marissa insisted on her own place, only crashing at mine when she was too hammered to drive home.

Grandma came to my house in the evening to tuck the girls in. The spare room was hers while I worked nights.

Meanwhile, Marissa partied late, slept in, and spent a good part of the day getting dressed up and made up.

"Isn't it a bit early for a drink?" I arched a brow.

"Never too early." She set her glass on the end table, stood, and wrapped herself around me. "Hello, darling."

My mouth found hers and her fingers slid up and into my hair.

A few minutes later, I pulled back. "You need to stop drinking."

"I thought Catholics were allowed to drink." She purred against my neck.

I shivered. "We're leaving at four."

"Where are we going?" her velvety tone hit every nerve center in my body.

"To church."

"Why would I go to church?"

"It's the Christmas Eve Cantata. I've been talking about it for a month. You would know that if you'd stop drinking."

"Now why would I do a thing like that?"

"Like what?" My eyes dropped to her mouth, and I lost my train of thought.

I didn't know if church was the answer, but I didn't want the girls growing up like Marissa. I tried thinking back to what had attracted me to her in the first place.

She gave me a sultry smile.

I remembered then, and we shared a kiss that had me following her to my bedroom and the promise of her body.

***

"Tomorrow's Christmas," I said, straightening my tie in the mirror. "Mother invited us to her house."

"They won't remember any of it." Marissa sat up in bed, sheet wrapped around her.

"But I will." I sighed. "Are you coming or not?"

"Not."

"I think we ought to do the right thing," I told her. "I think we should get married."

She laughed. "Now why would we go and ruin a perfectly good relationship by getting shackled?"

"For the girls." I struggled in the mirror with the tie. "And because it's right."

She stood and made her way over. Pushing my hand out of the way, she began to fix my tie. "I was never cut out to be a mother."

"But you are one," I said, even as I saw the resolve in her eyes. I pulled away, yanking the tie from my neck. "I don't want you drinking all night."

"I'll be a good girl, don't worry."

"I better get going." I turned toward the door. "I'm picking up the girls on the way. Grandma will want to be early."

"Of course she will." Marissa rolled her eyes.

"I'm leaving now."

"Don't worry," she gave a cold smile. "I'll be gone by the time you get back."

On my way to pick up the girls, I pondered the fact Marissa didn't act like a mother and seemed to have no interest in being one. The memory of her driving drunk with Shawn Vitense came rushing back.

Now Shawn was dead. Not from an accident, but dropped dead in his kitchen in front of his wife and sons. A heart attack at 35. His end, disturbing. He had a gorgeous wife, twin boys, and had lived his life partying and sleeping around.

My twin girls were still too little to understand, but soon they would know their mother didn't care about them. Or me.

Yeah, that's pretty bad. Things are going to get a lot worse unless you repent. Everything had been perfectly fine until an old man at a gas station announced it was the end of the world.

Everything is not fine.

Everything had not been fine for a long time.

69

Florence

The winter sun hung low in the west on the drive to the Christmas Cantata.

The service was good. Father Paul brought life to the church, talking about King Saul, how he was a good-looking, empty-headed donkey finder. "The Lord regretted he made Saul over Israel. The next king won't come from your family. Sin makes you stupid."

I even found myself smiling a time or two.

In a borrowed black sweater two sizes too big and several inches too short, black slacks that Andrew called flood pants, I sat next to Leah and her clean-cut boyfriend, Jared.

Admitting to Sophia I had nothing to wear was hard enough. In the end, I couldn't find the words to refuse the outfit. Anyway, not like Alex would be there.

Leah was wearing a dress the color of ripe cherries, her platinum bangs pinned up from her not-too-big forehead.

Jared seemed nice. They met when she started working at Gate City Bank. He was the manager, cute if you liked the office type.

Andrew stood next to me, and I leaned over, "Is my hair okay?"

He shrugged. "I hadn't noticed."

I smiled and sat back. A sensible man.

"Leah says men want women with long hair."

"Better than pants that are too short."

I frowned.

"Hey Florence. I didn't know you'd be here," Norman said, making his way toward us. He wore a dark blue suit jacket with a crisp white shirt beneath, the top two buttons undone, and no tie. His blue jeans were dark enough to pass for slacks. Two little girls with dark curls had his hand at either side. One in a velvet dress of green, and her twin, matching red velvet.

"Hi Norman." I stood, squeezing Eddy's hand.

"Mama, you're holding my hand too tight," he said.

"Sorry." I released it.

"Florence, Eddy, I'd like you to meet my girls Hildegard," he glanced down at the girl in red, and motioned toward the other in green, "And Gertrude."

"I like your dresses," I said.

"How come you're not wearing a dress?" Hildegard asked.

Norman frowned. "Hildegard."

"She's just telling it like it is." Was my belly showing? I resisted the urge to tug the borrowed sweater down.

Norman's eyes caught mine. "I've never seen you wear a dress, Florence."

"Andrew tells me you are a Corporal for the Jamestown Police Department."

"Yeah." He ran a hand over his hair.

"I didn't know Alice Wilson had a baby," I murmured as she caught the corner of my eye.

"Eighteen and senior in high school and he's as old as dirt," Andrew mused. "I wonder if she knows where they come from."

"She's a natural beauty," I said, recalling a girl that spent more time on the back of a horse than on the ground.

The scowl she wore was new.

"Did I tell you Dad's hiring Leo Nelson?" Andrew asked.

Norman chuckled. "Seriously? What does he know about bees?"

At bedtime, I tucked Eddy in and read him a story before getting ready for bed in the guest room. I caught a glimpse of my reflection in the mirror.

I was too tall, too frumpy, and too trashy.

No dress was going to change that.

"Provided that any of those neighbors sing out of tune or have boots that squeak, or double chins, or odd clothes, the patient will quite easily believe that their religion must therefore be somehow ridiculous." —Uncle Screwtape

C. S. Lewis, *Screwtape Letters*

70

Florence

Sunday morning Eddy and I were in church with Andrew.

John and his fiancée, Polly Landers were there along with Aunt Sophia and Dad. Norman, his girls, and his grandmother Elsa Martin, but not his parents. I suppose they still attended Catholic Mass.

Marvin Baker's wife Josephine was there with a little girl with blonde hair. Her daughter Irmgard? I didn't see Marvin. I couldn't help but notice Josephine's dress was short enough to ride high on her thigh as she sat down.

She turned and caught me staring. I looked away, bowing my head, unable to look forward for fear of seeing she was looking back.

Or if she saw what a good excuse Eddy provided me.

"Jesus straightened up and said to them, 'Let him who is without sin among you be the first to cast a stone at her.' And again He bent down and wrote on the ground. The people crowded around him were so touched by their own consciences that they departed…'" Reverend Alder read from the book of John.

"Praise to you, oh Christ," the congregation murmured.

In my comfortable place next to Eddy, I couldn't help but wonder what Jesus wrote on the ground that day. Or if the adulterous woman was any different than Josephine Baker, who sat alone, put in her place by the congregation.

By me.

How different were the Pharisees than I, on this second Sunday of January 2001?

Most definitely different.

They dropped their stones.

***

Waves of snow were carved in hard crusts around us.

A bitter breeze sliced through my clothes. "Rats. I forgot my coat at church." I laid a hand on Andrew's arm. "Wait here. I'll be right back."

Retrieving the forgotten item didn't take long. I buttoned it up and exited the church.

Josephine sat on the top of the steps, wearing only the thin dress she wore at the service earlier. Irmgard sat next to her, shivering.

My breath caught.

Her face was swollen, her eyes hollow. It was the timid-looking woman who was with Darrell at my surprise birthday party. Deep crow's feet surrounded her empty gaze as she stared into the distance.

"Are you okay?" I leaned closer, raising my voice above the howl of the wind, "Pretty chilly not to be wearing a coat."

"I can't take care of Irmgard. Will you? Carmen told me about her son. How good you are with him." She laid a hand on my arm.

It was cold and clammy. "Where's your husband?"

"You were always nice to me."

My mouth went dry and I glanced around. "I don't know what you mean."

She met my eyes. "I'm sorry for that party."

"I don't know what you're talking about." But I did. And I was sorry that she sat here. Sorrier that I knew the party she was referring to. "I can't just leave you here."

"You must believe me." Her voice cracked, tears trickling down her cheeks. "He said he was a guest. All he told me was that it was a birthday party for his friend's wife."

"You know her?" Andrew drew alongside me, pulling his collar up around his face.

"We better not leave her," I avoided a direct answer.

"I don't see Reverend Alder. Probably went home."

"I suppose we should call social services." I climbed in the passenger seat. From the corner of my eye, I caught Andrew's gaze fixed on my face. "What?"

"Nothing," he faced forward and pulled out of the parking lot.

From the rearview mirror, I saw her frail silhouette on the horizon. Why did she have to come here? I folded and unfolded my hands until I finally sat on them.

After arriving home, I called the police department. "She asked me to take Irmgard." I told the officer over the phone.

"I'll talk to her. Thanks for calling."

"You alright?" he asked.

"Yeah," I said, suddenly afraid Alex had come for me after all.

71

Florence

The phone was ringing when I entered the kitchen the next morning. "Hello?"

"She's in town."

"Good morning, Andrew."

"The woman from the church steps. You should bring her some kuchen. Marge Garms made enough to sink a..."

"No."

"It's not like you to be so…"

"…Stubborn?"

"Uncharitable."

"Why me? She's not my problem. There are plenty of people in the parish. Let one of them do their Christian duty and be the least of these brothers, because I don't want anything to do with her."

"Reverend Alder says she's pretty cognitive now. Brought her in and fed her. Said she's from Belfast, Maine. Her name is Josephine. She's Marvin Baker's wife."

"I see."

"You thought you knew her?"

"Yes. No. I don't know, I'm tired." I yawned loudly into the receiver.

Silence.

He cleared his throat. "Florence, you're the bravest woman I know."

"Hmph."

"So what are you afraid of?"

After I hung up the phone, I pondered my options.

My wedding ring.

I looked at the rock on my hand, reluctant to part with it. Perhaps it was a chance out of poverty. A way to figure out how to work and take care of the kids without having to go to Dad, who in turn, would check with Aunt Sophia. I had my suspicion she was behind selling the lake house. That is, her spending.

I picked up the phone and dialed Mr. Money.

"Everyone then who hears these words of mine and does them will be like a wise man who built his house on the rock. And the rain fell, and the floods came, and the winds blew and beat on that house, but it did not fall, because it had been founded on the rock."

Matthew 7:24-25

Part III

72
June 15, 2001

Florence

ExxonMobil and Qatar Petroleum signed a letter of intent for a natural gas to liquids (GTL) project that would be the largest in the world.

Aunt Sophia met me on my way downstairs with a work list. "Good morning," she sang, handing me a long piece of paper.

I frowned. "I haven't even had my breakfast."

Her fine brow arched. "I thought you liked lists, but if you'd rather not..."

I held up my hand. "No, no that's okay."

After all, I did prefer lists as opposed to endless orders. Even with a list as long as the Amazon River, I saw the end for myself instead of being ordered about and followed around.

Still. It made for an incentive to find a job. Today, I'd check the paper. Aunt Sophia…I really didn't want to leave Eddy when she was around. Then daycare. How would that work? I'd need a high-paying job and low daycare costs. What would happen if Eddy bit someone?

My mouth, dry as the desert, wished for a peppermint.

The aroma of fresh coffee wafted toward me. I made my way to the kitchen and halted.

Damp dark blond hair curling at the collar of the clean gray t-shirt he wore, Norman sat at the dining room table with his back to me. "If you know of someone with a boat, I'll check out…" he was saying.

Dad's eyes lifted when he saw me.

Norman glanced over his shoulder. His eyes traveled down and then back up, lingering a moment on my face before he turned around.

Making my way to the coffee pot, I was suddenly shy. Pouring a cup of the steaming black liquid, I saw his gaze on me from the corner of my eye.

"Good morning, Norman." Did he think my clothes were too small? That my half-sleeve tattoo of roses looked trashy?

"Mornin'." His eyes reverted to his coffee cup.

"Check this out." Dad pushed the paper over to him.

Eddy came out, copper curls falling over his forehead. He glanced at Dad, then Norman before he dashed over to me, wrapping his arms around my legs.

"Good morning, little man." I smiled.

I felt Norman's eyes on us as he sipped his coffee, and wondered what Andrew had told him.

Dragging Eddy along with my leg, I washed and dried breakfast dishes. Norman stood, and brought his plate and cup to the sink. "Thanks for washing my dishes."

I cleared my throat and said what was upmost on my mind, "Leah lent me these clothes."

"You look nice," he said.

Flustered, I asked, "What are you doing here?"

"Your dad invited me to go to an auction sale near Galesburg." A pause. "You?"

Good question. "Helping Dad."

"You're staying then."

"Maybe."

"Might be a job at the post office in Spiritwood if you're interested. They're going to put it in *The Jamestown Sun* this week."

"Thanks for the heads up."

"Nice little fella you got there." His eyes landed on Eddy clutching onto my leg with his life.

"Thank you. Your girls are sure pretty."

"Yeah." He rubbed the back of his neck. "Look Florence, I..."

"Norman it isn't..." I began.

We shared a laugh.

"You first," I said.

"I just wanted to say it's good to have you home."

"Thank you."

"What were you going to say?"

"Nothing important." My eyes shifted to the kitchen window.

"Expecting someone?" Norman asked, his gaze following mine.

"N-no," I stammered. "I better get Eddy ready for school."

It wasn't until after lunch I was able to look through the paper. I circled all of the jobs and pulled out my notepad.

Hi-Acres Manor was hiring Certified Nursing Assistants. Minimart a cashier. Paradiso, waitresses.

I put Hi-Acres at the top of the list because they likely paid the best.

Paradiso next. A waitress might provide enough tips plus the hours might prove to be less daycare.

Minimart on the bottom.

I paused when I came to the one in Spiritwood at the post office. A federal employee would get good benefits, but what did I know about mail? How had Norman known about it? I suppose he might hear if I applied and didn't get an interview. I circled it anyway and moved it to the top.

A chance was a chance.

73
March 2, 2002

Norman

U.S. conventional forces first deployed as part of Operation Anaconda in its invasion of Afghanistan.

Nickelback "How You Remind Me" was playing on the stereo as Florence moved about the kitchen.

The aroma of bacon and pancakes wafted through the air.

"Good morning," she said, and pulled a cup from the cupboard, pouring it three-quarters full, topped it with heavy whipping cream and sugar, and set it in front of me.

"You're going to spoil me." I removed my cap.

"I'm the one who's spoiled," she said. "By the time Eddy's done playing with the girls, he's worn out and ready for bed, no argument."

Swallowing a sudden lump in my throat, I found myself enjoying company, conversation, and a woman.

Did she care for me? She had once. In the fifteen months since her return, gone was the sallow look on her face. Her eyes still held the weight of sadness. I longed to bear her burden.

"They are outside battling to the death as we speak."

"Eddy has become much more gallant since he's been around you." Florence poured herself a steaming cup.

"And Hildegard and Gertrude are more attentive to details since your influence. So I was thinking..." I took a sip of coffee. "I'd like to get married."

She gasped.

"I don't have the biggest house in town, but there's room for improvements." I hadn't meant to propose, but catching her eyes, my resolve strengthened. A flicker of inner fire was in their green depths. They were eyes like no other—wise, knowing, and oddly innocent, showing a beguiling purity of spirit that belied the sophisticated armor she wore so well.

"I'm up for promotion to sergeant. The girls love you. I think of Eddy as my own."

"You want to marry me?"

"Yes." My neck grew hot and I ran my hand down it. "I'm not saying this right, but I want to take care of you. All of you."

"But how are we going to…" she stammered.

"Make a difference? Change the world?"

"I was going to say feed everyone, but there's that." She frowned. "This doesn't sound like a very modern way to do things."

"Thank you." I smiled.

"You're Catholic. You need to marry a good Catholic girl."

"I'm no longer Catholic," I said, "Or good for that matter."

"No." She shook her head.

My throat tightened. "I-I haven't taken you out on dates or wooed you, but if you..."

"It's not that."

"What is it then?"

"I don't want to get married again. To anyone."

Suddenly I felt like I was nine years old explaining that her mother really died. This had to be a lot easier.

"But your marriage wasn't valid."

Her eyes caught mine. "It was to me."

74
June 10, 2002

Florence

The first direct electronic communication experiment between the nervous systems of two humans was performed by Kevin Warwick in the United Kingdom.

"Eddy awake?" Dad sat at the kitchen table with the newspaper.

"He's playing in his room. I told him if he was really good today I'd take him to the Bismarck Zoo on Saturday."

"Nice." Dad looked up from his paper and folded it. "I got four men coming for lunch. We're going to be separating honey. Norman too. The girls will be with him."

"Oh good. Then Eddy will have someone to play with."

"Norman's been good to those girls." Dad held up his coffee cup.

I topped it off. "I meant to ask, what is their mother like?"

"She's out of the picture. Norman hasn't said much, but last I heard, she moved to Minot with a fella who has a ranch out there."

"Who takes care of them when he's at work?"

"Elizabeth's mother, Elsa." Dad stood. "I better be going. They're spraying chemical over at Spick's tomorrow."

"Sounds good."

After he left, the front door opened, and in blue jeans and matching sweaters, Hildegard and Gertrude stood in the doorway.

"Our daddy said we could come in and play with Eddy," Hildegard said. It had taken me two weeks to figure out who was who. Now even wearing the same clothes, I could tell them apart.

"Eddy? The girls are here."

"Be right out," he called, the sound of shuffling followed a thump.

I opened the door. "What are you…?"

Guilt was written all over his face. "Hi Mama."

"What do you have behind your back?"

He took a step back. "Nothing."

"It's not nothing." I took a step toward him.

Then he turned, ran past me and out the door.

"Eddy!" I turned around, dashing after him.

He laughed. I chased him into the kitchen, grabbed the edge of his shirt, and he slipped away, laughing as he ran in the opposite direction.

"Edward Lee, when I get my hands on you…"

The front door opened. "Hildegard, you forgot…" Norman stepped into the doorway.

I slammed into his side. Caught off guard, he stumbled back, and I fell with him to the hard linoleum floor.

Silence, heavy and awkward, followed.

Towering over him, an idea came quick as a flash and I hocked up phlegm in my throat.

His eyes widened, a surprised laugh burst from his lips.

"Mama are you going to spit on him?" Eddy asked.

Rolling off him, laughter started to roll over me.

Still chuckling, Norman picked the backpack off the floor. "Hildegard forgot this."

Giggling, I said, "Eddy smuggled in a kitten."

Norman sat up. "Eddy."

Eddy halted in midstride.

"Come back here."

He hesitated.

"Now please," Norman's voice wasn't hard, but firm.

"I didn't want her to squish Fredrick." Eddy held the kitten up with both hands. "He's my kitty."

Norman nodded. "Did you have permission to have Fredrick in the house?"

"No sir."

"It's okay," I said.

A smile worked its way across Norman's face as he handed the backpack to Hildegard.

Eddy looked up at me with pleading brown eyes. "Mama, can Fredrick play with us? Please?"

"Grandpa doesn't like kitties in the house." I shook my head. "Take him outside. I'll be out in a bit. We'll pick up sticks in the yard."

After they disappeared, Norman turned to me. "I heard you're going to foster Irmgard Baker. Is everything working out with your job?"

"It will." I drew a breath, letting it out slowly. "I know you might not get it. Aunt Sophia doesn't. Dad doesn't, but life isn't just about making money and keeping house."

"Change doesn't come without sacrifice."

"Just trying to shine a little light in my corner." The sound of splashing on the stove in the kitchen reminded me I set the potatoes to boil. "I better go."

"See you at lunch."

A batch of fresh homemade buns should go nicely with ham and potatoes.

The men arrived with a noisy outburst, and one by one, washed their hands at the kitchen sink.

Dinner was potatoes, ham, and buttered carrots.

Three heads dropped to their plates, and the men began shoveling in food.

Aunt Sophia arrived shortly before dinner and began cleaning cupboards I'd cleaned, wiped counters I had wiped, and seasoned food I had prepared.

All in front of Dad and his hired hands.

When I'd taken my wedding ring to the pawn shop, I discovered another thing about Alex.

He was a cheapskate.

A cubic zirconium. I knew from my grandpa giving such a ring to grandma it was fake, although that was during the Depression so I'd always excused him. I was running out of excuses for Alex. "Surely it was worth something," I had asked. Would they give me a hundred dollars?

In the end the salesman offered me a ten dollar bill, and I think he offered that just because he felt sorry for me.

Suddenly getting married to Norman didn't seem so bad.

75
July 2, 2002

Florence

Steve Fossett became the first person to fly solo around the world nonstop in a balloon, and Aunt Sophia was in a glorious mood. It didn't take long for her to begin intelligence gathering.

"Good morning, Florence. I made coffee," she said, pouring the steaming black liquid into two mugs. "Marvin Baker took off."

"Really?" I sat down at the table.

She set a steaming cup in front of me. "Gloria said Sheriff Miller found Baker on his way to Canada, stopped him at the border in North Portal. He said he didn't think Irmgard was his."

"Josephine is unable to take care of her."

Aunt Sophia said, "You bit off too much."

"What else could I do?"

Aunt Sophia reached over, laying a hand on my arm. "You okay?"

"I'm fine," but wasn't, instead ridiculously close to tears. "Josephine didn't want a paternity test," I said. "She signed off on her parental rights."

"Who would give a single mother custody of her four-year-old daughter?" Aunt Sophia took the chair across from me. "Doesn't say much about her being fit."

"I've got my foster care license." I realized then I would keep Irmgard.

"Why didn't you tell me you're getting another kid?" Aunt Sophia asked, incredulous. "Not everyone is against you. You have friends."

"I didn't think it was any of your business."

***

Norman and the girls arrived at breakfast. Irmgard was sitting next to Eddy at the table eating a piece of peanut butter toast.

Hildegard strolled up to her. "Are you Eddy's sister?"

Irmgard glanced at me.

"She's staying with us for a while. Until her daddy comes back. This is Irmgard," I told them, laying a hand on her head, smoothing her blonde curls down.

I didn't care what Sophia said. Eddy might have been the reason I took classes for foster care, but there was no reason Irmgard couldn't benefit.

Hildegard cut in, "This is our daddy."

Norman smiled. "How do you do, Irmgard?"

"We're six," Gertrude and Hildegard said in unison.

"Do you like to play with dolls?" Hildegard smoothed the ratted nest on her baby doll.

"We could bake," Gertrude suggested.

"Why don't you kids go downstairs to the playroom?" I said.

After they disappeared in a whirl, I glanced at Norman.

He had removed his hat, fingering the edges. A determined look in his eyes belied his nervous hands. "I was just going to grab a cup of coffee."

I stood, made my way over to him and lifted my eyes several inches to meet his, which made him a little over six feet next to my five foot ten inches.

He searched my face. "I came to help your dad move bee colonies. Andersons are spraying chemical tomorrow."

"Why did you leave the Catholic Church?"

"I haven't gone off the deep end." He blew a sigh. "Look, Florence. A lot has happened since we were kids. I'm not the same person I was then."

I knew he was talking specifically about that summer everything changed. I couldn't ask. Wouldn't ask. I knew some things were better left alone.

"Yes."

He blinked. "What?"

"You asked me to marry you and my answer is yes," I said. "Unless you changed your mind."

His eyes searched mine. "When?"

"Yesterday. As soon as possible." I rubbed my hands together, searching for the words. "I'll ask you for loyalty and in turn you'll have mine. Also, I don't know if I can have kids. I mean, I've never been pregnant."

He tugged his cap on. "What are you doing Saturday?"

"Not sure yet. Why?"

"You want to go look for rings?"

"Yes."

After he left, I thought about what just happened.

I'd accepted his proposal and he didn't kiss me. There was no hug or even a handshake. I suppose that would have been quite awkward.

It was time to accept the things I couldn't change.

The toughest challenge yet.

A house without woman and firelight is like a body without soul or sprite.

-Benjamin Franklin

76
July 6, 2002

Florence

In Wimbledon Women's Tennis, Serena Williams beat older sister Venus for her first Wimbledon singles title.

With a determined jawline, Norman stood next to me at Zale's Jewelry.

For the first time since the day I threw my boot at him, I thought about what he would look like without a shirt. How would it feel to be in his arms? His attitude was friendly and casual toward me, and I couldn't see it happening.

We weren't even married yet, and already life together seemed complicated and awkward.

So..."I was thinking Eddy could sleep in the laundry room until the addition is finished. That way the girls can keep their room and Irmgard could have the spare. I hope it won't be too hard on your grandma."

"Which is your favorite ring?" he asked.

"Not sure. Which is yours?"

"I like this one," he held up the simple ring with a square cut diamond. It was the one I liked, but the price tag was outrageous.

"What about this one?" I reached for the other, much cheaper selection.

"It's nice," he said, still holding the other one, "But if you're asking me, I like this one better."

"Me too," I sighed. "But it's so expensive."

"It's a wedding ring. It's supposed to be."

"I feel funny about having you pay for it," I said, wringing my hands. "Maybe I should pay for half."

He arched a brow. "I asked you to marry me. It's tradition for the groom to pay for the ring. You can't break tradition."

But this wasn't really a traditional marriage. I should have spoken to him about the matter of sex when I agreed to marry him, but I hadn't allowed myself to consider the logistics of it.

After he purchased the ring, we got into his black Chevy Suburban, and he glanced over at me. "Want to grab a bite to eat?"

"I've got a roast in the Crock-Pot."

"Dairy Queen then. I'm dying for a peanut buster parfait."

"I don't know…"

"Come on," he said, "You don't have to order lunch. I'm sure you wouldn't turn down a strawberry Dilly Bar."

"I can't eat those anymore. I gain weight just looking at them."

"So when has that mattered?" He turned, following my gaze. "You see someone you know?"

"No." I glanced away.

After a strawberry Dilly Bar for me and peanut buster parfait for him, Norman drove north out of town, up hospital hill, and turned on Highway 20.

"Where are you going?" I asked.

"I thought we'd take the long way home." He went east on 42.

The sunset splashed brilliant shades of gold and violet across the western sky. He headed north around the lake.

The trees and landmarks were familiar, and my heart kicked up as I recognized the driveway.

At last, he pulled up in front of our old lake house and shifted into park.

"Want to take a look?" He glanced over at me.

"I don't even know who lives here now."

"Michael Gibbs was the last owner. Before him, your folks. Clyde Anderson was the one before that." He exited the Suburban. "Come on."

The setting sun cast long shadows off the rippling lake.

"This wasn't here before," I said as we passed a double stall detached garage. The old shed and blacksmith shop full of farm tools was still there.

The *for sale* sign was new.

The lake house was painted white, the deck was hardwood that continued into the house, replacing carpet of days past. The kitchen was open with a center island.

"At least they took the carpet out of the kitchen," I said, eyeing the center island. "Why people in the seventies thought carpet in the kitchen and bathrooms a good idea was beyond me."

The windows were large and the fireplace still inviting.

In the living room sat a baby grand piano.

"The owner must play," I mused, running a finger along the smooth edge.

"I thought the kids might want to take lessons."

"You mean...?"

"I bought the lake house," he gave me a boyish smile. "For us. I know I should have asked you first, being that Sophia took it over. I wasn't sure if you had any hard feelings, and I…"

Without thinking, I threw my arms around his neck.

His eyes widened briefly and he chuckled. "I take it you like it."

"I love it."

77
August 19, 2002

Florence

A Russian Mi-26 helicopter carrying troops was hit by a Chechen missile outside of Grozny, killing 118 soldiers.

Our house was nestled on the beautiful shores of Spiritwood Lake. Sixty-five people lived around the lake, and another twenty-seven in town.

Our wedding day was a simple event at the lake house. I made cupcakes. Attendees were Reverend Alder who married us and his wife Ruth. Dad and Aunt Sophia. Sue Ellen Henke and Marge Garms. Andrew, John and his fiancée Polly. James and Renee were in Europe. Norman's mother and Sheriff Casey. Elsa Martin, Norman's grandmother.

The kids went home with Norman's grandmother. Elsa offered to take them, and I couldn't refuse without raising eyebrows.

After the guests left and the food was put away, I sat in our master bedroom. It had a mahogany door and matching window sills. The walls were teal. There were three egress windows facing gentle grassy slopes.

The walls were adorned with pictures of the prairie, sunflowers, and one of a bee hovering over a lily.

A braided rug lay on the floor alongside the poster bed. There was a shelf of paperbacks.

A man who reads?

I realized I didn't know Norman as well as I thought.

In pajama pants and a tank top, suddenly the room seemed small. The bed, smaller.

Other than the light, dry peck on my mouth at the ceremony, he hadn't touched me. There were no dreamy looks from his eyes. I supposed we would eventually have sex, but not tonight.

I grabbed the Buffalo hunter from beneath my underwear in the dresser drawer where I'd stashed it earlier. Hurrying over to the bed, I scrambled under the covers, gently turning off the sphinx lamp. If I was careful, it didn't spark.

He wouldn't expect me to get up, would he? We already ate. What if he brought me something to drink?

The door opened and floorboards creaked.

The mattress sank beneath his weight.

Icy fingers of fear raised the hairs on my spine. Pretending to be asleep, I caressed the marble handle of the skinning knife. In the silence of the moonlit bedroom, I waited for him to make a move.

Every little movement on his side of the bed seemed sinister.

Slumber was a sweet friend, beckoning until I could no longer deny the deep sleep coming for me.

***

I woke to a body pressed against mine, a hand on my hip.

In one quick motion, I rolled over, pressing the blade beneath the man's chin. "The next hand you lay on me is getting cut off."

A low sound erupted in his throat.

I lifted the blade.

He swallowed visibly. "Florence."

I blinked. "Norman?"

"Yeah." His gaze lowered to my breasts flattened against his chest. The thin white tank top wasn't much to separate skin on skin.

Gray eyes lifted and held mine. "Mind removing the knife from my throat?"

"Sure. Sorry." I moved back and flipped over. Sheathing the knife, I prayed he wouldn't push the matter, listening to the silence until the rumble of snoring erupted.

The scene played again in my wide-awake thoughts.

Good, Florence. Real good. He was going to want to talk about it in the morning. I should have made a casual comment about waiting at the wedding supper. Or when we got our rings. Or anytime, anyway besides pulling a knife on him.

Tomorrow was soon enough to clear matters between us.

At last, I started to drift.

Sleep, the elusive beast, was a long time coming.

78

Florence

The peaceful rise of the August sun was a glorious start to a new day. Welcoming the heat, I sat on the deck, staring out at rippling waters.

I glanced over at the sound of the sliding door.

Norman stepped out and smiled.

Maybe everything will be alright.

"Mind if I join you?" he asked, coffee mug in hand, cheeks whiskered with the new growth of a beard

"Of course not."

Norman sipped his coffee alongside me. "Looks like it's gonna be a nice day."

"Remember when we used to go fishing here?" I rubbed both my arms. "Maybe the girls and I will catch walleye."

"I'd like to take Ed with me to gather honey. We won't be home for lunch."

"Hopefully fresh fish for supper then."

A few more minutes passed.

"The wedding was nice." His eyes were fixed on the lake.

"Yes it was." I flicked him a sideways glance. "Not much of a honeymoon."

His eyes remained focused ahead.

I turned my gaze to the sun blazing across rippling waters. "I guess I'm not really sure how to explain about last night."

He sipped his coffee, sleek muscles rippling beneath his cotton shirt

More peaceful silence.

"Anyway, I want to be a good wife."

He stood and reached for his cap. "Do you need anything from town?"

"Not that I can think of."

His gaze met mine and the tenderness I saw there took my breath away.

After he left, I sat alone for a few more minutes, blinking back the sudden swell of emotion.

It was the start of a new day.

79
August 20, 2002

Florence

A group of Iraqis opposed to the regime of Saddam Hussein took over the Iraqi Embassy in Berlin for five hours before releasing their hostages and surrendering.

In my ugly brown sweater, I went to the pantry to perform inventory. Canned food, boxed dinners, sardines, two bottles of sherry.

Beyond that, a Bible.

There was a knock on the door. Grabbing the Bible and two jars of peaches from the pantry shelf, I hurried to the kitchen. After setting the peaches on the stove, the Bible on the top of the fridge, I went to answer the door.

Crock-Pot in hand, Sue Ellen Henke from the north had an expectant smile. Next to her was Marge Garms with kuchen, the neighbor to the south.

Here for inspection.

"Hello Florence." Marge said. Her blouse was crisp and ironed, and her slacks neatly pressed. I was certain, intended to put me in my place.

"Thanks for the hotdish," I said, taking the Crock-Pot from her grasp. "Won't you come in and have coffee?"

"Marge, how are you doing?" Elsa Martin, Norman's grandmother, came in behind them. "Sue Ellen. Nice to see you."

"Nana!" The girls shouted in unison, bounding down the stairs.

Elsa gave Gertrude a hug. "Nana loves you, sweetheart," she turned, giving Hildegard the same treatment.

Irmgard trailed down behind them and over to me.

Elsa turned, glancing at my sweater and pajama pants. I ran a self-conscious hand over my hair.

"You've been very busy." She glanced around the kitchen, and crossed to the stove. "Can I help with breakfast?"

"Sure. I was thinking of bacon and pancakes." I glanced at the neighbor ladies. "And Marge's famous kuchen."

The ladies exchanged looks. "We better be going. We don't want to interrupt breakfast."

After they left, I told Elsa, "Thank you."

I often wondered how Elizabeth managed after Sophia and Casey. Yet, she stayed married to him. I didn't know if that made her the biggest idiot or a hero. It was unnerving having her mother in my house.

Edward emerged from his bedroom, cradling a ball of fur. "I've got a kitten, Nana."

"I see that."

"Her name is Sassy."

"He hears the girls call you that," I rubbed my hands together. "I hope you don't mind."

Elsa smiled. "I don't mind."

The kids dug into their eggs. I poured milk and water glasses, and helped cut pancakes into triangles.

After breakfast, I dragged a stool over to the sink. "Who wants to do dishes?"

Eddy came over. "I will."

"Thanks but I was thinking it might be the girls' day to do them."

His eyes brightened and he held Sassy closer.

"In fact, if you get ready, you might be able to go with Grandpa and do bee chores."

"Yay," he ran off.

Irmgard climbed up on the stool. I turned to Hildegard and Gertrude. "You two can dry."

Gertrude made a move to grab a dishtowel.

Hildegard reached for her arm. "We're too little."

"Alright," I said, and felt Elsa's frown more than saw it. "But next time, you don't get to eat."

"What?" They cried in unison.

I shrugged. "If you don't work, you don't eat."

Hildegard raised her hand. "I'll do them."

"Thank you. Maybe next time you can even help cook."

Gertrude came over. "I want to cook."

"Everyone wants to cook and no one wants to clean up," I said. "That's why we take turns."

As the girls washed the dishes, I wiped the table. "I can guess what people are saying."

"About what?" Elsa stacked plates in the cupboard.

"What do you think? About us getting married and all these kids."

"You care what other people think?"

I took a step back. "I don't."

"Florence?" Elsa said.

"Yeah?"

"I'm glad you two got married and have all these kids."

"Make full use of the fact that up to a certain point, fatigue makes women talk more and men talk less. Much secret resentment, even between lovers, can be raised from this." - Uncle Screwtape

C. S. Lewis, *Screwtape Letters*

80

Norman

The horizon was ablaze against the glass lake.

Breakfast was noisy and tempers were short. The children quit squabbling long enough to wolf down eggs and sausage.

Florence picked at hers.

"Your dad really has a thing going with the bees," I said, "I'd like to get into the bee business. I have thirty colonies now, but I'd like to make a living at it."

"You'll likely need five-hundred colonies. You could probably start with three hundred fifty and still quit your job," Florence took a drink of water. "After five hundred, you'd want to hire extra help."

"If I had you and the kids we could do it. I suppose there is the part about shipping the queen. She's fragile." I smiled. "At least that's what the girl I grew up with told me."

"You remembered."

"Yeah, I remembered. They ship them from California. That's going to be expensive and tricky since the queen doesn't like to move around."

"Raise your own queens."

"What would that entail?" I arched my brow.

"Start with the nucleus colony, a small one where the egg hatches after three days and becomes a larvae. On the fourth day, graft it from its cell and put it into a queen cup.

"From there, put that queen cup into a queenless colony. The bee colony will finish the queen cells by filling it with royal jelly and sealing it off with wax.

"Then before they hatch on day fourteen, put the cells into queenless colonies. She'll hatch and go on mating. She'll fly away and return to the colony as an egg-laying queen around day twenty four and start to lay eggs because she has been mated." Florence sat back in her chair. "She goes on many flights, not just one. The process takes about a month."

"I had no idea you knew so much about bees."

"Don't forget who my dad is," she smiled softly. "Between ten days and two weeks they'll be really sensitive so you don't want to disturb them."

"I'll mark the top producers. Hildegard, I'll show you how it's done." I took a bite of eggs.

"Okay, Daddy," she said.

Eddy's gaze burned a hole through her. "I'll help too."

"Seconds?" Hildegard popped the popular question.

Florence dished up another helping of sausage and eggs.

"Girls shouldn't eat seconds." Eddy scowled.

"I'll need you to haul honey," I told Eddy, hoping to diffuse a bomb. "The boxes are too heavy for Hildegard."

Eddy stuck his chest out. "You don't have muscles like I do."

Hildegard stuck her tongue out. "I'm just as strong as you are. Right, Daddy?"

I searched for a response that wasn't a lie and wouldn't make my daughter cry.

"You're strong, Hildegard," Florence came to my rescue.

"See?" she said to Eddy.

"But not the same way he is."

Hildegard's face fell.

"You see," Florence added quickly. "Girls are often forced to grow up quickly and bear more than we think we can. Our strength comes from inside."

Hildegard kicked the air. "I didn't choose to be a girl."

"God chose you to be one."

It was my turn to sit up straight, proud to have such a wife.

81
March 12, 2003

Florence

Elizabeth Smart was found after having been missing for nine months. The wind whipped across the land, blowing dust and dirt against the bedroom window pane.

The house shook beneath gusts. Windows rattled, the screen door opened and shut.

The school bus had come for the kids, and I was going to Hugo's to buy groceries. I arrived at the crowded grocery store.

Good thing I'd made a list.

Hamburger

Eggs

Sausage

Cheese

I stared at the different packages of ground beef. Ten pounds? Probably. I reached for the closest one, bumping into the guy next to me.

"Excuse me." I withdrew my hand and chose the one next to it.

Ticking off one at a time, I finished, and made my way outside. Searching the parking lot, I remembered parking by the east side door. When I found the Suburban, I made my way over.

I packed groceries in the hatch and got into the driver's seat, wind whipping around me. The scent of coconut oil flooded my nostrils.

My heart kicked up, slamming in my throat.

It couldn't be…? Alex! An image of the man with the hoodie in the meat aisle flashed through my mind. Shaking, I got out of the SUV, scanning the parking lot.

Alex was nowhere to be seen. Of course he wasn't. He was in Minneapolis, not in Hugo's parking lot in Jamestown, North Dakota.

I gave a nervous laugh, the wind carried it away.

Back in the driver's seat, I started the engine and backed out of the parking space. Should I tell Norman about it? What would I say?

Alex hadn't even bothered with me when we were married. Silliness led me to the altar after knowing him a whole four months, and pride kept me there even after I found out about Carmen. Alex was a voyeur who had taken care of his own needs at a party or in a hotel room. I had only bits and pieces of memories for what kind of parties those were.

Norman wouldn't understand and I couldn't blame him.

Loose lips sink ships.

The threat went around and around in my head.

Even if Norman was sympathetic about our marriage not being real, I never told him about the parties. How would I explain the blackouts? And when he had needs, I pulled a knife on him.

Would our marriage survive such a truth?

The truth.

Norman had never spoken about that summer after the weekend ride. I had never asked.

The only thing left in my memory was his indifference.

He'd think I was paranoid. *I* thought I was paranoid. Would he even believe me? I drew in deep breaths, checking the air for the scent of coconut. I couldn't smell it now, but I had when I'd first gotten in the Suburban.

Hadn't I?

By the time I reached my driveway, I had myself convinced I'd only imagined the whole thing and guilt made me jumpy.

What will you do with your guilt?

I pushed the thought aside and hauled groceries into the house.

82

Norman

Squeezing in a couple of hours every day working with the bees had been my sanity.

Watching Florence moving about the kitchen with determination was now the highlight of my day. She treated the girls like they were her own, and they shined beneath her care. I found myself looking forward to seeing her every morning, reluctant to leave for work.

She was never far from my thoughts as I patrolled the streets.

Today, she wore a yellow t-shirt with a picture of a bee on the front and faded blue jeans. Her face was makeup free except a hint of mascara on her long lashes. Her mouth…

I shifted my thoughts from the path they'd taken, and kicked off my boots.

She stilled at the sound, and then continued to move about the kitchen, avoiding my eyes.

At supper, I asked, "How are you doing?"

"Good."

"Uh huh." I passed the peas. "Anything happen in town?"

"Nothing special."

"Uh huh." She was hiding something.

Around the dining room table with the children's eyes on me, I decided it wasn't the time to dig.

"I'm going for a walk." She pushed away from the table and away from me.

I started to get up.

Let her go.

I sat back down. "We'll clear the table and wash the supper dishes."

From the entrance, she called, "Where's my jacket?"

"I'll help you look for it." I stood and made my way over.

"N-no, I'll find it," she stammered, her eyes darted toward the door.

I took a step closer, searching her eyes. "What are you afraid of?"

"N-nothing."

I stepped back. She used to be so frank. I wished with everything inside me for that honesty. By her nearness, I felt the urge to surround her, protect her, shelter her from whatever demons drove her to independence.

"Can I go with you?" Eddy asked.

I laid a hand on his shoulder. "Not this time, your mama needs to think."

Clearing the table, I thought about her fire and passion, no longer burning for me, brimming beneath the surface. Something was eating away at her. She didn't speak of it, but from her reaction, Alex Diestrum had done a number on her. She didn't trust me either. I felt defensive, yet defenseless.

I had to get a grip.

By the time the sun colored the western sky a brilliant shade of orange and violet, she returned.

Wild with worry, I met her at the door and pulled her body against mine. Wrapping my arms around her, I said, "Where have you…"

She buried her face against my chest.

I held her tightly.

"You can…take care of your own needs if you want." She hid her eyes from me. "I'm sure by now you maybe even prefer to."

"No."

Her head came up. "But you…"

"I'm not going to live in my own world, in my own head, or take care of my own needs." I held her away from me, giving her a gentle shake. "And you aren't going to retreat into your own world where you hate my touch," I swallowed hard, "my hands on you."

"I just want to be left alone."

"I can't do that."

"Why not? You never had trouble ignoring me before."

Frustrated, I snapped, "I was a stupid kid."

"I'm tired." She covered her mouth, faking a yawn. "I think I'll go lay down."

I scooped her up in one smooth motion.

Caught off guard, she threw her arms around my neck. "What are you doing?"

"What does it look like? I'm taking you to bed."

"No," she began to struggle.

"What did he do to you, Florrie?" Both sorrow and pain settled in my chest. I entered the bedroom, crossed to the bed and laid her down.

She pulled away, and I sighed, turning on my back.

My mind reverted to days of old where her eyes danced and her lips had a ready smile. I might have done something to save her. At the time, I'd been too wrapped up in my own bitterness. Losing myself in shame, I slept with everyone I could.

Now her innocence was lost. I couldn't go back and save her, but more than my next breath I wanted to find words of comfort and love where there was silence.

Then, between her and me. The same, now here in our own bedroom.

I reached over and slipped my fingers through her hair. She sighed, moving closer until there was no space between us. The soft snore told me she was sleeping.

In your sleep, you're not afraid of me, even welcome my touch.

I laid my head back on the pillow.

She had the kind of passion that made me feel alive. I hadn't felt like this since…that day on the porch when she kissed me.

I'd never felt so unbalanced.

83
March 16, 2003

Florence

The largest coordinated worldwide vigil took place as part of global protests against the Iraq War.

Wind gusts blew dirt around the house for the fourth day in a row.

"Eddy, don't pick your nose, little man. Kids, let's finish cleaning the bee shed," I said, "Hold my hand and we won't blow away."

Together, the five of us worked on organizing the bee shed. Gertrude swept dead bees, Hildegard organized tacks, and Eddy hauled boxes.

When we finished, we made our way to the house, passing a black Chevy car in the driveway next to the Suburban.

We continued toward the house. Norman was at the front door talking to a beautiful woman with long black hair.

I felt like I'd been punched in the stomach.

"Hi," I said, my voice cold as the morning.

Norman motioned to the woman. "Florence, this is Marissa Potter."

She laid her hand on Norman's chest and laughed, it sounded lilting and made me want to scratch her eyes out.

"Hello." I forced a smile.

She smiled back, her lips, full and perfect. Her hair, dark and long and looked to be her own. Her teeth too. She was by far the most beautiful woman I'd ever seen. Now I knew where the twins got it from.

"Won't you come in for something to drink?" I asked. "My neighbor brought peach kuchen."

Marissa glanced at Norman. "I better not. I was just leaving."

"I'm going to head in and start supper." I walked past them.

"I'll be right in," he said.

Ten minutes later, Norman made his way into the kitchen. Lean muscle rippled on his arms from hauling hundred-pound boxes of honey.

"Skunks have been known to eat poisonous pests such as rattlesnakes. They're unaffected by doses of venom higher than those that could kill a cat," I said.

"Did you see a skunk?"

"Not today, although they prefer insects and grubs, skunks are not picky eaters. Especially during the colder months, they'll stumble upon small rodents in wooded areas or near the garbage."

"Why do I get the feeling you aren't talking about the famous furry pest?"

"I have no idea." My lack of enthusiasm was pushing him to the edge. He had no lack of women before me. How long would he put up with my aloof manner?

Do you want to be ugly.

The thought was unsettling. I laid a flat hand on my belly and sucked in. I didn't want to be ugly.

84

Norman

The wind stopped. Calm ensued, more unsettling than the violent gale. It was close to midnight.

I sat at the edge of the bed.

Florence crawled in next to me and shut off the lamp.

Something was definitely wrong with her.

"What is it?" I asked, laying down.

"Nothing," she snapped.

Silence.

"Have a good visit with Marissa?" Her angry tone carried the force of the wind.

"What's that supposed to mean?" I pulled the covers over us.

Florence tossed them off. "What did she want?"

"Just to see how the girls were doing." I paused. "Did you know Marvin Baker before he moved here and took a job with Andersons?"

"Why? Did she say I did?"

"She alluded to it."

"I didn't know him before he came here."

"Don't get so defensive. I'm just telling you what she said."

"And you believe her instead of me."

"You don't tell me anything so there's nothing to believe."

"Fine."

"She is their mother," I said, realizing what was going on. "Besides, that was before us."

"She looked at you like she wanted you to take all her clothes off with your teeth," anger slashed each word.

"What am I to do about the way she looks at me?"

"Not smile," she flipped over and turned the bedside lamp on. A spark shot out. She ignored it, her green eyes glared at me, snapping like a crackling fire, "Talk, be polite, but for the sake of all that is good don't you dare smile. And for your information, no one forced you to marry me."

"Nothing I say is right so I'll say nothing."

Then she was on top of me, her face inches from mine.

Beyond frustrated, I reached for her arms to set her aside and reason with her, and suddenly her mouth was on mine.

My head hit the pillow.

It took all of a millisecond to realize what she was doing. Then my hands came up to her cheeks, through her hair, and she kissed the socks off me. Until my head spun and my heart drummed in my ears.

It was an angry kiss, one meant to punish. She was mad. Why was beyond me, but oh, what punishment!

A new direct communication sizzled between us.

My hands ran along her back. I kissed her right back and knew very well the reason—for being a woman and dominating me, my thoughts, my heart.

She stopped, her face inches from mine. We dragged in breaths, glaring at each other.

I fumbled for reality. She slid under the covers once more, flipping away from me.

I was unhinged around her, and yet, the world had never felt more right. Drawn to her, I wished I could reach her.

I felt the choice taken away from me in an instant. She was a rare find in my world of choices. Warmth spread through my entire body from the tips of my fingers down to my toes.

She was a beautiful woman, fierce and strong.

85

Norman

The wind picked up on the way home from work.

Florence met me at the door. "I tucked the children into bed. I'll heat your supper."

"Sorry I missed it."

"It's okay."

The air between us felt odd. Unsettled like prairie dust. Nerves made me famished, and I ate the last few slices of flatbread along with cheddar cheese.

She set coffee to brew.

"Late for coffee," I noted.

"Yeah."

"Chilly out there. Bees are likely in their hives shivering. Did you know they rotate like penguins do in Antarctica? They move in different positions to stay warm."

She didn't respond and grabbed two mugs.

"You mad?"

"Nope." She sat across from me.

We ate our bread and cheese in silence.

Stood in unison.

"I'll do dishes." She reached across the table for my plate.

"Let me," I said, stopped and cleared my throat, "I'll wash, and you dry."

At the sink, we stood side by side. I reached across her to set a dish on the towel. Who knew washing dishes could feel so intimate. She reached over and took a cup from me. I couldn't tell if she felt it too, because she went about her task in the same manner as always.

The wind whipped across the land, and I was wide awake in the living room. The walls of the structure groaned. A gust shook the window facing lakeside. I sat in the high back living room chair and picked up my Bible.

My boots were still on. *I should go take them off.*

My eyes grew heavy.

I woke at the sound of a creak in the wooden floor.

Florence was kneeling in front of me.

"Florence? Is it the kids?"

"Sleeping like babies."

"Did you need something?" I sat up, pushing my hair down with a flat hand.

She began unlacing my boots and tugged them off. Then she did something so unexpected, I dragged in a breath. She began rubbing my feet.

It felt like heaven but awkward as well.

"You don't…" I started to pull my foot away.

Florence looked up and caught my eyes. "I want to."

Any further protest died on my lips as she massaged from my toes to heel. When her fingers reached my arch, I let my head fall back on the chair. Then she worked on the right foot and by the time she was done, all tension in my body fell away.

Then she was crawling over me, running her hands over my chest. Bursts of desire wiped reason from my mind. I memorized the angles of her face, her mouth, close and tempting.

I held my breath for fear I was dreaming.

In her eyes, longing reflected in the lamplight mirrored my own feelings. Her slumberous eyes dropped to my chest. "I should go."

"Please don't," I whispered, not caring if I sounded desperate, and reached for her hips.

She reached for the lamp. It sparked as she shut it off and we shared a nervous laugh.

I stood and scooped her up, strolling to the bedroom.

I lay her on the bed we shared but never consummated, following her down. "I'm going to kiss you now," I said in the time it took for my mouth to reach hers. I pulled away briefly, gazing into the green depths of her eyes.

"Norman?"

"Yeah?"

"I like kissing you. Do you like kissing me?"

"I love it."

86

Florence

In uniform, Norman was sitting at the breakfast table the next morning when I entered the kitchen.

Last night, lovely sensations enveloped me. Then night faded to day, and where darkness hid, daylight now exposed. I wished he would say something.

Anything.

I poured myself a cup of coffee and sat across from him. "The kids are going to Nana's so I can do some spring cleaning without having to pause every two seconds to be referee."

Norman sipped his coffee as any other day. Read the newspaper like he didn't touch me last night until I could no longer pretend I didn't love his hands on me.

Everything was just how it was, but somehow different.

Permanent.

We were married, so I guess it didn't get much more permanent than that.

"Cold one out there. Snowed last night," he said, and stood. "I think I'll check on the bee shed thermostat on my way to work. Can't be more than five degrees." He pulled on his winter jacket and reached for the blue stocking hat marked *JPD* in yellow.

"Norman?" I bolted from my seat and rushed him.

Hat in hand, he stopped. "Yeah?"

I drew a blank, and when I could think of nothing else, I said, "I'll make steak and twice-baked potatoes for lunch."

"Yeah?" His eyes held mine, and the look in them was new, like he was seeing me for the first time. "I'll be in around noon."

At lunch, Norman arrived on time. I was glad because the steaks were cooked perfectly, medium rare. The twice-baked potatoes were whipped to perfection, topped with a dollop of sour cream.

He said grace and we ate in peaceful silence.

After lunch, he stood and held out his hand. "Come with me."

"But the dishes…"

"Can wait."

I followed him into the bedroom. "What did you …?"

He pulled me inside and shut the door, his hands slid up the back of my neck. "You smell good." He pressed his face against my hair and inhaled.

"It's the middle of the day," I whispered.

"Just a kiss." His mouth found mine until I couldn't think. What I felt for him was longer lasting than lust. More powerful than desire. At last he lifted his head and caught my eyes. Taking my hand, he guided me across the room.

"The kids…" I fell back on the bed.

He came down over me. "Are at Nana's."

He gave me a smile, a warm, affectionate one that made my heart thud and my stomach flip.

All the lonely days melted away.

87
July 22, 2003

Florence

Members of 101st Airborne of the United States, aided by Special Forces, attacked a compound in Iraq, killing Saddam Hussein's sons Uday and Qusay, along with Mustapha Hussein, Qusay's 14-year old son, and a bodyguard.

In North Dakota, the hot summer sun beat down on me in the garden alongside Eddy and Irmgard. Norman, Hildegard and Gertrude were at Dad's helping with bees.

Winter was long and spring, brief.

I welcomed the heat and the work. Somehow, I was also irritated with both, and tired.

The shoots were up, asparagus was tall, turnips, which no one liked but me. They'd been something Momma always planted because they grew fast.

A garden tomato was ready. One really beautiful and perfect.

I reached for it, and Eddy swiped it off the vine, sinking his teeth in. "Delicious."

I swallowed back tears. "Why did you do that?"

"Do what?" He squinted at me, tomato juice dribbling down his chin.

"Nothing."

I pulled the last of the weeds around the row of peas and stood. Spots danced before my eyes. The world spun and the garden faded.

At a shock of water in my face, I came to, blinking droplets from my lashes. Eddy and Irmgard's worried gazes peered down at me.

"You fell asleep, Mama," Eddy said.

At supper, Norman sat across from me, his eyes alight with the news of the day. "We moved the red 22 colony over to Peterson's west quarter. He planted Hard Red Spring Wheat. Then over at Beck's, sunflowers. I want to move one to the outside of Spiritwood. There's quite a few different types of fruit trees."

He tightened the lid on a honey jar. "Eddy said you fainted in the garden."

My head came up. "He told you that?"

"Actually, he said you fell asleep and you filled in the blank just now."

At bedtime, Norman sat in the chair alongside the bed, a thick book open on his lap. I'd never seen him read in the bedroom.

I halted in the doorway. "I didn't mean to bother you."

He turned the page. "You're not bothering me. It's your room, too."

"What are you reading?" I crossed to where he sat.

"The Bible," he said, "I used to read bits and pieces here and there. Pop in and out, ya know? Dare to be a Daniel, fight my giants like David…"

"Be beautiful like Queen Esther."

He smiled. "Then I thought if I read all other books from the beginning to end, why not the Bible?"

"What book are you on?"

"Galatians. But I read it all the way through for the first time last year and discovered something."

"Which is…?"

"The whole Bible is about Jesus."

"And the Old Testament…?"

"Is about Jesus."

The room tilted and I laid a hand on the footboard.

Norman caught my eyes. "Still not feeling good?"

"I think I should probably make an appointment to see the doctor."

He stilled. "Oh yeah?"

"I'm pregnant."

He didn't respond.

"You don't have to act so shocked," I sighed. "Things might be tight for a bit, but they'll get better, and…"

"I sorta hope it's a boy," he said, a foolish grin spreading across his face.

I smiled. "I sorta do too."

88
December 14, 2003

Florence

U.S. President George W. Bush announced the capture of Saddam Hussein.

The north wind raged outside. Frost gathered on the inside of the window. Norman went out to the bee shed to check the thermostat.

I tucked the children in bed, and dashed to our bedroom, scurrying beneath the covers.

Norman returned, crawling in next to me.

"What did you find out?" I shivered beneath the blanket.

"It's at forty-two in there."

"We should build a fire in here."

"I thought pregnant women were always hot." Norman's arm came around me, his hand parked beneath my breast. My belly was swollen, large as a summer squash.

I trembled.

"You cold?"

"No. Not anymore."

He made a sound of pleasure. I thought of others without warm houses, good food to eat, and a husband to hold them.

He didn't try anything, lying next to me. A lot was said about passion running strong in men. Even more about good wives who took care of them. But I knew nothing about a man who made room in his bed for his pregnant wife.

***

"Your face is puffy." Elsa frowned at me during breakfast the next morning.

I frowned back. "I throw everything up."

Her eyes filled with concern. "I'll get Norman."

"I don't need your sympathy. I need food that stays down," I grumbled.

She reached for her coat and secretly I was glad. Elsa had proven to be a good grandmother. Gertrude and Hildegard the best of helpers. Eddy was protective and Irmgard an angel, but none were Norman.

Norman walked through the door. I didn't play it cool or aloof, instead, flung myself at him, burying my head in his chest. "You're here."

"Yeah." He stroked my hair.

To my horror, I started to cry.

Norman patted my back. "We need to go to the doctor."

"I'm okay," I sobbed. "I know I'm a mess, but please…"

Norman turned to Nana. "We'll be back," he said, holding my coat up for me. Together we headed for the car.

The nurse checked my pulse, temperature and blood pressure.

"There's no fetal heartbeat," Dr. Hodges announced.

"What does that mean?" Norman ran a shaky hand down the back of his neck.

My chest burned, like someone lit a fire inside. I turned and hung my head over the side of the bed. "I'm sorry, I think I'm going to be sick."

***

There was no cry of a newborn. Memories were clear as day yet, muddled as a dream.

"She didn't make it," Dr. Hodges said.

Reverend Alder was there with a solemn expression.

"Should she be baptized?" I asked.

"I can."

It was cold in the room. I wrapped her body in baby clothes I planned to bring her home in, then in warm blankets.

"My baby. My poor girl," Norman lamented.

She was to be Mary.

My heart a stone in my chest, I pondered the child we hadn't even been given a chance to know.

Norman reached for my hand. "You ready to go home?"

The ride home was quiet.

At bedtime, Norman laid down next to me.

"Florence?" he asked so much saying my name.

"It was a gray, dreary day. Everything's dirty. The outside, the inside. I don't know what the point is."

He didn't answer.

"I want to feel sad, furious…something. Not this cold, gray inside, like the winter sky." I shut off the lamp, ignoring the flicker from it.

I pondered a little girl with strawberry curls and a life that didn't get a chance to live, not even an hour or a day. What made me so special I got so many more days? And that I would give up all of mine if it meant she could have one of hers.

89

Norman

"Reverend Alder dropped off a pie," Florence said when I walked in the door. "He didn't stay long."

The wind howled across the frozen prairie, shaking the walls and windows, blowing waves of snow around us.

Temperatures were close to zero.

"We spent the better part of the afternoon making more lefse and flatbread," she continued. "All except Irmgard who sat quietly on the rug playing marbles.

"I told Eddy he could keep the kitten. Clara Ziggledorf hoards cats. Did you know Clara had thirty felines in her house at one time? A few were dead by the stench emitting from her trailer house. And the smell…Uff Da."

Florence rolled out pieces of lefse. "Is there such a thing as good fruit cake?"

Before I could respond, she continued, "I never liked it either, but Aunt Sophia made it every Christmas for the down-and-outers that came.

"I've got to finish supper," she turned her back to me.

Knowing I'd been excused, I headed for the shower.

Dinnertime was a noisy affair with forgotten manners as one child out talked the other.

Eddy sat across from me, plowing through his food like it was going out of style.

"I want to join 4-H," Hildegard said.

Florence opened a carton of milk. "Hildegard, don't talk with your mouth full of food."

"Me too," Eddy said. "The club is called Spiritwood Stars."

Florence filled his glass with milk. "Don't lean on the table, Eddy."

"I don't like milk," Hildegard grumbled.

"I know," Florence reached for the pitcher of water.

Eddy gulped his milk, and set his glass down. "Grandpa said I can show honey at the fair. Can I join?"

"Eddy, you have a milk mustache." Florence handed him a napkin.

"Jay Higgins is a 4-H leader," I cut in. "Children ages ten to twenty-one do projects together for prizes. Good, friendly competition."

"Better learning than dumb ol' school," Eddy said.

"School is bad. 4-H is good," Gertrude chimed in.

I wiped my face with a napkin. "So I spoke to Carlton and Sherrie Spick."

Florence sighed. "I feel bad for them."

"He said their thinking it'd be nice to have a girl, preferably." My eyes shifted to Irmgard. "They're nice people."

"No," Hildegard said.

I set my fork down. "I beg your pardon?"

"Can I speak?" Gertrude's hand came up.

"May I speak," I corrected.

"But I want to." Her lower lip stuck out.

Florence giggled. "Yes, go ahead."

Gertrude folded her hands on the table in front of her in a grownup manner. "I don't think we should let Irmgard go to the Spicks."

"Why is that?" Florence took a sip of water.

"We've decided to keep her." Hildegard leaned forward.

"We can't keep her," Florence said.

Hildegard sat up. "Why not?"

"Because she isn't ours. She's company. You can't just bring someone home like they're a dog. Or a cat."

"Why not?" Eddy took a bite of his beans. "You did."

Florence's face flushed pink. "I know I did but that's different."

"We like her and we all agree." Hildegard circled her finger around the table, "All us kids."

"Besides, we need her." Eddy used his finger to guide the last of baked beans onto his spoon.

"Eddy, use a knife instead of your finger," I said.

"Looks like I'm outnumbered." Florence leaned back in her chair.

"Can't blame the kids for turning out like you," I grinned.

A lock of red hair tousled over her forehead, her liquid green gaze caught mine, and I felt like I was coming home.

I took care of the dishes while Florence tucked the kids into bed. Afterward, I sat in the stuffed chair in our bedroom and opened my Bible.

Florence entered the room. "You were the one who asked me to marry you."

My head came up. "What?"

"You can't be upset we have all these kids when you said I could make a difference. In a way you said I should make a difference. And I couldn't leave her or Eddy. Let them be ignored or punished." She shivered. "And if…" she wrung her hands. "…I forgot your birthday."

"Yours too," I closed the Bible. "Florence, I'm happy Hildegard and Gertrude are yours. That Eddy and Irmgard are mine." *And that you are mine,* but she wasn't ready to hear that quite yet.

90
Christmas Eve 2003

Florence

The sunset came early across the lake. This, the loveliest of days marked our first family Christmas.

Irmgard played "Hark the Herald" on the piano while the other kids played marbles on the living room floor.

Eddy leapt to his feet. "I'm done playing marbles with you. Forever."

"You're just mad I'm better at marbles than you are." Hildegard set her hands on her hips.

He punched her arm. "Better at cheating."

She kicked his leg. "Take it back."

Eddy grabbed her hair and yanked.

I took a step back as they tumbled to the floor.

"Hey kids, come help me with the table," Norman said.

They broke apart and raced to Norman. Together, they pulled the center leaves from the table, and pushed it against the wall.

"Irmgard, will you play 'Happy Christmas Eve'?" Norman asked.

Irmgard sat at the piano, her fingers moving across the keys.

In my head, I began to sing, *"The snow is fallin', look out the window with me…"* "I guess I better clean up the supper dishes."

"Dishes can wait. Dance with me." He pulled me toward the kitchen floor and spun me around.

The children broke into giggles.

Then he pulled me close for a slow dance. The song lasted forever, yet was over all too quickly.

I stepped back as it ended. "Time for bed."

"Aw. Do we have to?" Hildegard whined.

"Hildegard," Gertrude admonished. "Santa's watching."

Eddy cut in, "There's no such thing…"

"Eddy," I sliced his words off. "You'd hate for him to hear you. You'd be a sad boy Christmas morning without a visit from St. Nick."

Irmgard remained silent, but her eyes were on me.

After tucking the children into bed, I sat in the Jacuzzi tub, thinking of the evening. I couldn't recall a Christmas Eve I'd been more excited for Christmas morning. Against my better judgement, I'd gotten Norman a novel and hoped he hadn't read it.

I stepped out and into the bedroom.

The door opened.

Norman walked in and time stood still.

A hot flush spread all over my body.

In all my glory, I refused to cover any part of me with my hands, though was dying to. Not that we hadn't been intimate, but it had all been with the lights out.

Never had I felt so exposed.

He said, "I should have knocked."

"I didn't think you'd be in so soon." I shivered, keenly aware the chill.

"I came to see if you wanted to watch *It's a Wonderful Life*."

We stared at each other before I said, "I do."

"Great." He made no move to leave.

"Do you mind?" I asked.

"Right," he turned and walked out.

Feeling safe and exposed all at once my heart thudded in my ears as I dried off and then fumbled with my clothes. I caught a glimpse of my reflection in the vanity mirror. My face flushed at the look in my eyes. Mature. Adult.

Above all, womanly.

91
Christmas Day 2003

Florence

The kitchen counters were filled with an assortment of Christmas goodies. Gingerbread men, krumkake cookies filled with whipped cream and, of course, kuchen.

The table was filled with mashed potatoes and yams, roasted chicken at the center. Hot apple cider and coffee for drinks.

The wonder of the magic of the holy day was alive in the children's eyes as they opened their gifts.

Irmgard nearly squeezed the stuffing out of her baby doll.

"I told you Santa's real. I told you," Hildegard said.

Eddy opened his new marble bag.

"Santa always comes." Gertrude set furniture in her new dollhouse.

Nana arrived before lunch, bringing gifts for everyone including Irmgard and Eddy. I thought back to Christmas with Aunt Sophia. Elsa was a wonderful grandma.

Norman scanned the back of the James Patterson novel I gave him.

"Have you read it?" I asked.

"It's brand new." Norman turned the hardcover over. "Thanks, Florrie."

"Santa forgot Mama," Eddy said.

"No, he didn't," Norman said, digging into his pocket, pulling out a box. "He didn't want her peeking, so he gave it to me to give to her."

"What is it?" I asked, taking it from his grasp.

"Open it."

I popped the lid, and a pair of sunflower earrings with diamonds in the center twinkled back.

"Are they real?" I whispered.

Norman grinned. "Of course."

I retreated to the bathroom, fastening them in the mirror.

There was a soft knock on the door.

"Come in."

Norman entered and made his way over to me. "They look good on you."

"Thank you." I placed a hand on my ear.

"I need to talk to you about something."

My heart kicked up. I wracked my brain to explain about the knife. That was so long ago though. Surely it wasn't about that.

Elsa.

But she'd been nothing but nice to me.

People aren't always as they seem.

"Did she tell you I bossed the girls around? I don't. I mean, I did, but that was ..."

He gave me a puzzled look.

"I don't like lists," I prattled on. "I mean, I do but I don't like when other people make them for me. I own only one dress."

His brow came up. "I don't expect you to wear a dress."

"I need to talk less, listen more. Your grandma is an excellent cook and I burn water. I'm a terrible housekeeper, and say things I shouldn't..." I blew a curl from my forehead.

His brow came up. "What's this about?"

"What do you think it's about?" I stepped away from the mirror. "You said you wanted to talk to me."

"There's a New Year's party at Greg and Susan Hamill's place. I thought it might be nice if you'd like to go. Grandma will watch the kids if that's okay with you."

"I'd like that."

He pushed a lock of dark blond hair from his forehead, "Are you opposed to wearing a dress?"

"No. Are you opposed to a shave and haircut?"

"Not at all." A grin worked its way across his face.

"Why are you being so gregarious?" I chewed my lower lip.

"You know, too many times, after time goes by, you realize later just how rare one is. How meaningful spending time with them should have been. More appreciated. Special."

"I suppose..."

"And maybe I'm waiting for you to look at me like you used to. Like when we were kids."

"How did I look at you?"

"Like you'd just come out of the desert and I was water."

I shrugged. "That was a long time ago."

His gaze caught mine. "But there's nothing to keep me from trying."

***

From the bedroom window, I watched Norman emerge from the shed, puffs of frosty breath transpiring from his lips as he made his way toward the house. He was dressed in a black shirt beneath his gray coat, and moved easily in his steady, determined gait. He had shaved, his smooth cheeks ruddy with the cold.

Inside my closet was Momma's royal red dress, akin to the early ruddy sunset, sleek and low-cut in front and back. I remembered how Momma liked the way her back looked in it. I turned around, studying my reflection in the mirror.

I searched the closet, and only came up with sensible black shoes. Digging a little further, I found my black high heel boots.

I stepped out of the bedroom, and Norman's gaze stopped on me. Every place his eyes touched came alive.

He reached out, running a hand down the side of my hair. "It's the color of fall apples."

"You like the dress?" I was close enough to smell pinewood and soap.

"That's nice too."

At the Hamill household, streamers decorated the living space, and couples mingled about. Beneath curious gazes of guests, I stuck close to Norman. He didn't disappear.

"I've always wanted to be my own boss," he said alongside me. "I did some figuring. We don't need a lot of land. Farmers around need the honey bees, and will let us put twenty colonies in one area. Up the colonies to four hundred or so, and we can make a living with the bees."

"And quit your job?"

"Yes. At five bucks a pound, we could sell honey in fifty-five gallon drums to distilleries, LDL freight companies, and factories. Not to mention the wax," he said. "You and the kids could help with the business."

"It wouldn't be perfect. There's foreign dumping and tariffs always mucking up business."

His eyes met mine. "That's why I have you."

"I heard you bought Mark's lake house," Susan Hamill said, making her way over, wine in hand. "I've always liked that place." Susan was a well-dressed woman with manicured nails.

"Me too. It belonged to my folks back in the seventies." I pressed my lips together.

"What was your maiden name?"

"Solberg."

"Right." She glanced down at my hand. "Where's your drink?"

"Oh, I don't drink."

"I meant soft drink," she laughed. "So what did you do after Bible School? Sophia tells me you lived in the Twin Cities."

Norman reached for my hand. "Thanks for having us over. We had a nice time. Right, Florence?"

"Right, Husband," I said quickly.

In the Suburban, he gazed at me in the darkness like he'd never seen me before. "You called me husband."

"Aren't you?"

He started the engine. "Yeah, just never heard you say it."

92
April 22, 2004

Florence

Two fuel trains collided in Ryongchon, North Korea, killing around 150 people.

Aunt Sophia stopped by with lefse and news. She didn't know how to act about the stillborn birth. I didn't know how to act either, with a piece of me missing.

She kept her distance like I was diseased. Last I heard, death wasn't contagious.

"Where are the kids?" she asked.

"Helping gather honey," I said, "How's Leah?"

"I don't see much of her." She buttered a piece of lefse. "You know she's expecting."

"I didn't."

"Due in four weeks."

"That's nice."

"Jared is doing well." She squared her shoulders. "Goes to meetings nearly every night now, stopped drinking, and doesn't gamble."

"How is Lana doing?"

"Lana is a gynecologist and lives in Florida. She never married, and is having a baby in vitro."

"How is…" I started to ask how that worked and decided I didn't want to know.

Sadness engulfed me, empty and vast as the prairie. I was out of tears, and imagined climbing up on the table and screaming. "Do you want to bake bread? I'm almost out."

Aunt Sophia blinked. "No, I should be going."

Thank God. "That's too bad. It's been a nice visit."

***

At supper, Norman dug into his potatoes.

The children chattered away until I told them to get busy eating. I imagined the same table, Norman holding another daughter. I pushed those thoughts aside.

Some days, I hated my imagination.

After tucking the children into bed, Norman was getting comfortable in his chair with a book. Lately, I caught his eyes on me, like he was sharing my grief. He didn't coddle, avoid, or pity me.

He treated me the way I wanted to be treated.

What I felt for him was deep, a part of me. The joy I experienced in his company…I didn't remember it not being there. He didn't expect anything from me, rather accepted me.

Lying in bed, I realized I could live without him.

But I didn't want to.

***

Norman's eyes lifted when I walked into the living room. He shifted in his chair. "Everything okay?"

"I can't sleep."

His eyes returned to his book. Like he knew what I needed to say was difficult.

"Losing Mary brought sorrow beyond anything I've ever experienced. The months I carried her, though all too short, were of the sweetest. Worth the heartache of losing her."

Norman's gaze lifted from the page and met mine.

"That day you asked me to marry you, remember? I don't even know exactly what you said, but the way you looked at me, like you are now, is how I see myself." I folded and unfolded my hands.

"I know I'm messing this up. The way I feel…love isn't the right word…" There was a flicker in his eyes, but he remained silent. "…it's bigger than that. Deeper. Like you…" I forced myself to hold his gaze, "…The children, are a part of me. Like you always have been."

I blew a long breath.

"What I mean is, I'm glad. My life before you had dark places and bad things. I always wondered if Momma hadn't died, if things would have been different. And yet, here I am, with you."

He closed his book. "Are you ready for bed?"

"Yes."

***

I laid in bed, staring up at the ceiling.

On his side, Norman snored softly. He shifted, his leg brushed against mine, hairs scraped my smooth skin, drawing a shiver. I considered him drawing his own pleasure in mine.

"My love," he had whispered against my face, kissing my forehead.

My love, the words echoed through my thoughts as I lie awake, unable to comprehend what I had done to deserve such a man.

93
April 29, 2004

Florence

Oldsmobile built its final car ending 107 years of production. Spiritwood's spring weather had three forecasts: cold, windy, dusty…make that four:

Today was lovely.

Norman sat at the kitchen table with a piece of toast, a cup of coffee, and *The Jamestown Sun.* "I got an email from John today. Sounds like they love it there."

John and his wife were in China teaching English. We heard more from them than from James and Renee who were in Edina, Minnesota.

James was a bank manager, and Renee just got promoted to Best Buy assistant manager.

I sat across from him with my own coffee mug, studying his features. Not what one would consider classically handsome, but Norman had a determined jaw and knowing eyes.

He looked up from the paper. "Do I have food on my face?"

"No." Heat rushed to my cheeks. "From the matted hair on the crown of your head, down to your dusty jeans, I never want to forget what you look like."

His mouth dropped open and before he could respond, Eddy emerged from his bedroom.

"That room of yours needs cleaning, Eddy," Norman told him. "And no fighting with the girls."

"Aw Dad."

Norman thrust out his hand. "Give me a gentleman's agreement you'll get along."

Eddy sighed, reached over and shook his hand. "No fighting with dumb ol' girls."

Irmgard made her way over and threw her arms around me. The embrace was welcome and I hugged her back.

Gertrude and Hildegard bounded down the stairs. "What's for breakfast?" they asked in unison.

Norman stood. "Never a dull moment with four kids."

"Soon to be five," I said casually.

His eyes met mine. "Seriously?"

The disbelief in his tone pushed me to my feet. "Look, this isn't all on me. It takes two…" And before I could speak another syllable, he dragged me against his chest, holding me so tight I could hardly breathe.

After a long, perfect silence, he stepped back and reached for his cap. "I'm headed to town this morning if you need anything."

94
August 3, 2004

Norman

The pedestal of the Statue of Liberty reopened after being closed since the September 11, 2001 attacks.

Beneath the hot summer sun, Gertrude and I made our way over the dirt path to the slough at the edge of the shelterbelt of trees.

It was sweltering, waves of heat radiating from the ground. In the distance beyond evergreen trees against the horizon, a brand-new silver Corvette pulled into the yard.

Gertrude tugged on my arm. "Who is that?"

"Not sure." My underarms were sweaty, my heart kicked inside my chest.

Gertrude stepped closer to me. "Is he a salesman?"

"Looks like it."

She blew a dark lock of hair from her forehead. "What is he selling?"

"Not sure."

She reached for my hand. "He looks like a bad guy."

"Who does?" Hildegard made her way over, carrying the box of honey samples.

"Why don't you kids head into the house and bring the samples to your mama." I guided the girls toward the house.

They obeyed without another word.

The Corvette came to an abrupt halt.

The driver's door opened, and a man got out.

His dark hair glistened in the sunshine. He wore a crisp white shirt and green paisley tie. Shiny leather shoes peeked beneath the cuffs of his gray tailored slacks.

He had the look of a man who liked to drink too much and work not very much at all. He also looked vaguely familiar.

He studied me and thrust out his hand. “Florence around?”

I ignored it. “Who’s asking?”

He withdrew his hand. “Alex Diestrum.”

“What do you want?”

“Hot out, isn’t it?” He reached into his pocket for a handkerchief, dabbing beads of sweat from his forehead.

Florence exited the house and made her way toward us, drawing alongside me. “Hello Alex.” She stepped closer to me. “This is my husband Norman.”

“Bates?”

Here we go. “Miller.”

He chuckled. “Probably heard that one before.”

“What are you doing out this way?” Florence asked.

“Nice place you got here,” he said with an easy smile. “I see Spiritwood Resort hosts a campground with a public boat ramp. Might check out the campsites. Looks like a nice place to visit. What are the rates?”

“They’re seasonal,” I said.

“Maybe I’ll look into a seasonal lot.”

“You do that,” I said, knowing there were none available. In fact, there was a waiting list.

"I thought maybe we could talk, Florence," Alex said, his gaze on me. "In private. I passed a resort restaurant bar. Maybe you wanted to grab a bite so we can discuss Eddy. You don't really want me discussing matters in front of your new man." There was a gleam in his eyes.

That's when I remembered a guy in the parking lot at Perkins when I was at Alexandria Technical College.

It couldn't be.

"No." I said, clenching my jaw, anger slamming through me in a scorching wave. "No. Double no. No a million times over no."

Did she still have a thing for him? Florence would likely be furious. Didn't matter. I wasn't going to sit at home while he schmoozed my wife.

To my surprise, Florence said, "You heard him, Alex. I'm not going anywhere with you."

Alex chuckled. "Did she tell you she likes watching?"

Florence paled.

Rage swept through me. Where did he come off talking like that? And why did I get the impression they shared a secret? I took a step toward him.

A smile worked its way across his pretty boy face. "Oh, do you have the sads because the delicate little flower has a bruised petal?"

"Alex, I think you'd better leave," Florence said.

"Baby, can't we talk about this?" He reached for her arm.

She snatched it away.

The sound of tearing echoed in my ears.

In a flash, I had him pinned against his shiny sports car.

"This is the last time you are going to talk to her. No more surprise visits to our place. No cornering her when she's out in public." My nostrils flared, "...This is the last time you look at her. Leave her alone. Period. Do I make myself clear?"

I released him with a sound of disgust. "Get off our property."

Alex flushed beet red, looking like he swallowed a grapefruit. Casting one last doleful glance toward me, swallowing several times, he gasped, "I'll have your badge."

We watched him drive out of the yard.

"Well, that's done." I brushed my hands on my pants. "I suppose it's my promotion too."

Florence frowned. "You were protecting me."

"I'm up for a promotion for sergeant. Threatening a civilian could take me out of the running."

"Really?"

"We'll see. I think I'll head over to your dad's place." I tugged my cap down, catching her green gaze beneath the brim. "You floored me by standing up to him."

"Is flooring you a good thing?"

"Yes."

95

Florence

The sun was a pencil of orange in the western sky.

The children finished their baths and were in pajamas when the Suburban pulled into the yard.

"Wait here. I want to talk to your dad for a minute," I told them.

I met Norman in the yard and took the box of honey samples from him. "He'll get a lawyer. The law is on his side and he has a lot of money."

"We'll cross that bridge when we get there."

"Eddy isn't mine. I shouldn't have taken him..."

"Andrew told me he left you without a word for a week right after your birthday. And it wasn't the first time, was it?"

I shook my head. "But I don't know if the courts will side with me either. I forgot things and hallucinated. But the part I'm most guilty for is my silence. Letting him go about doing what he was doing, and I…" Something brushed my leg, and I cried out, jumping back. "A snake."

Norman smiled and picked it up. "A garter."

I waved a wild hand at him. "Get it away."

He laughed. "Not the first snake you've encountered."

"I always thought of Alex more as a skunk."

"Really," Norman chuckled. "You didn't happen to relate me to that animal?"

"No, just Marissa," my smile turned upside down.

"I stopped in at the police department." His eyes searched mine. "I resigned. I'm happy about it. The job, I mean. I bought three hundred colonies from your dad. That makes three hundred fifty."

"You're officially self-employed?"

"That depends." He grinned. "You looking for a job?"

"Yes." I threw my arms around his neck.

He laughed, holding me close.

I pulled back. "Is it too late to make ice cream to celebrate?"

"Nope. Let me grab a shower."

When I reached the kitchen, I asked, "Kids, you want to help make ice cream?"

"Really? Ice cream?" Eddy shouted.

"Yep."

Twenty minutes later, Norman strolled in, damp blonde hair curling against his neck. He was wearing a red shirt and a happy look.

Irmgard rushed him. "Papa, we made ice cream. Want some?"

The room came to a halt. It was the first time Irmgard had spoken since coming to live with us.

"Hold on, hold on." He laughed, glancing over at me. "What's this about ice cream?"

"She let me help, and I…" Irmgard stopped, looked at me and smiled, "Mama. Mama let me make ice cream."

Norman ruffled her hair. "Ice cream sounds real good."

We ate our treat, the clinking of the silverware the only sound breaking the silence. A quiet that was appropriate and right.

And enjoyed.

96

Florence

John Elway was inducted into the Pro Football Hall of Fame and 3 Doors Down "Kryptonite" was on the stereo."

I sat at the kitchen table with a steaming cup of coffee in front of my laptop. I was definitely not going to call Alex Superman.

There was an email from DAlex@gmail.com

TO: Florence Miller

FROM: Alex D

SUBJECT: Re: Eddy

DATE: August 4, 2004

I'm not trying to be difficult. I'm just doing what any good father would. I didn't go to the police when I came home and you were gone, taking my kid. If you want to continue to raise him then let's talk. I want to be a part of his life and I am working hard to make things right. As for questioning my beliefs I am a believer and want what's best for my family. I am more than willing to communicate without anger and discuss what's best.

Cheers,

Alex

P.S.—That skunk? You've got my imagination running wild. Would you mind divulging its location? I'd sleep better at night knowing it.

TO: Alex D
FROM: Florence Miller
SUBJECT: Re: Re: Eddy
DATE: August 9, 2004

I had no contact with Norman until I returned. May I remind you, it's been years since we left? Something a judge would find interesting. I guess it doesn't matter in the big scheme of things.

TO: Florence Miller
FROM: Alex D
SUBJECT: Re: Re: Re: Eddy
DATE: August 10, 2004

Well if he needs something I am willing to help the best I can. Just let me know.

TO: Florence Miller
FROM: Alex D
SUBJECT: Re: Re: Re: Eddy
DATE: August 15, 2004

Everything you told me was a lie to get me to marry you, then you bad-mouthed me to my son which was wrong and created a strain in my relationship with him. That's not being difficult that's the truth. You were okay with AFF. Don't act all innocent. I was willing to make things right. Are you? If you're willing to actually communicate without anger, I would welcome that and call it a step in the right direction....

I laid my forehead in the palm of my hand.

AFF.

I'd forgotten about Adult Friend Finder. The account had been set up and run by Alex's constant pressure. I'd gone along with it to appease him and had told no one.

What would Norman think? My face burned at the thought of him ever finding out. I closed my computer and stood.

Norman was in the doorway.

How long had he been there? I hadn't told him about emailing Alex. I'd been scared Alex would take Eddy, and thought I could reason with him. Now, I'd only made things worse.

"Just finishing up a few emails."

A new silent communication settled between us.

Outside, the wind continued to howl. Inside me, another blew hotter, terrified.

Far more unsettling.

97
August 22, 2004

Patrick's Bakery
Southdale Square
2928 West 66th Street
Edina, Minnesota

Florence

Two paintings by Edvard Munch, "The Scream" (1910 painted version) and "Madonna" were stolen at gunpoint from the Munch Museum in Oslo, Norway.

We dropped the kids off at Nana's and Norman took me on a honeymoon.

The silence between us disappeared on the six-hour car ride to the Twin Cities. Mapping our adventure, the atmosphere was filled with easy conversation and sharing fond memories of our childhood, and more recent ones of our children.

On the docket, the Saint Paul museum and Mall of America. We finished at the Farmer's Market in Saint Paul.

"You just wanted to buy illegal cheese and meet with vendors," I teased.

Illegal cheese was what foodies referred to as cheese that wasn't pasteurized. We found a vender Norman knew who made the treat in a cave. A dollop of honey on top, it made for a sweet tart delight that had the taste buds singing.

The sun twinkled over the skyscraper, and he caught my eye. "Shall we go to Patrick's Bakery?"

"Oh! That place in Edina? I'd love to."

At the bakery, we ordered our food and sat outside. There wasn't a speck of wind. I enjoyed a ginger beer and Norman nursed a Miller Draft.

"What do you suppose the kids are up to?" Norman ran a finger along the side of his bottle.

"Well, Irmgard is likely doing dishes, Gertrude's sweeping, and Eddy and Hildegard are fighting."

"Nah. Grandma says they don't fight for her. It's a kid thing. They only fight for their own parents."

"Lucky us." I took a sip of my spicy drink. "Did you ever think we'd be here? I mean, married and on our honeymoon?"

He smiled. "You told me we would be once. I should have believed you."

"My dreams always meant something back then."

A stereo resounded in the distance, *"Oo there must be magic in that..."*

"Oh not this song," I said.

"I love this song," Norman said in unison.

"Do you want to know the last time I heard it?" I asked. "It was that day in Walgreens when you were hot and bothered over the new girl."

He smiled. "That was a tough day."

"Tell me about it. My heart definitely spilled onto the floor watching you drool over her."

His eyes caught mine. "I was such a fool."

"You're my husband now, so not that much of a fool."

"I want to talk to you about something."

"What is it?" My heart gave two hard kicks.

"It's time I told you about that weekend and the coach."

The air around me buzzed as he started with his parents. "You know Mother and Dad did the best they could, but there was always tension between them. It flared up mostly when we went over to your house.

"As a kid, I thought it was because I liked it there so much, more than home. I suppose there was that between both of them as I was an only child.

"Right before the accident, I saw the way my dad looked at your momma. And then after she died, Sophia. Mostly because she looked like her sister. Their fling didn't last long. It ended after the coach drama."

He drew a deep breath. "So now we're up to the part where Coach Ted offered me a ride. I didn't want to take it, but my mother thought he was the greatest thing since sliced bread and I wanted to be in hockey. I suppose there was part of me that thought he was my ticket."

Norman told me how his memory about it was blank, then later came back like film bites. And finally, not wanting to remember anything at all.

When he was done, he gave the briefest of smiles. "There was so much shame for so long. I tried to prove I wasn't gay by sleeping with every willing girl. And now, as much as talking about it makes it seem real somehow, it's a relief to tell you."

Without a word, I stood, walked around the table and sat on his lap. Placing my arms around him, I tucked my face in his neck, silent tears streaming down my cheeks.

He stroked my hair, and I couldn't think of anything to say. A bond had been formed. I knew he understood my grief. Like me, he had felt guilt for things not his fault and forgiveness for things that had been.

"People are staring," he whispered against my hair.

"Let them."

"After we were married, you gave me a few sleepless nights." There was a smile in his voice. "The light in your eyes had gone out. I couldn't help but think I had something to do with it."

"Don't you see?" I lifted my head and caught his eyes. "It was necessary. We were dead in guilt and shame. For what was done to us, for what we'd done." I paused. "We were dead, our hearts and souls. The dead can't be saved."

"Christ breathes into them and gives them life." He rested his face against my neck.

"Thank you for sharing your nightmare with me."

"Thank you for listening."

98
August 29, 2004

Florence

28th Olympic Games closed at Athens, Greece.

On our drive home, Norman and I played the state game, and both agreed it wasn't as fun without the children.

The wind stopped by the time we arrived at the lake house. The space outside was dark and silent.

When we reached the front door, I turned to him. "Shall we get the kids tomorrow morning?"

"It is pretty late." His eyes locked with mine.

The same feeling arose in me. I wanted one more night to be alone with him. I glanced at my watch. "It's already nine. The kids are likely to be in bed."

Inside the lake house, the kitchen smelled stale.

A thought popped into my head. "What if Alex comes looking for me or comes for Eddy?"

"The day he sets foot in this house will be his last." Norman pulled me by the hand toward the bedroom.

A nervous giggle erupted from my lips.

Outside the bedroom window, a twig snapped.

We froze, our eyes caught.

"What is it?" my hushed voice sounded explosive in the stillness.

Norman held his finger against his lips, and mouthed, "Someone's out there." He reached into the nightstand next to the bed, and pulled out the Taurus revolver.

"Get behind me." He pushed me back and moved toward the front door. "I'm as far as anyone's going to get."

Taking hold of his shirt, I peered over his shoulder and hovered.

Norman turned around and we collided.

"What?" I whispered.

He shut the door. "There's no one there."

We made our way back to the bedroom. He returned the revolver to the nightstand, and turned around, running into me. Laughing, we landed on the bed, me on my back, Norman above me. His eyes were flooded with love. His mouth dipped to mine, and that's when I smelled it. *Coconut.*

"Norman," I whispered against his lips.

His mouth moved to my neck. "Hmm?"

"Something's not right." I moved my face away.

"Want me to check?" He continued to kiss me.

Then I saw a man in the doorway. His silhouette took up the entire frame. Terrified, I placed both hands flat on Norman's chest and pushed hard.

"Someone's here."

His head came up and he reached for the lamp.

Fear clenched my gut. I laid my hand over his. "Don't touch it."

He stilled. "Why?"

The man turned and walked out.

"We need to leave. Right now." I grabbed his hand, tugging him toward the door.

Norman rolled off the bed, following closely. "What's going on?"

Together we hurried out the door and down the stairs to the edge of the lake.

There was no one there. I scanned the area. "Where did he go?"

Norman trailed behind me. "Where did who go?"

"No one I guess. Let's go to Nana's and call the cops." I pulled on his hand. "I don't think we should go back in the house."

"Why?" he asked, even as he headed toward the Suburban.

"Could just be ghosts. A hunch."

But it wasn't.

99
September 3, 2004

Florence

The Beslan school massacre ended in the deaths of approximately 344 people, mostly teachers and children.

The lake house had been flooded with propane gas.

Sheriff Casey initiated a search of the vicinity and found Marvin Baker wandering the property near the shed.

Uncle Don identified him as the new guy he hired at Solberg Plumbing & Heating.

Baker had tampered with the furnace the day before we arrived home. For nearly thirty-six hours, propane gas filled the entire structure.

After getting five CO2 detectors, we invited Sheriff Casey and Andrew over and discussed it over coffee and kuchen.

"Marvin Baker had a bad gambling habit. If he made a dollar, he gambled two," Sheriff Casey said, sitting down at the table. "After his wife Josephine was committed to the State Hospital, he said Irmgard wasn't his kid. Then he moved to Watford City."

He picked up his fork. "He said he was paid to do it."

Norman straightened. "Okay, you have my attention."

"Did you talk to Alex Diestrum?" I wrapped my hands around my coffee cup. "He knew my bedside lamp tended to flicker. Maybe he thought if the place was full of gas, and there was a spark…" I shivered. "I didn't have the heart to get rid of the lamp. Momma got it from her daddy."

"I brought you that lamp." Andrew ran a shaky hand over the back of his head. "Last time I'll ask anything from Uncle Don." Andrew completed law enforcement academy, and was a deputy for the Stutsman County Sheriff's Department.

Sheriff Casey took a sip from his mug. "Alex was staying at the Buffalo Motel with his girlfriend and admitted to knowing Baker from the oilfield."

Norman glanced at me. "I didn't know Alex worked out west."

"Me neither," I said.

"Diestrum said he knew nothing about Baker working for your uncle, but wasn't surprised to hear about the propane gas. Said Baker was obsessed with you. Figured if he couldn't have you, no one could." Sheriff Casey took a bite of kuchen.

"Me?" Fear prickled my skin, knowing I had to tell them. "Marvin Baker was at my surprise birthday party."

Andrew sat up. "Whoa. I didn't see him there."

"It must have been after you left." I swallowed hard. "I wasn't introduced to him, but I thought his name was Roger."

"What was his last name?" Andrew asked.

"I don't know. Alex called him Roger. I thought he looked familiar when Dad hired him that summer. Then he left and I forgot about it."

Sheriff Casey's brow came up. "Is it possible he had a thing for you, Florence?"

"I'm not sure," I said honestly.

"That would give motive." Andrew leaned back in his chair. "You two could have been singing with the angels. All it would have taken is for one of you to turn on the stove."

"Or a lamp." A shiver ran through me.

***

Norman

The next morning, I woke before dawn.

Florence slept soundly next to me. By the light of the moon, I reached for the shirt I discarded the night before.

Movement from her side told me she was awake.

Suddenly, light flooded the room without a spark. The new lamp was on the top of her list when we went shopping for CO2 detectors.

"What time is it?" She yawned.

"A little after four." I stood.

She sat up. "You getting up?"

"Yeah, can't sleep. Mattsons are spraying chemical tomorrow. Thought I'd get a head start on moving boxes."

"I'd like to talk to you before you head out."

My eyes caught hers. "You don't have to. It won't make any difference how I feel about you."

"I want to. I realized after what you told me about the coach, we should bear one another's burdens."

"All right, I'll start the coffee," I said, and as I reached the bedroom door, she called, "Norman?"

I halted and glanced back.

"How do you feel about me?"

I smiled. "I love you."

She smiled back. "Good. 'Cuz I love you too."

At breakfast, Nana fussed over Eddy and the girls.

Florence sat across from me. Her eyes met mine when she reached for her glass, then the butter. She picked up her fork, and our eyes held for what seemed an eternity. The words she'd spoken earlier made my heart kick hard in my chest. Now I felt respect just looking in her eyes.

In their green depths, love burned like a blazing fire.

100
January 15, 2005

Norman

An intense solar flare blasted X-rays across the solar system. The wind howled outside, pelting ice against the window.

The children played marbles on the rug.

Florence was sitting on the couch, her feet propped up on the stool.

I was in my chair finishing Harlan Coben's *Play Dead.* "The guy in this story faked his death on his honeymoon," I told Florence. "He came back, but had to keep his new identity. The man he had been before had to stay dead."

"Do you think people can change?" Florence asked.

"What do you mean?" I closed my book and set it on the end table.

"Like bad people. Hitler. Satan," her voice dipped to a whisper, "Alex."

"He abandoned Eddy." I shot a glance toward the children who were out of earshot. "Not to mention what he did to you. You don't just snap your fingers and be good."

"But I can't help feeling sorry for him."

"I'm not sure it's up to us. Besides, I've come to think of Eddy as my own. Second chances are fine, but children are a high ante."

A soft smile flooded her face. "God has mercy upon whom He'll have mercy and compassion on whom He'll have compassion."

"Sounds like someone's been reading her Bible."

She winced. "It's probably time."

"For the baby?" In a flash, I was on my feet, looking out the window. "Not a good one by the looks of it."

"Don't think this one cares," she groaned. "Good or bad it's coming."

***

Florence

Gunter Karl Miller was born December 15, 2005.

The early morning sunshine poured through the window. Outside, fresh snow glistened.

Norman rocked his son, a foolish grin plastered on his face. His eyes grew heavy and soon he was snoring softly.

Gunter slept on his chest.

Like eager children, we gathered around the newest family member.

Eddy brushed Gunter's nose with a gentle finger. "He's my brother. Right, Daddy?"

Norman's eyes opened. "That he is, son."

"Mine too," Hildegard jumped in with her usual fighting response.

"Duh, yours too," Eddy draped his arm around Hildegard. "'Cept me and Gunter are both boys."

Her face broke into a grin. "Right."

"And mine," said Irmgard.

"All of ours," Gertrude smiled.

101
June 20, 2018

Florence

U.S. President Donald Trump signed an Executive Order ending family separation at the border for illegal immigrants.

At the edge of Merle Anderson's soybean field, Norman, Gunter, and I pulled boxes from the back of the pickup, placing them on a ready pallet.

"Let's set up the small colony right here, Gunter," Norman said.

Gunter was a bright kid just finishing up his first year of school at home.

A black pickup pulled onto the approach. Andrew got out. Dad was with him.

"Stacey seems nice," I told Norman, watching them make their way over. Andrew had been on a total of two dates with Stacey Wilson, which was one more than most other women.

"Yeah."

"I guess I always felt responsible Andrew's still single."

Norman glanced over at me. "Why would it be your fault?"

"He always considered me his responsibility."

"He's had eighteen years since we've been married."

"Hey," Andrew said, keeping his distance from the bee boxes. He'd been stung once, one time too many according to him. "I stopped by and saw Gertrude and Hildegard on my way home from Aberdeen. They say hi."

Gertrude and Hildegard were dating brothers at Trinity Bible College in Ellendale and both had summer jobs.

"Check this out," Dad said, making his way over to a nearby cottonwood.

Bees swarmed about the tree trunk.

"It was later in the day when I moved red colony boxes yesterday." Gunter's eyes were on the tree. "What should we do about them?"

"Make note of it," Norman said. "It'll explain any reduction in honey production for the colony."

"They can return to the small colony we set up," I said.

"The colony will just accept whatever bees show up?" Gunter asked.

"Why not? They'll be carrying resources like honey and pollen."

A car closed the distance, dirt and gravel kicking up behind it. As we watched it approach, I quickly realized it was Aunt Sophia.

She pulled up along the approach and got out, stepping delicately through thick grass in high heels.

"Bruce, are you ready to go?" she called.

Dad's eyes dropped and he appeared shamefaced. "Be right there." He turned back to us. "I promised Sophia I'd take her to Fargo. She wanted to do a little shopping. I suppose we'll go out to eat afterwards."

"Have fun," I said, compassion swept over me. I couldn't imagine an evening with Aunt Sophia doing anything, even dinner and a movie being fun. But he was a grown-up. Besides, there was no use shining the light for someone who chose to live in the dark.

"I'll stop by tomorrow, Pop." Andrew clamped a hand on his shoulder.

Dad nodded and headed toward the car.

After they drove away, I turned to Andrew. "Shall we expect Stacey to be with you on Saturday?" No point in beating around the bush.

Andrew gave an innocent look. "What's Saturday again?"

"Irmgard's piano concert at Valley City State University."

"Right. I'll probably show up by myself."

"Sad," Norman said.

Andrew chucked his shoulder. "Not everyone can be as happy as you two lovebirds."

My pocket buzzed. A text from Eddy who was attending summer classes at North Dakota State University for engineering. Can I get a ride to Irmgard's concert? I need a new alternator for the Chevy.

I looked up. "Or you can pick up Eddy on your way."

"That's out of the way," Andrew grinned, "But I'd be happy to."

"We must tell people what we have learned here. We must tell them that there is no pit so deep that He is not deeper still. They will listen to us, Corrie, because we have been here." - Betsy Ten Boom

Corrie Ten Boom, *The Hiding Place*

102

October 15, 2020

Florence

Thai government issued an emergency decree banning public gatherings amid increasing pro-democracy protests and criticism of the king, and Ed Sheeran sang "Castle on the Hill" in the kitchen.

From the picture window, I saw a black Ford Charger pull up and two men in business suits got out. The men wore face masks. I didn't like the way Norman kept glancing toward the lake house.

At last, Norman nodded and they turned, making their way toward the house.

Uh oh. My mind flew in every direction.

The door opened and all three stepped in.

"Florence, these men are with Homeland Security," Norman said.

"I'm Special Agent Carter," the shorter man said, and I imagined a smile behind the face covering.

"I'm Special Agent Greg," the taller, younger man said.

I remembered a text I'd ignored earlier.

Ms. Miller my name is Daniel Carter, I'm a Special Agent with the Homeland Security. You're not in trouble, but I need to speak with you about a case you might be a witness to.

"Hi." The tips of my ears burned. Was I under arrest? What happened? I searched my brain for what I'd done wrong.

"You're not in trouble," Special Agent Carter read my thoughts. "We're here about an incident that happened back in 2000."

My face flushed hot. "I did get a call and text from you. I'm sorry I didn't answer."

"No problem. A lot of people don't answer because they don't recognize the number so they think it's a telemarketer or spam."

My heart thumped in my ears. "What case are you talking about?"

"It's one involving Alex Diestrum."

"Our marriage wasn't legal."

"We know that Ms. Miller."

"Won't you have a seat?" I motioned to the couch. "I'd offer you something to drink, but you might have trouble drinking it through your mask."

They chuckled.

"We're good," said Special Agent Carter.

"Do you want me to wear one?" I asked.

"No. They make us wear these for work," Special Agent Carter said.

I glanced at Norman. His presence calmed me.

I returned my attention to Special Agent Carter. "What do you want to know?"

Special Agent Carter had a manila folder. He opened it up, withdrew a photograph and showed it to me. "Do you recognize him?" He held up a picture of Darrell from the surprise birthday party.

"Yes."

"His name is Darrell Hardy." He showed me a few more pictures, all of them Darrell. "This is a case regarding an incident that happened back in 2000. It was at a strip club in Minneapolis. Do you remember it?"

I flicked a glance at Norman.

"Do you want me to leave?" Norman asked.

"No, you can stay," I said, both calmed by his presence, and yet, terrified.

"Yes, we were there," I told the special agents.

"Does the name Alice Hardy ring a bell?"

"Yes. She was a stripper. I don't remember much at the strip club. Alex kept drinks in front of me. He always said they were to help me relax. I didn't remember a lot afterward."

"Were drugs involved? Besides the alcohol."

"Alex gave me something to relax. The doctor prescribed oxycodone for a bad bladder infection I had around that time. I remember him saying it was the remainder of the prescription.

"We went to a hotel room. The four of us rode in Darrell's pickup. I was upset with Alex for making me sit in the back with Darrell. I had to push Darrell off the entire time as he kept trying to push his hand up my skirt," I said, keenly aware of Norman.

"Was the hotel the Radisson?"

"Could have been? I don't remember."

"Tell us what happened when you arrived at the hotel room," Special Agent Carter said.

Focused on my lap, I gave him my brief recollection of events and the images of unfamiliar men and couples afterward.

"Flashbacks," Agent Carter said.

They asked detailed questions about the sex, and I did my best to answer, wishing the entire time to be anywhere but there.

"Were you coerced?" Special Agent Carter asked.

"Alex had a way of making you want to do what he told you to." I told them the part about the deodorant and how it hurt a little but mostly scared me. How he'd leave for hours, and later days on end.

"How did you meet Alex Diestrum?"

"It was when I was in Bible School." I told them how I was going to be a missionary and before that, about Jason Waverly and how Alex seemed my advocate at first. I even told them about finding the picture of me with the name Daisy Richards on the back.

"Were there any drugs?"

"Sometimes. Prescriptions mostly. Once I woke up and I thought one of his friends was having sex with me."

The special agents exchanged glances. "That sounds a lot like what Alice claimed happened to her."

Special Agent Greg said, "If I'm understanding you correctly, it escalated. First threats, then deodorant, and giving you a child to threaten to take him away. Are all your children your husband's?"

I went on to explain how all of the children came about.

"You lacked money?"

"No. In fact, we lived very well. Alex was an interior decorator for a corporation."

"What corporation?"

My cheeks reddened. "I'm not sure."

"Did your husband threaten you? Say he would lose his job if you told anyone?"

"Once. I freaked out and wanted to leave. But mostly, he threatened to take Eddy away." I told him about Carmen and how I found out they weren't brother and sister. "She left, and he was really nice to me after that. At least for a while." I told them about the surprise birthday party.

"My brother was there and left late afternoon. He had a long drive. All the guests left after that except three men. Darrell Hardy was one of them."

"Go on." Special Agent Carter nodded.

"I was thirsty and Alex brought me some water. The rest was hazy."

"Did you see any money exchanged?"

"No."

"Were drugs involved?"

"I don't remember. I thought he put something in my water."

"It sounds like abuse that escalated," Special Agent Greg said.

"I was an adult. What happened when I was a kid with Jason Waverly wasn't my fault, but I married Alex willingly in Las Vegas, and I went along with all he asked me to do."

"He brainwashed you, Florence," Special Agent Greg said.

I continued, reaching the part where I overheard the conversation about Eddy.

Special Agent Carter interrupted once again, "Did they do anything to Eddy?"

"I don't think so." I shook my head. "I found Eddy in the basement where his bedroom was. We played Sardines to hide from them. Sardines is..."

"I've played it before," Special Agent Greg said.

I imagined he smiled. "Marvin Baker, one of the guys at my surprise party went by the name Roger, tampered with our lake house furnace back in 2004. He served prison time. Last I heard, he got out on parole in 2016."

"What about Alex?" Special Agent Carter asked.

"They investigated him," I said, "but in the end, it was Baker's word against his. Alex had a better reputation, better connections, and a whole lot of money."

Special Agent Carter glanced at Norman. "How did you two meet?"

"I was good friends with her and her family growing up. We were married in 2002 after she came home when Alex left her."

"Did you know Alex Diestrum?"

"No." Norman's jaw twitched, and if I didn't know better, I would think he was hiding something. "He showed up for Eddy one day in 2004. Then he disappeared and hasn't been around since."

The special agents exchanged glances.

Special Agent Greg nodded. "I think that's all."

They stood.

"Thank you for your time," Special Agent Greg said.

"Did you want us to investigate Alex Diestrum?" Special Agent Carter asked.

"I was an adult."

"You were brainwashed." He handed me his business card.

"Let me know if there's anything else I can do to help Alice." I stood and saw them to the door.

"If you're needed to testify on Alice's behalf at the hearing, is that something you would be willing to do?" Special Agent Carter asked.

"Yes."

After they left, a long moment of silence passed.

Finally, I snatched a glance at Norman.

A mixture of emotion flashed in his eyes, tenderness, anger, and love. Without a word, he stood, strolled over and wrapped his arms around me. "I'm sorry you had to go through that."

"That was the old me." I laid my cheek on his chest.

"It doesn't change the way I feel about you," he said, "How I love you."

I smiled. "Shall we start coffee?"

"I'd love some."

103
December 13, 2021

Rosemarie

Germany announced a strict lockdown until January 10 after looser restrictions failed to prevent COVID-19 numbers from surging.

Post Malone's "Circles" playing in the background, I put the finishing touches on a birthday cake. *Happy Birthday to Us.*

The theme was bees. The customer was a woman named Florence who had a house on Spiritwood Lake.

The phone rang. I set the tube of frosting down and wiped my hands on my apron. "Hello, Celebrate You. How may I help you?"

"Hi Rosemarie? This is Florence Miller."

"Oh, hi Florence. Your cake is ready. You can pick it up anytime. We close at five."

"Five," a frown was in her voice. "Rats. I'm still in Fargo…Can I pay you with a card over the phone and have my brother pick it up?"

"Sure." I reached for a pen next to the cash register.

"Oh great! Thank you. Let me get my purse." There was a rustling of papers in the background. "Norman will be so surprised. We were born in the same hospital on December 13, 1975. Well, he was early and I was right on time. Our fathers were best friends."

It wasn't uncommon for customers to tell me their life story while picking up a cake, but this one intrigued me. "Really? What hospital?"

"Mercy in Valley City. Oh here it is. Ready? It's a Mastercard…"

Both born at Mercy Hospital in Valley City in 1975. Same as me. What kind of coincidence was that?

"Are you still there? Rosemarie?"

"S-sorry," I stammered. "I'm ready to take the number."

After she gave it to me, I ran it, and said, "Happy birthday."

"Thanks. I'll tell Andrew you close at five. He'll be early. He always is."

After I hung up, I went back to work.

The phone rang again. That would be Victor. He was picking me up after work and taking me to Paradiso for supper for my birthday. His mother Pearl kept asking when I'd have a ring. I told her I'd have one when I'd have one. Truth was, Victor would have given me one a year ago. He seemed to know not to push it, and I never brought it up again. Our friendship was easy and warm.

I answered the phone. "Hello, Celebrate You."

"Hey Rosemarie," Victor said.

I smiled. "I was just thinking about you."

"Good thoughts, I hope."

"Of course."

"Say the reason I'm calling is the cows got out."

"Oh no."

"I still want to go out if you do, but I'm going to be a little late."

"No problem. Call me when you're done."

"Thanks, Rosemarie. I knew you'd understand."

"Okay, see you then." After I hung up, I eyed the cake. It was perfect.

The jingle of the door had me setting the tube down. That must be Florence's brother to pick it up.

"Coming," I called, wiping my hands on my apron and made my way to the front.

A man stood wearing a red down coat, dark hair flecked with gray, and he was clean shaven. My breath caught in my throat, my belly flopped and my heart kicked up.

"You must be Florence's brother here to pick up her cake," I said, my voice coming out in a squeak.

He turned, his dark eyes caught mine, and I knew in an instant he felt it too.

How long we stood like that, I wasn't sure. Seconds ticked by, seeming an eternity.

"Are you here for Florence's cake?" I asked.

He shook his head as if to clear it. "Yeah. Sorry. I was just busy..."

"Busy?"

His cheeks flushed. "Watching you."

My cheeks burst into flames. "I'll go get it." I turned, rushing to the back for the cake. Reaching for a box to put it in, my hands shook. *Get a grip, Rosemarie. You're acting like you've never seen a man before.*

But I hadn't. Not like him. He was something out of a book.

He's probably married. Have you learned nothing?

He didn't act married.

He did nothing other than lock eyes with me.

It was nothing, and I was...hopeless.

I taped the box, picked up the cake, ridiculously disappointed I didn't have a reason to keep him here a little longer.

I walked back out to the front of the store.

His eyes met mine once more, and he smiled. "There's a light display in the park. They serve hot cocoa. Would you like to go with me? Tonight I mean."

"You're asking me out?" Was this some sort of dream?

"Well yeah." He smiled sheepishly. "Truth is, I rehearsed it in my mind the whole time you were in the back getting the cake. I guess maybe it sounded better in my head."

"I don't know, it sounded perfect to me." *Rosemarie, what are you saying?*

His eyes lit up. "Is that a yes?"

Reality hit me at once. Even if I wasn't going out with Victor tonight, I couldn't. We might not be officially engaged, but we were sort of engaged all the same.

"I can't. I'm sorry." A war waged inside me as I felt a strong desire to take back the words.

Disappointment flooded his features. "Is there someone else?"

"Yes."

"You're married?"

"No." I turned away before I did anything stupid, like crying or throwing myself into his arms. "I've got to go. It was nice meeting you."

Meeting you?

But he seemed to get the hint all the same. "Good night then." He turned and walked out into the night.

Preparing to close, I couldn't help but think there was a lot more hope in good night than goodbye.

104

Florence

Andrew dropped off the cake, brushing past me. He appeared flustered. I'd never seen Andrew flustered.

"What's wrong?" I asked, opening the box. "Oh, it's perfect. Look at the detail on the bees. Did you ever see such a perfect sunflower?"

"It's her," he burst out.

"Who's her?"

"The cake lady." He rubbed the back of his neck.

"Who, Rosemarie? What's wrong with her? She seemed nice enough on the phone."

"There's nothing wrong with her. She's perfect, that's the problem."

"Oh, I see," I said slowly. "You like her."

"Doesn't matter. She's with someone."

"You asked her?"

"No. I mean I did ask her out but she said no."

I closed the lid on the cake box, turned, and stared at my brother. "You asked Rosemarie on a date when you picked the cake up?"

His face flushed red. "I know, I shouldn't have, but I was sideswiped. Flummoxed."

"No, it's okay, but that must mean…" *you love her,* but I wouldn't say that out loud. "Well you know what they say. There's a whole lot of fish in the sea."

"Florence. How old am I?"

"Forty-five. Why?"

"I've never met anyone who intrigues me as much as she. It's not even her looks really, although she's quite pretty. It's everything about her. I felt good just being in the same room. I suppose you don't get it."

"No, I do. It's how I feel about Norman. But Andrew, if she's with someone else that's it. You know that."

"Yeah." He sighed. "Happy birthday."

"Thanks." I gave him a hug, my heart breaking just a little.

He caught the look in my eyes. "Okay, let's not both feel sorry for me."

I laughed. "I love you, Andrew. Have I ever told you that?"

"I love you too."

***

The silver moon was a sight to behold, hanging against the winter sky as Norman pulled alongside the curb in Oakes.

"Where are we?" I asked, glancing up at the large brick restaurant. "The old House of 29?"

"It's Simon's Place now. Did you know it was featured in *Eating Well* magazine?" Norman shifted into park and cut the engine. "I made reservations."

We walked in and sat down. A kid who appeared to be around Eddy's age took our orders.

The steaks were cooked perfectly. The chef emerged from the kitchen. He wore an eyepatch.

"The finest this year," he said, a bottle of wine in hand.

"Thanks," Norman said.

He filled our wine glasses. "What's the occasion?"

"Our birthday." Norman's eyes were on me.

The chef smiled. "Which of you is the birthday boy or girl?"

"Both of us," I said.

"Funny," the chef said, "Mine too."

"You think that's funny," Norman said. "We were born at the same hospital. Mercy in Valley City."

The chef blinked. "I was too. What year?"

We exchanged glances. "1975."

105

Rosemarie

Victor ended up canceling. It was nearly nine o'clock by the time he got all the cows in and the fence fixed. He brought me a present, a set of cake-decorating tools, and gave me a tired kiss on my forehead.

"You go home," I told him. "I'll take a raincheck."

"You sure?"

"I'm sure."

Alone, I glanced at the clock. It was nine. I thought about the Christmas lights in the park and grabbed my coat. I didn't really want to go to bed early, my emotions in turmoil.

It really was okay Victor couldn't make it. I knew if I married him, there would be many nights and days where the cows were out or fences were broken.

I stopped at Minimart to fill up with gas for the ride through the park.

"Rosemarie?" said a deep voice behind me.

I turned around. It was Andrew, Florence Miller's brother.

"Hi."

"Funny running into you."

"I was just on my way over to the park." My heart hammered in my throat.

"Seriously?" he said. "Me too."

"I thought…well it sounded Christmassy and my other plans fell through."

"By the way, I'm Andrew Solberg." He smiled. "I realized I never introduced myself."

"Rosemarie Hamill."

"I don't suppose you want to ride through the park with me."

"I suppose I do," I said, but before he could say anything else, I added, "But I won't."

He nodded. "Have a good evening."

I smiled. "You too."

"MY DEAR WORMWOOD,
The most alarming thing in your last account of the patient is that he is making none of those confident resolutions which marked his original conversion. No more lavish promises of perpetual virtue, I gather; not even the expectation of an endowment of "grace" for life, but only a hope for the daily and hourly pittance to meet the daily and hourly temptation! This is very bad." –Uncle Screwtape

C. S. Lewis, *Screwtape Letters*

Florence

The pink horizon was pencil thin in the eastern sky. The lit propane canister gave off a sufficient amount of heat.

"Nice morning," Norman said, sitting on the deck next to me.

"Yeah it is."

"In the spring, I was thinking we could head to Central Valley, California. The Almond Corporation will pay two hundred thirty dollars per colony."

"That would be fun."

"I applied for the license needed to certify where the bees go across country. They're supposed to get back to me, but Gunter is pretty excited about it."

"He's a good kid." I took a sip of coffee.

"You had another nightmare last night." Norman's eyes were fixed on the rising sun.

I shivered. "Everyone I knew was a demon and they were laughing at me. I tried to exorcise them, but they just laughed when I called on the name of Jesus."

"Hopefully I wasn't among them."

"No. It did get me thinking about my life, though. I lived so much of it selfish, lost, and desperate. Every day I still struggle with bitterness, pride and…even loving you the way I should."

"I know you love me."

"I mean showing you." I sighed. "I wanted so much to change the world. Make a difference."

Norman took a sip of coffee. "But that's what He does."

"Right." My phone buzzed in my pocket. "It's Special Agent Carter." I touched the screen. "Hello? When? January 21?" I caught Norman's eyes. "Yes, I think I can work that out. Okay thank you." I hung up.

"Well?"

"He wants me to testify in the case involving Alice Hardy."

"How do you feel about that?"

"The thought scares me, but that person I used to be? I don't even recognize her. It's like I'm a completely different person. I didn't change, more like I died."

"Crucified with Christ."

"And yet, I live." I studied the sunrise. "Being a mother and raising a family is the highest calling a woman can have. It wasn't always easy, especially when you have a husband working long hours, and five kids under the age of ten.

"But now I consider how it turned out with Eddy and Irmgard. Children who had a mother and father to raise them."

"Gertrude and Hildegard too, don't forget," Norman said. "They are lovely young women, strong in their decisions and relationships. You made a difference. They are who they are because of you." He caught my eyes, his gaze tender. "I am who I am because of you."

"And who are you?" I teased.

His gaze returned to the lake. "A self-employed man who's in love with his wife."

Contented, I sighed. "You take my breath away."

Leah Meisch Photography

Hazel Mattice is the author of 5 novels, including *The Green Door*, *Where there is no Whisper*, and *Thirsty Ground*. When she isn't writing books, she can be seen on her porch in the summer enjoying the outdoors or riding her motorcycle. She is a sucker for cookies, cleverly written romance, and anime. *Sinking Sand* is book 4 in her series *The Chosen Five*.

Made in the USA
Columbia, SC
17 September 2022